MW01482759

ISBN: 978-1-7780658-5-9 (Paperback)

ISBN: 978-1-7780658-7-3 (Ebook)

Any references to historical events, real people, or real places are used fictitiously. Names, characters, and places are products of the author's imagination.

Front cover image by Mibl Art

Book designed with Vellum

First printing edition 2023

Shale Empire Press

388 Sumac Road East

Kelowna, BC

www.tammytyree.com

TAMMY TYREE

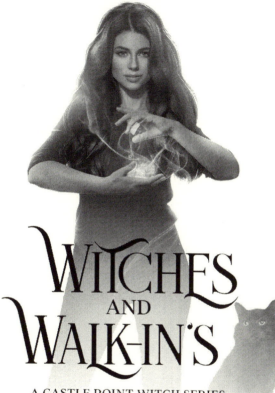

WITCHES
AND
WALK-IN'S

A CASTLE POINT WITCH SERIES
BOOK 1

For Hallie

ACKNOWLEDGMENTS

There is always more than one person involved with birthing a new creation. In my case, several people.

With deepest gratitude for your help, support, love, and encouragement, thank you to Jennifer for your expert eye and sense of perfect prose. Chloe Leah and Joanne for your professional, tactical, and organizational savvy. Carissa for your support, encouragement, and coaching.

Thanks to my cheering squad: Darren, Cass, Carrigan and Connor, and my friends, I appreciate and love you all.

WITCHES & WALK-IN'S

A CASTLE POINT WITCH SERIES

BOOK ONE

TAMMY TYREE

Shale Empire Press

AUTHORS NOTE

This is a work of fiction.
The demons, however, are real.

PROLOGUE

The Earl Dagon and Castle Point History

In 1608, the Earl of Newberry came to America from Bristol, England, in pursuit of his greatest love, Evelyn of Cumbria, herself a practicing witch. Legend has it that the "Evil Evelyn" cast a love spell over the Earl, used him for his money and title until the Earl was penniless, and his title stripped from him.

This was untrue.

The Earl was an abusive man, irresponsible with his money, and took advantage of his subjects. Evelyn escaped the Earl's grasp, fled England, and crossed the ocean to what is now known as the State of Maine.

The Earl attested to be deeply in love, but more so, relentless in his desire to 'possess' Evelyn. He followed and found her, settling in a small village on the ocean's edge. Evelyn patiently waited for her opportunity to escape and did so, placing a curse upon the Earl that would prevent him from ever leaving.

Devastated and angered by her betrayal, the Earl

summoned the Demon, 'Vine'; Builder of Towers and Identifier of Witches. Vine appeared as a lion, riding a black horse and carrying a viper.

He granted the Earl's requests to build a castle on the highest point, overlooking the ocean, and find Evelyn.

Vine did so, also granting the Earl exceptional strength and powers, in exchange for the Earl's eternal soul.

Once the castle was built and Evelyn exposed, the Earl - now calling himself Earl Dagon; "Devil of the Sea" - burned her alive at the stake in the castle courtyard.

He swore to purge the world of witchcraft and witches, instilling a fear that witches were the bane of existence and harbingers of all things evil, and implemented a law against the practice of witchcraft.

To this day, the punishment for such a crime is to burn on the pyre within the castle.

The Earl formed the Order of the Witch Hunters. Instilling the core belief that all witches are evil, and must be purged from the earth, their powers stripped and given to the rightful owners - the Witch Hunters.

The Witch Hunters became pupils of the Demon Vine, who granted the Witch Hunters the power to absorb a witch's power just before taking their life. Vine agreed to teach the Witch Hunters and grant them this privilege, in exchange for their souls.

The Witch Hunters were sent forth to form thousands of branches throughout the world, to instill the belief that witches were evil, and enforce the law against the practice of witchcraft, or being a witch. To any non-mage they granted generous rewards, should they find and expose a witch or their coven to the Hunters.

The Earl later married Madeleine Bavent, a Catholic

nun who renounced her habit for the love of the Earl. Under their hand, the community of "Castle Point" flourished.

The exceptional strength and powers for evil granted by the Demon, Vine, ran through Earl Dagon's lineage.

As time went on, the witches had to be more and more inventive in remaining undetectable, and an 'underground society' was formed. The members of the society, now hundreds of thousands strong, discontinued coven meetings and became solitary practitioners.

By maintaining a strict 'no coven' rule, they could still function as witches and work their magic for the benefit of those who were pure of heart and intention and who sought their help.

This law against the practice of witchcraft remains in effect in the present day.

And that is where my story begins...

Alexandra Heale

CHAPTER
ONE

BETTY

The cool air tickled my arms. Tiny hairs rose with the gooseflesh. Small mounds of pimpled thermometers popped up over my arms, chest, and neck.

I heard a beeping sound, faint at first, then slowly it became louder and closer. The scent of cleanser assaulted me, harsh and chemical.

My eyes stayed firmly shut as if glued at the seam, or tiny weights held the lids down. My breath came in rhythmic, even bursts.

What was that in my mouth? My tongue wiggled and slammed against the hard plastic. I couldn't taste anything other than stale, rotting breath, but I could tell something was firmly lodged in my mouth.

What the hell was it?

Why was it there?

I forced my eyes open a fraction. Moonlight filtered through the splintered cracks of my heavy lids and shattered against my eyes. Too bright! I closed them again, only long enough for my tongue to push up against the plastic in my mouth.

I could feel it now, not just in my mouth, but going down my throat. A swell of panic ran from my toes to my nose. I wanted to gag.

Spurred by the beeping beside me, louder now, my eyes flew open. I tried to sit up. I couldn't move. I laid back against the softness of what must be a bed and peered around the room.

A hospital room.

I felt a heaviness as if underwater, the weight of my arms, legs, and chest making it difficult to see or breathe. The scent of cleanser pierced the back of my nose as I tried to breathe.

What was that thing in my mouth and down my throat? I forced my eyes to open wider, but they burned and felt gritty like someone had sprinkled fine sand under the lids. I blinked several times to clear the grit. My eyes took a while to adjust.

I looked down and saw a tube coming out of my mouth. My heart rate sped up. The beeping beside me kept pace as it beat faster and faster.

Why did I wake up in a hospital?

Was I in an accident?

The beeping sped up again, fast enough to send a wail of high-pitched signals through my room and into the adjoining hallway.

The large door burst open, startling me, which made the beeping speed up yet again. A nurse with short dark hair, dark-circled eyes, wearing pink scrubs with multicolored cartoon puppies on her shirt rushed in.

Puppies? Was this a hospital or a vet clinic?

"Betty! Oh my god, she's awake!" she practically screamed, to whom I couldn't imagine. I assumed she was talking about me, however, as she leaped to the beeping machine and pressed a button to stop the noise.

Much better.

But... Betty?

Was that my name?

"Quick, call Dr. Holloway!" The pink puppy nurse barked to another nurse with long, curly red hair and a generous dose of junk in the trunk who had joined the party.

She was wearing sensible dark green scrubs that I thought complimented her curly copper hair, curvy body, and green eyes nicely. That nurse left the room quickly, her long copper hair trailing behind her.

I eyed the other nurse as she started fussing over me. "It's ok Betty, calm down, nice and slow breaths. You have a tube down your throat that's helping you breathe. Just breathe with it."

No shit, Sherlock. Did I have a choice?

I tried to focus on breathing in and out with the rhythm of the machine. I felt tiny beads of sweat spring from my temples. My heart charged ahead, clearly not on board with my brain and the rhythmic breathing tube.

I squeezed my eyes shut, willing my heart to slow down. Tears, mixed with sweat, streamed down my cheeks, some running into my mouth. The sharp, salty taste assaulted my tongue.

So many body parts had forgotten how to operate, and others were running wild. I felt a darkness fall over me, almost willing my brain to return to its vacation - wherever it had been - and my body to slip back to where I'd be safe.

So much of this didn't feel right.

That included this body.

Or being in one.

Everything was confusing. Least of all the name I heard the nurse call me. Betty, was it? I tried to focus, to remember how I got here, and who I was. 'Betty' sounded foreign. It didn't fit.

Was that weird?

I should know my name, shouldn't I?

Copper-haired booty nurse rushed back into the room. "Doc Holloway's on his way. Can you extubate her?" she asked the pink puppy nurse.

"Yes, of course," she snapped, rolling her eyes and huffing a breath so large I half-expected a jet stream of fire to follow it.

Pink puppy nurse was a bit of a bitch, apparently.

I noticed the booty nurse step back, slightly behind the pink puppy bitch nurse, narrowed her eyes, then twirl one index finger at the back of the pink puppy bitch nurse's head.

Did she just cast a curse on the bitch?

I decided I liked booty nurse a lot.

"Betty, I'm going to remove the breathing tube for you now, but I'll need you to breathe out hard while I do. Do you think you can do that?" Pink puppy bitch nurse barked - *funny* - as she pulled on sterile gloves and removed the two strips of white tape securing the breathing tube against my face. I grimaced as the nurse yanked at the tape.

Ouch!

Settle down there, bitch.

She grasped the breathing tube.

Was that a freaking smile on her lips?

My heart skipped a beat. I changed my mind. Just leave the tube in, and I'll learn to live with it. But the bitch nurse apparently couldn't read minds and therefore wasn't giving me a choice, so I summoned some nerve from somewhere inside this foreign landscape and nodded slightly.

"Ok, now, take a deep breath... ready... blow out!" As I blew, the nurse dragged the long tube from its position down my throat.

An intense burning sensation welled up from deep inside my chest. Bile chased the feeling up my throat. A damp taste of age-old dirt and grit stopped short of exploding past my teeth.

"That's it! Great job, Betty!" Bitch nurse's praise sounded hollow, and her smile faded - torture time over. Booty nurse clapped and even bounced a little, an action that made her my numero uno.

I coughed and retched, gasping for fresh air.

"Penny! Don't just stand there! Give her a sip of water. Her throat's gonna hurt."

Somebody must have pissed in the bitch nurse's bran flakes.

I'm guessing it was a copper-haired booty nurse, Penny.

Copper Penny. How annoyingly adorable and appropriate.

Penny placed the breathing tube on a nearby tray and turned off the breathing apparatus, then offered me water through a straw. I could feel a cool flush down my throat and land in the pit of my stomach. The small sips were invigorating.

I managed a smile.

It was the least I could do.

Bitch nurse cooed at me and rubbed her hands up and down my legs.

My smile faded.

Uh-uh, no thanks, lady.

9

Your bite is worse than your bark and the cute pink puppy shirt you think makes you look Shih Tzu adorable is just fabric covering up a Pit Bull of a lie.

I wanted to giggle.

I think I'm funny!

Except, I think I like Pit Bulls, so comparing one to a pink puppy bitch nurse was an insult.

I definitely like Shih Tzu.

But how I even knew this was beyond comprehension.

My head pounded.

Penny removed a white, plastic clamp thingamajig from my middle finger. I assumed it was there to track my heart rate. There was a coolness around the area where the clamp had been. How long had it been there? It left a red mark.

I didn't recognize the fingers attached to hands that also looked incredibly unfamiliar. I glanced at my other hand, somehow thinking perhaps it would be different, but it wasn't. I had never seen these hands before, nor the arms attached. My skin was sallow, but also loose, wrinkled, and saggy. I rested my eyes, then opened them and glanced at my hands again.

No change, and definitely not mine.

I felt certain about it.

Which meant that things just got weirder.

I noticed a heavy weight on my chest, but, peering down, the only thing I saw was a rather large hump in my hospital gown....ohhhhh.

I had big boobies.

Nice.

Just then, a tall, slender man entered the room. His grey hair was slightly mussed and off to one side, glasses barely resting on the tip of his nose, and the white coat he was wearing was miss-buttoned and floating behind him as he rushed in. There was a hunch in his shoulders and a slight limp in his step that revealed the wear and tear of his age.

This must be Doc Holloway, that pink puppy bitch nurse told Penny to call. He spoke quickly and quietly to both nurses before turning his attention to me. He smiled a robust, wide smile.

I was instantly annoyed.

"Welcome back, Betty! You've been with us for quite some time! Can you try to speak? Maybe even a whisper? Do you know where you are? You were in an accident nine months ago. Do you remember?"

The doc's rapid-fire quiz made me feel like retreating under the covers if I could only move my heavy, saggy arms to pull the covers over my face.

The assault on my senses continued when he clicked on his penlight, pulled at my eyelids, and checked for pupil dilation. I blinked in rapid succession, eyes tearing up and overflowing onto my cheeks once again.

This man I didn't like, I decided.

I glared at him, or at least I glared in his direction, as bright white dots floated across my vision.

Doc Holloway stood back, waiting for me to speak, but I took a few minutes to focus on his face and then on the nurses and around the room, moving my head slightly.

I felt like a circus animal in a cage.

Wait, had I ever been to a circus to see caged animals?

I assumed I must have since I suddenly felt like one.

'Everyone look at the freak who just woke up from a coma! Praise be! Oh, and by the way; her name is Betty!'

Except it wasn't, was it?

I took another look at the three expectant faces awaiting me to perform my next miracle. Then I focused in on Doc Holloway and wet my lips, preparing to speak.

My saliva tasted like blood and bile. I felt a wrenching swelling from deep inside me but I swallowed it down and took a ragged breath.

Doc Holloway leaned in slightly as I parted my lips to speak. My voice, merely a raspy whisper after what I now understood was months of hibernation, announced what I was suddenly very sure of.

"I'm not Betty."

CHAPTER
TWO

JACK

I t was nine months ago while I was at work on the docks of the Castle Point shipping yard, unloading the fresh catch of the day, when I got the bad news about Betty's accident from Doc Holloway, and I just up and left. I couldn't think, and could barely breathe. Droppin' the bushel full of fish right there on the damn dock, - not caring that I spilled the damn fish everywhere. I jumped into my old Ford pick-em-up, screeching m' tires all the way through town and straight into the "Emergency Vehicles Only" parking area. I blasted out the truck door then, leaving it running and the door wide open behind me.

They issued me a ticket for that. Can you friggin' believe it?

The Good Doc Holloway did everything he could for Betty, right from ground zero. The entire town of Castle Point knew he was the 'Good Doc', simply because he was a good doctor and had the track record to prove it. But now, where Betty was concerned, he had his doubts 'n he was honest with me from day one.

"It doesn't look good, Jack. With her injuries... I just don't know if she'll pull through," he said. "You might take her off life support, and see if she can survive on her own, once she's through her surgeries and her broken bones have healed up some."

Bad day, that day, the worst I ever had.

I shur'nuff appreciated Doc's honestly, but I refused to take Betty off life support as long as there was a tiny trace of brain activity left in 'er body. I just knew in my heart that she would come back to me, no matter the damage the semi-truck had done when it collided with her minivan.

The 'Mom-Mobile' - as Betty used to call it - had been crushed at the auto-wreckers shortly after the accident, and I had been there to watch. In fact, I stayed 'til I could no longer see the "Proud Mom of an Honor Student" bumper sticker.

And I cried.

With every crunch and pop of the van's body, I cried harder.

Our life had changed in the blink of a sleepy trucker's eye.

Our nine-year-old daughter, Alana, visited Betty in the hospital once a week, less often than me, but our sweet baby girl couldn't handle seeing her mom all full of tubes' n stuff, so she usually stayed home.

Who could blame 'er?

I stopped by every day on my way home from work and sat with my Betty for a good hour, holding her hand, telling her 'bout my day. I didn't care that the staff said she probably couldn't hear me because I knew she could, and talking kept me from cryin'.

Every day I'd ask Doc Holloway how my Betty was doin', and every day the answer was; "no change".

Today, however, I got the news I'd been dreaming of from the day they wheeled Betty into the emergency ward.

I was wheeling a crate of today's catch into the warehouse for processing - just like I was when the accident happened - when my cell phone jangled in my back pocket. Somethin' in my heart just knew this was gonna be good news, and shur'nuff I was right.

My Betty woke up!

I shoved the crate of fish into the warehouse, lickety-split-like; a couple of them slimy suckers spilled out and fell onto my boots, but I didn't care. I yelled at my manager - ol' Thomson, we call him - and ran out to the parking lot, my feet barely hitting' the concrete.

I couldn't get the ol' pick-em-up moving fast enough, praying' I would see no cops on my way, and whoever lived up in them big ol' clouds heard my prayers. I drove my ol' Ford, tires screeching off the last of their tread - into the hospital parking lot, this time - stopping short of hitting a 'Visitor's Only' sign. I slammed the ol' gal into 'park', mindful of turning it off before I blew open the truck door, slamming it behind me, and rushed to the hospital entrance.

No issuing me tickets this time, no sirree.

I raced up the stairs to the third floor and pulled open the door. A blast of canned air and the faint smell of cleaning' stuff assaulted my nose. I ran down the hall to room #319, the room Betty had occupied for nine long months.

My work boots, still stinkin' of fish and just as slippery, were not accustomed to being on shiny clean hospital flooring. My feet failed to stop at Betty's door and I slid past, grabbed the door frame with one hand, and slip-sliding into Betty's room, breathing hard.

There she was, laying on the bed, none of them damn tubes' n such coming' out of her. She was the best thing I'd seen in such a long time.

"Betty! Oh, my God," I yelled.

My tears came in a rush, running down my cheeks and onto my smelly fish boots.

Betty, who looked to be resting, had her eyes closed. But when she heard me, she opened her eyes - wide - and took a good ol' look at me.

I must have looked a sight!

I was too excited to stop at home and wash up and change out of my plaid work shirt, jeans, and work boots, but I quickly ran my hands through my hair which, shur-r'nuff skewed to one side of my head, but I knew my Betty wouldn't care.

I collapsed onto her, forcing her breath out with a 'whomp'.

She was a lot skinnier than I liked, but I didn't mind that right now. I was just so happy to hold 'er and eat 'er good food - she made the best Clam Chowder in Maine - and watch our favorite game shows and' laugh with 'er again.

She wasn't so happy to see me, however.

"Get off me!" she rasped in my ear. I backed away, grinning' like a mad fool, streaks of clean skin shining where my tears had been.

I ignored 'er. She was always joking around with me.

"Oh, Betty! I knew you'd come back to me. I just knew it. I told the Doc from day one - 'my Betty will come back to me, I just know it!'"

She quirked one of them adorable eyebrows at me and rasped;

"Who are you?"

My stupid grin slid off my stupid face.

I sniffed and ran the base of my palm across my eyes and down my cheeks. She was joking' with me again, wasn't she?

"What do you mean, Betty? It's me. It's your husband, Jack!" I sniffed again, reaching' for her hand. Betty slid 'er hand away from me, with some effort, then squished up her lips 'n rolled her eyes back. She looked like she was trying to search deep in 'er brain for something, but that something never came.

"Nope, never heard of ya." she croaked.

"Well, what the hell, Betty? Don't you recognize me?" My heart dropped into my belly with a thud like a deep-fried turkey on Christmas.

I was sure the entire hospital could hear. I stepped closer 'n looked her in the eyes. "It's me, Betty. Please tell me you remember me!" I was pleading now, and the damn tears revved up again, but the Betty I thought I knew wasn't listening.

"Stop calling me Betty," was all she could muster.

She shifted a little in the bed as if she was trying to roll over and avoid the sight of me, but she couldn't. She just lay against the pillow and closed her eyes.

I wanted to crawl into a hole and die.

"Leave me be," she rasped.

Bad day, that day. The worst I ever had.

THREE

ALEXANDRA

"Ok Mrs. Twillinger, just relax on the chaise." Sweet little grandmother of four, Evie Twillinger, laid back on the comfortable chaise lounge in my office. "Good, now close your eyes and take a deep breath." Evie was under a court order to attend sessions to resolve her sudden, rampant anger issues. Thankfully, Judge Adams had been lenient on the kindly widow, despite the thousands of dollars of damage caused when the tiny Grandma took a Louisville Slugger to her neighbor's beautiful '57 Chevy Bel Air. The Judge's initial assessment of Mrs. Twillinger was that she 'snapped', but, from experience, I knew that odd, unexpected behavior from a sweetheart such as Evie was likely *not* from running out of Metamucil, or from the paperboy throwing the news a little too hard and ruining her petunias.

No. I knew it was something far, far worse. And I would bet my mother's expensive antique china on it.

An entity attachment.

Lucky for Evie, I was the therapist Judge Adams assigned to her case. In part, because Evie and I are neighbors on Ocean View drive, as is Judge Adams, but also because I was the only therapist in Castle Point who would recognize an entity attachment.

Which means I was the only person capable of releasing it.

Because I wasn't just a therapist, I was a natural-born witch.

Entities were kinda my thing.

Not that there were a ton of therapists to choose from in our small part of Maine, and none with my reputation. So, I had a full client list, and sometimes, being a witch came in handy for said practice. None of my clients knew about the witchy side of me, however, and it had to stay that way.

I've cataloged that information deep in my cauldron of secrets for almost 38 years.

The best way to extract an entity without the client being totally freaked out by the experience is through hypnosis.

And not the cluck like a chicken and bark like a dog kind, no. Stunts like that are reserved for showmen who couldn't get into clown college.

I grabbed my notepad and pen off my desk and sat in a comfortable chair beside Evie. Being eighty years old, she was already in a state of light sleep, as most eighty-year-olds were when they've been horizontal for a mere thirty seconds. I counted her down into a deep, hypnotic trance. When I was sure she was relaxed, but not sleeping. I asked.

"Evie, can you please go back to the day that you picked up the baseball bat and went to your neighbors?" After a few moments, Evie's soft voice replied.

"Ok... I'm there..."

19

"Good. You're doing great. Can you tell me what was going through your mind at that moment?" Evie took a few moments before replying.

"I... uh... I... nothing... I don't know... I don't remember... I just kind of woke up and was standing there with the baseball bat in my hand, and poor Thomas's car smashed to bits!" she cried. I placed a hand on her shoulder.

"It's ok, Evie, you're safe, you have done nothing wrong. Just relax, that's it... nice deep breaths, feeling calm, relaxed, and safe. Good." Once Evie had settled down, I continued. "Evie, I'd like you to scan your body, kind of like that MRI machine Doc Holloway put you in last year, remember that?" Evie nodded. I had driven her to the appointment myself.

"Great, Evie. Now, slowly run the scan down your body. Is there any part that feels a little strange to you?"

"Yes."

"Good, ok, can you describe where you feel that in your body?"

"My tummy." Evie's voice was a little peep as she patted her belly.

"Ok, Evie, if you could assign a color to that feeling, what color would it be?" Evie took a minute before responding.

"Green."

Bingo.

Entities essentially showed up as black, red, or green "feelings." The green ones were usually smaller and referred to as 'Imps'. The good ones could take the shape of small animals or insects and, other than eating tomatoes from your garden or ending up in your shower, the little bastards were practically harmless, doing nothing worse than making people scream.

The bad ones were jokesters who wanted to possess innocents, mess with people's Ouija boards, and play nasty practical jokes.

A giddiness welled up inside me and I did a little happy wiggle in my chair.

I loved this part of my work.

Entity bashing was the most excitement I had in our sleepy town. For me, it was better than any Friday night alone, at home, perfecting potions and coffee foam art.

"Ok, Evie. You're doing great. Now, I'm going to talk directly to the green feeling you have in your tummy, okay? You can listen if you'd like, but it's okay if you'd rather just step aside and relax." I gave Evie a few seconds to settle deeper into the couch, her breathing shallow but regular. "I want to talk to whoever was really in charge of the baseball bat that day. *Now*." I snapped my fingers.

After several moments, a low growling rumble came from deep inside Evie's chest, moving past her throat and bursting from her tiny mouth, which had screwed into an evil snarl.

"*It was me, witch.*" A deep, resonant bark had replaced Evie's tiny voice. Spittle flew from her lips, landing at various places on the couch and Evie's clothes. I gripped my pen a little tighter, amazed that a voice that big could come out of little Evie Twillinger.

This had to be quite the evil little Imp.

Nothing I couldn't handle.

I recalled the time that a nasty, red, wanna-be demon clung to Mr. Geary, who came to see me for a sudden onset of violent behavior. The normally quiet, respectable tenth-grade history teacher would never hurt a fly until he woke up one morning and started hitting.

Himself.

Repeatedly.

And couldn't stop.

As far as I could decipher from my session with Mr. Geary, it was likely the evil little Imp found a 'in' and attached itself to the man after he had taken four of his wife's Vallium by mistake - thinking they were his prescription arthritic medication. Then, as he often did on a weekday evening "to relax from his day of trying to teach our nation's history to ungrateful deviants" downed the drugs with a double rye and coke. He promptly passed out, giving the mini-joker its opportunity to weasel its way in and wreak a little havoc.

Raise a little hell.

When Mr. Geary woke up the next day - with a wicked headache and a pool of drool - he got super slap-happy, thankfully hitting no one but himself.

Expelling that little joker was the most fun I'd had on a sunny Friday afternoon in this dusty one-broom town.

Hopefully, the green sponge soaking up Evie's sunshine was less of a challenge.

I refrained from rubbing my hands together, eager to send the slimy green sucker back to hell, and Evie back to her sweet self.

"And who are you, exactly?" I asked calmly, watching as Evie's facial features scrunched and twisted.

"*Wouldn't you like to know...*"

"Oh, I think I do, but why don't you tell me, *Imp*?" Evie's head slowly spun toward me, then her eyes flew open. They were completely green, with black slits for pupils. The green was a harsh contrast to Evie's sallow, white skin.

Her mouth opened into an "*O*".

Calling the jokester demon out apparently shocked the shit out of him.

"*You don't know me, witch, and you cannot release me from this vessel!*" More spittle shot from Evie's mouth. Her arthritic hands curled and knotted together as her tiny, stockinged feet flailed on the chaise, the Imp demon having a toddler's tantrum inside of her.

"You're wrong. You have no right to attach to this woman and play your vicious little games." I'd had enough of this cranky tool.

Time to work my magic.

I stood up and retrieved my wand from a drawer in my desk. Standing over Evie, still flailing and whining like a small child, I pointed the magical weapon above her chest. A beautiful sliver-blue ball of light expanded from the tip and moved over Evie's chest. It hovered there as I began the incantation to expel the jokester demon;

"*Goddess of the North, South, East, and West, help this woman, do your best, remove this demon from her chest, send him to his place of doom, remove all traces of his gloom.*"

Evie's body quivered, then she shrieked. The ball of light dipped into her chest, and came out again, the dark green entity attached. It was small, green, and ghoulish, with large, bat-like ears and a small tail.

"So long, sucker," I said, holding my wand steady.

The Imp, firmly encased in the wand's ball of light, eyed me and sneered. "*You can't hurt me, witch!*" it sputtered.

"No, but I can send you back to where you came from!" I raised the wand and flicked it at the tiny ghoul. It shrieked in pain as the electric shock wave streamed from the wand.

This was just too much fun.

"*Demon Imp, begone and do not return, I banish thee!*"

I flicked my wand again and watched as the ball of light grew to the size of a basketball, rising higher above Evie, then burst. Tiny sparks of light fell around the room and dissipated, the green Imp vanishing with the sparks. The light scent of sulfur remained.

Evie stirred.

"Evie, just relax, you're safe. I'm going to count from one to five, and when I reach five, you'll be perfectly peaceful, and happy, and not remember a thing that happened here today." I started counting, reciting a simple forgetting spell under my breath as I did so. "Ok, here we go. One... *Goddess grant* two... *this woman grace* three... *embrace her in* four... *your protective cloak* five - *of forgetting. Thank you, Goddess,* and awake!"

Evie opened her eyes and smiled. "Oh, hello dear. Did I fall asleep? I'm so sorry." Evie blushed, false teeth clattering slightly as she spoke.

Her sweet smile warmed my heart. *This* was why I loved my work. Helping people like Evie.

I smiled, "Oh, that's perfectly ok Mrs. Twillinger. Understandable with everything that's been going on." I patted her hand. "Everything will be fine now, though. Do you remember anything? Dream anything?"

"Oh, no, nothing at all. Just needed a good nap, I guess," she shrugged." Am I all fixed up? I won't have any more of those crazy ideas, will I?"

"Nothing of the sort, I can assure you." I helped Evie up from the chaise.

"But do you know why I did that in the first place?" Her rheumy eyes glistened with tears.

A little jab hit my heart. "Let's just say... it wasn't you. Can we leave it at that?"

"I'm good with that, if you say so. Will you tell Judge Adams I'm all fixed up?"

"Oh, yes, I certainly will. Just leave that to me," I assured her, assisting with her coat. The floral scent of

White Shoulders perfume wafted through the air, reminding me of my mother. A bittersweetness settled on my chest.

"Do you think I'll still have to pay for the damages? I have little money..." tears dripped onto her sunken cheeks. I placed a hand on her shoulder.

"Don't worry about that, Mrs. Twillinger, okay? I'll deal with Judge Adams now."

We walked into the reception area and said our goodbyes just as Penny rushed through the door, her copper-colored curly hair flowing behind her. She nodded at Mrs. Twillinger and fast-walked through reception, into my office, breathless, barely glancing in my direction.

I followed, closing the door being me. "Hey, Penny, what's the rush? Is there a fire? Cauldron overflow again?" I giggled, my curiosity piqued. Penny's batty behavior never surprised me. She was a special, talented witch and psychic with her own brand of weirdness that I adored. She was also my oldest and best friend, the only one who knew everything there was to know about me.

Almost.

Some things I kept in the cauldron.

"Mrs. Burke - Betty - she's awake! But she's not Betty!" I studied Pen for a moment, narrowing my eyes at her. Then sat down at my desk, tucking my long, wavy black hair behind my left ear and fidgeting with the tiny vial of ashes hanging from a short silver chain earring.

"Penny, slow down. What are you saying?"

"I shouldn't be telling you this, so if Doc Holloway calls you, act surprised." Penny practically panted, her words coming out in a rush. She took a seat across from me. Her freckles, normally tinged a light copper, were practically glowing - like a pile of teeny pennies on her skin.

"Make sense, woman! Why would Doc contact me about Betty Burke, and what do you mean, she's not Betty?" I asked.

Penny explained the morning events, finishing with Betty's refusal to admit she was the same Betty Burke who went into a coma after a car accident nine months before.

"She flat-out refuses to recognize her name or her husband." Penny slapped the desk, making me jump. "And poor Jack! He's been beside himself all day."

"That can be quite common in coma patients, Penny, you know that." I quirked my brows and sat back in my chair, unsure why she was practically in hysterics about something that was likely to happen, anyway.

"This is different, Alex. When I touched her... well, I... I couldn't see anything. It was just blackness and pain, a lot of pain... it practically burned me." Penny could see a person's past, and sometimes their future, with just one touch. Because of this, she stopped shaking people's hands years ago. It made her job tricky, as patient care was - well - her *job*, but she somehow managed.

"But that makes sense. There would have been a lot of pain and darkness when the accident occurred," I argued.

"No, it's something different. *She's different*," Penny insisted. "She says her name is something else, but she can't quite figure out what. She won't listen to reason, and she doesn't even recognize her own face when we brought in a mirror!" Penny's face flushed, her freckles disappearing..

She was definitely more animated than usual.

A bee lodged firmly in her bonnet.

I studied her for a minute before replying. "Ok, Penny, I believe you. Something weird must be going on with Betty Burke, but I can't really do anything about it unless Doc

Holloway wants me to consult on her case. Did he mention whether he would?"

Penny shook her head, copper curls bouncing. "I told him he should, but why would he listen to me? I'm just an RN, not a specialist. And I can't reveal my psychic insights, you know that." She took a breath. "I know he is planning to consult with a coma specialist, but I don't know who."

"Well, there's not much I can do, Penny," I said, softly. "I appreciate your bringing this to me, but if I'm not invited to consult, then I really don't have any business checking into Betty's case."

Panny slapped the desk again and stood up, glaring at me.

"I know you can help her, Alex! You're probably the only person who can! *There is something wrong.* I just know it goes beyond textbook post-coma behavior," she said, wringing her hands together.

I stood up and calmly walked around the desk and stood next to her. Placing my hands on top of Penny's, I felt her energy, a tangled web of nerves and fear, when normally she was calm, funny, but serene. If that was the case, then I knew Penny was on to something. Her psychic visions and intuition were rarely wrong.

If there was an entity or demon or some other presence attached to Betty Burke, then I had more experience dealing with it than anyone. I would have to make up some excuse for Doc Holloway and needle my way into Betty's case.

"Ok Penny, I'll head over to the hospital this afternoon to check on my other patients and see what I can find out. In the meantime, keep this to yourself. We don't need the entire community freaking out."

Penny blew out a breath and hugged me. "Thank you, Alex." She gave me an extra squeeze.

"No problem. I have to head next door to the shop and check on a few things, then I'll make my way to CPM. I'll call you later." A lightbulb flicked in my head. "Oh, I almost forgot! Can you do me a favor?"

"Of course, anything."

"Can you send a secure email blast to all the Dagon County witches and ask for anonymous monetary donations for Mrs. Twillinger? An Imp possessed her when she smashed up Thomas's old chevy. I released the Imp, but she still has to pay the court damages."

Penny clutched her chest. "Oh good Goddess, the poor thing! Of course! How much is the fine?"

I checked my notes. "$10,000 total."

"Oh good Goddess, ok, will do. I better go, though. I promised Cathy I'd pick up a few things before heading home."

I smiled at Penny's reference to her wife. The two of them were the perfect couple. To be honest, I was a little jealous of their relationship. "Say hi to Cath for me? And thanks for coming in." I gave Penny another quick hug before she left, grabbed my coat, and headed through the reception area to the front door.

"Maggy, I'll be out for the rest of the day. Please hold all calls - unless it's an emergency, then put them through to my cell." Maggy, my long-time receptionist, nodded in agreement and went back to transcribing client notes for the files. "C'mon Blackjack, let's go next door." My black familiar rose from his position on the reception lounge, arching his back in a big cat stretch, farted, then sneezed before jumping off to follow me out the door.

"Good grief, Blackjack. Really?" I looked apologetically at Maggy, who was already spritzing air freshener around the room.

I heard Blackjack's voice float through my mind. *"Oh woman, please. Like you don't pass gas as you walk up the stairs. I know, I follow you, remember?"*

"Hush, you mangy brat. Let's go." I smiled at Maggy, then followed my furry familiar to my other business.

The small brass bell above the Castle Point Apothecary Shoppe's door tinkled as we entered. Mint and lavender filled my senses, and I breathed deeply. The store, with white, floor-to-ceiling shelves filled with artisan-created bath, body, and natural health products, was a gift from my mentor, Mr. Waldo Cres ('Cressy') before his death some years before.

Although, when Cressy passed it to me, it wasn't an apothecary. It was a storehouse of the oddest collection of antiques and paraphernalia I'd ever seen. He called the store 'Wishful Things', and it's where we met, when I was only eight years old, and spent most of my time, without my mother's knowledge, learning to hone my skills as a witch.

After Cressy's death, I took most of the inventory home, then turned the space into an apothecary. As a hobby, I had perfected the craft of natural, organic face and body products, and enjoyed making them for my friends. It was Penny who insisted I clean up the old shop and start selling my goods. After a while, I invited other artisans to sell their products in the store too, and before I knew it, I had a thriving second business.

I nodded and smiled at the patrons, many of them repeat customers, then stopped in front of Theadora (Teddy to everyone who knew her), my apothecary ShopKeep. "Good morning Teddy. How's everything today? Did the wildcraft honey from Adam's farm come in?"

"Sure did-a-le-did! And the sample face cloths from the

weaver are on your deskaroonie." Teddy's colorful grasp on the English language matched her wild, tinted pigtails that shook as she nodded her head toward the back of the store.

"Thanks, I'll have a look. Nice boots." I commented, looking at the five-inch wedge combat boots that lent a few inches to her petite frame.

Theadora dressed in her favorite color, black, the stark opposite of the white surroundings of the shop. Her shirt sleeves barely covered her tattooed arms (a clever glamor that she altered almost daily). Despite the dark choice of clothing, and the face, ear piercings, and wild hair (also a glamor she changed almost daily), the apothecary patrons loved Teddy and her boisterous, childlike personality. She was a Master Herbalist by trade and a fledgling solitary witch who concocted the teas and natural herbal remedies for the shop.

Blackjack took up his usual position in a front window display, stretching out among the products. His raven black fur and deep green eyes shone in the sunlight streaming through the window. He and I bore an eerie match in the hair and eye department, lending truth to the 'people and pet's look-alike' argument. "I have to head up to the hospital later this afternoon. Ok if I leave Blackjack here with you? I'll come to get him later when I head home."

"Of course, no problemo!" Teddy gave Blackjack a good scratch behind the ears and shuffled a few things around him on the window display.

"Hey, nobody asked me if I'd like to hang with the wild witch and her idiot hellhounds." Blackjack's silky purr floated through my mind. I glanced at Teddy, grateful she could not hear the animal speak, although she practiced daily with her hellhounds.

"You be good for Teddy, Blackjack. And don't pick on

Draco and Lucius like you did last time," I said to my familiar, who merely opened one eye and glanced my way.

"I didn't spend all morning cleaning my coat just to have those two monsters drool all over it."

I giggled. The store patrons smiled at my furry black beast, almost as if they could hear what he said. *"Just be good. Is that asking too much?"*

"Not making any promises." Blackjacks sniffed, snuggled in, and closed his eyes.

I opened the door to the back room of the apothecary and stepped through, firmly closing the door behind me. The back of the shop looked the total opposite of the front. A musky scent of Sandalwood, Sage, and Palo Santo hit me - a collision to my senses from the gentle lavender and mint scent in the shop's front - but I breathed it in. The wood-paneled walls and floor were stained dark, with black floor-to-ceiling shelves filled with amber bottles and jars, neatly side-by-side on the shelves.

It wasn't just a stockroom for the apothecary - it was a secret storehouse of herbs, potions, and other ingredients - an exclusive supply chain for the county's practicing witch population.

Just one more secret in my cauldron.

Probably the biggest one.

I was living on the edge, risking my reputation, my livelihood - even my life - should that cauldron ever spill, pouring my secrets out. I practiced and lived alone because of it, but I liked it that way.

And I wasn't the only one.

All witches harbored secrets of their own, shared the same risk, and practiced in back rooms. We were all ancestors of generations of witches that practiced 'underground'.

The reason was simple. Practicing witchcraft was illegal.

And, in our county, to be caught and captured meant spending time in the bowels of Castle Dagon before being burned at the pyre.

I shuddered.

Draco and Lucius, Teddy's hellhounds, rose from their large dog beds to greet me as I approached the antique desk at the back of the shop. *"Mistress,"* they dipped their massive heads in acknowledgment, their deep resonant voices floating through my mind.

"Hello, boys. Thanks for watching the place." I stroked their coarse fur. Teddy had cleverly glamoured the hounds as Bull Mastiffs, which suited them perfectly and made it a hell of a lot easier to take them for walks. They settled back onto their beds. I enjoyed having them as protection for the apothecary and was grateful to have found Teddy and her hounds.

Teddy came to Castle Point on the run from a terrible relationship. Unfortunately, the jackass found her shortly after her arrival, and he, along with his gang of biker baddies, roared into town to find the poor girl and take her back to their domain.

Teddy's boyfriend was a demon.

Hence the running away part.

Because who wants a demon for a boyfriend?

Good thing I know a thing or two about demons. I expelled her badass b.f. back to hell, along with his demonic entourage.

Teddy kept the hounds.

I never asked how they got together in the first place - need-to-know basis and all that yadda-yadda - but I figured Teddy had dabbled where she shouldn't have and found herself between a rock and a hunky demon. And, since she was interested in all things magical and herbal, I hired her to work at the apothecary and started teaching her a few of my tricks.

So far, she had Glamor 101 perfected.

After filling a few orders for the underground witches, feeding the hounds, and having a quick bite to eat, I left the shop in Teddy's expert hands, gave Blackjack a quick scratch, and made my way through our quaint town toward the hospital.

The sun was slowly dipping, marking the lateness of the afternoon. Framed by the fading sun, I could see Castle Dagon, at the edge of town, high on a rocky point - Castle Point - sea churning far below. The castle's tall tower pierced the sunny sky while the bulk of the castle loomed darkly over the town below.

Blinded by the late sunlight, I placed a hand over my eyes, blocking out the view of the castle.

I wished I could block the view of that wicked place forever.

So many ancestors of the castle's namesake; the Earl of Dagon, still lived and thrived in Castle Point.

Me being one of them.

Not something I'm proud of. Namely because if it weren't for Earl Dagon, witches would be free. We wouldn't have to hide. We could live in the light.

Another of those ancestors - my mother - still lived, although not in Castle Point and not thriving. My thoughts of my mother were as dark as the shadow cast by the castle over the town. A slice of daughterly guilt tore through me, as I pictured her wasting away in a mental institution one county over.

Because her being there was kinda my fault.

The one case of possession I had yet to solve, not for a lack of trying.

I sighed. A momentous task for another day.

I arrived at the hospital, pushed open the front door, and stepped inside.

CHAPTER
FOUR

BETTY

"*Stop calling me Betty! I'm not Betty!*" I had regained use of my voice, screaming the best I could, but it came out more like the gravelly rasp of a chain smoker. I was currently shrieking at the tall Goofus Hillbilly named Jack Burke, the good Doc Holloway, and the surrounding nurses. My stupid hair, short, dark, and annoyingly curly, clung to the sweat on my face. I attempted to push the curls back, away from my forehead, but they would only spring back, landing over my eyes, which enraged me even more.

"Betty, sweetheart, I don't understand what you're saying! Of course, you're you! You're my wife, my sweet Betty. Don't you remember? We met in grade school, married after high school, and have a daughter! Oh, Betty, what's going on?" The man who calls himself my husband appeared to be beside himself with concern for me.

That really pissed me off.

"I do not know who you are, and no idea how I got here!

35

I keep telling you people that! I'm not Betty! *She's not here!"* I burst into frustrated tears. I truly didn't feel like I was this 'Betty' person they kept telling me I was, and their insistence was really pissing me off.

Why couldn't they just leave me the hell alone?

I cupped my hands over my face, pushing the stupid aggressive curls aside, and bawled for a few moments before reaching for the hand mirror the staff had given me earlier.

Maybe taking another look would jog my memory, as the 'who am I' question stared back at me.

"Oh, my God," I sniffled, talking to anyone who would listen, but mostly to myself. My hair clung to my pimpled face. The foul odor of sweat permeated the room as it popped from every large pore.

My cheeks were as red as beets from a garden.

I think I hate beets.

"This is not *me*! I'm not this middle-aged frumpy mess! And my name is not Betty! Stop calling me that!" I threw the mirror across the room. It hit the wall and shattered into a bazillion pieces.

Great.

My shitty day just got 7-years shittier.

"Hey! My wife is not frumpy!" The tall Goofus Hillbilly, Jack, defended… well, me, I suppose. "She's perfect and wonderful 'n sweet 'n kind. Whoever you are, I can agree you're not 'er!" Jack turned and stormed out of the room. The nurses and Doc Holloway followed him.

"Finally, we agree on something!" I screamed. I could hear a distinct thud from the other side of the closed door, and what sounded like someone sliding down the door to the floor.

Then I heard Hillbilly burst into tears.

CHAPTER
FIVE

ALEXANDRA

I heard a commotion coming from Betty's room, then saw Jack, Doc Holloway, and his staff storm out, shutting the door behind them. I watched as Jack leaned on the door, then slid down to the floor, hand on his face. His aura was a muddy avocado green - anguish and despair. I knelt beside him, resting a hand on his flannel-clad shoulder. "Hey Jack, it's ok, I'm sure she'll come around..." I whispered to the sobbing man. It broke my heart to see Jack - he and Betty, both well-known and well-loved people in the community - so upset.

"Th... thanks Alex, but I just don't know. She says she doesn't know me. What am I supposed to do?" Jack sobbed. I rubbed his shoulder, trying unsuccessfully to soothe him.

Doc Holloway approached, so I rose to greet him. His white coat was misbuttoned and crinkled, his name tag hanging crooked, and his hair askew. That was the Doc. Messy and rumpled, but a helluva good doctor.

"Alexandra! So good to see you!" He shook my hand. Exhaustion lined his aging face and bloodshot eyes.

"Hi Doc, good to see you too. Just coming to check on a couple of my clients. Err... Anything I can help with?" I motioned to Jack, still sobbing on the floor. The doctor scratched his head, eying me, then pulled me aside.

"Betty Burke has come out of her coma and gained full service of her voice. You can hear her screeching at the staff from almost every room in the hospital wing." The doc shook his head and rolled his eyes a little.

"That doesn't sound like the Betty Burke I know."

"I agree. Interesting case here, Alexandra. Betty claims she is not who we think she is. I think it's a memory block from the coma, but I've requested a consult from the psychiatric hospital in Lexington County. A Dr. John Middleton. He's a coma specialist. Do you know him?"

I eyed Doc Holloway cautiously. I knew Lex Psych well, as I've been visiting my mother there for the past twenty years, but didn't know Dr. Middleton. Doc Holloway was one of only two people in Castle Point - Penny being the other - that knew the story of my mother's mental illness and sequestering to Lex Psych.

He didn't know the entire story, however.

That part I kept in the cauldron.

"No, I haven't heard of him. Perhaps he's a new doctor there. When does he arrive?"

"Hopefully today." Doc touched a finger to his chin. "Say, in the meantime, would you mind having a chat with..." he nodded toward the room Betty occupied, "her?"

Predictably, Doc Holloway asked exactly what I hoped he would, and I didn't have to say a prayer to the Goddess to make it happen.

But it's best to thank the Goddess anyway, so I did.

"I'd be happy to." And I really was.

Also curious as hell to find out what was really going on.

Doc Holloway helped Jack into a chair before going to check on his other patients, giving instructions to the nurses to keep Mrs. Burke as calm as possible in the interim.When I was certain he was on his merry way, the rumpled doctor's coat flapping behind him. I entered Betty's room. I saw the Betty I knew and immediately noticed the strange color of her aura. It wasn't her usual cheerful pink and cheery, sunny yellow. It looked muddied, dull, and lifeless. I had never seen this color before, and it made me think that someone, or something, had to be attached.

I also noticed the weight loss on Betty's body and face. No longer as plump and cheerful as the 'real' Betty, the months of liquid diet via tube feeding showed. Although still holding some weight, her skin was slack, her brown curly hair scattered, dull, and limp, and currently clinging to her swollen, red face.

I gingerly stepped over what looked like parts of a shattered mirror and introduced myself. "Hello, I'm Alexandra Heale. May I come in?" I approached, cautiously.

Betty eyed me suspiciously, wiping tears and pushing at the mop of wet curls. "Wh-who are you?"

"I'm a therapist and a friend of Mr. and Mrs. Burkes."

Betty's eyes narrowed. "Well, Betty isn't here, and if I hear one more person try to tell me who I am, I'll tear this place apart."

Definitely not Betty.

The lazy "Burke drawl" she and Jack shared as southern transplants were gone. Where this person said 'isn't', Betty would've said 'ain't'. Although the voice was Betty's, her speech was more... refined.

"I know you're not Betty, so it's ok, you can relax."

A.k.a. Betty's eyes widened. "You know? How? Do you know what's happened to me?" Her voice, which was recently loud and bellowing, was now quiet as an unwelcome mouse.

"I can just tell, that's all. I've known the Burke's for a long time, and I know Betty. You're definitely not her. Question is, who are you?" I was at her bedside now and reached for her hand. She stared at my hand for a moment, then allowed me to take hers in mine.

Her energy was just as lifeless as her aura.

"I've been trying to figure that out, but it's not coming to me. I just know that I don't recognize any of these people." She waved a hand at the door. "That man that says he's my husband. I've never seen him before, and I feel like I don't belong in this body." She sighed and laid back on the pillows.

"Well, I think I can help you, but there are protocols in place. Doc Holloway has requested a Dr. Middleton from another hospital to assess you. He's a specialist." I explained.

Not Betty eyed me, indignant. "Do they think I'm crazy?" Her voice crept up on the screech meter.

"No, of course not. But Doc Holloway is being cautious, and wants the best care possible for you; hence the specialist." I smiled and stroked Not-Betty's hand, comforting her, and poured my energy into her. This didn't help shift her aura at all, however, she was still muddy.

"Anyone would be better than that bumbling fool who calls himself a doctor." Not Betty tilted her head toward the door. I assumed she meant Doc Holloway. "But how can *you* help me?" she asked, eyes wide.

"Well, let's just see what Dr. Middleton has to say first, shall we? Then perhaps we can go from there."

"When is he coming, and when can I get out of here?"

"I believe he's on his way, so hopefully they'll release you soon." I smiled, trying my best to comfort the person - or thing - inside Betty's body, while trying not to give her too much hope.

"In the meantime, what shall we call you? If you're not Betty Burke, what do you suppose your name is?"

"Gosh, I don't know... it's... fuzzy...," she replied.

"How about we try something that can help us find out? Would you be okay with that?"

"What though? What can we do?" She looked hopeful and sat up straighter.

She asked, so I assumed that meant she trusted me already.

Now was my chance.

"Just lie back, relax, and close your eyes for me. Can you do that?" Not-Betty settled back against the pillows. I turned, stepped over the broken mirror, and closed the door, but not all the way. I wanted to hear footsteps, should anyone approach. I turned back to Not-Betty, who had snuggled into the pillow, the blanket pulled up around her neck.

"Ok, you settled?" she nodded. "Good. Take a deep breath, that's it, relax... breath... relax..." Not Betty did exactly as I asked. I counted her down into a trance. After a short time, she completely relaxed, and her breathing was normal. "Open your mind, allow yourself to go back to a time before you woke up in this body. Go there, now." I snapped my fingers and gave her a moment to do as

41

instructed. "Are you there?" She nodded. "Ok, can you give me an idea of who you are? Where you are from or your name?" I watched as her eyes moved rapidly underneath her lids. She fussed a bit, her body twitching slightly. "It's ok, just relax, and tell me, what do you see?"

"There's just... blackness... I see nothing... but I don't enjoy being here. I'm scared." She fussed a bit more.

"Ok, you're doing really well, just relax. You don't have to try too hard to figure out what happened. That will come in time, and you're perfectly safe." I paused, watching her relax. "For now, though, can you get the sense of what your name might be?" I asked, hopefully.

The fussing stopped and she relaxed once again. It was several minutes before her reply came;

"I think I remember."

"Good, that's great. Can you tell me what you remember?"

"I remember my name."

A giddiness welled up inside me as I leaned in. "Go on, tell me what you remember."

"It's Sh... Sharon. Sharon M... Myles."

Amazing. "Are you sure? Settle into your body and mind, just to be sure. Are *you* Sharon Myles? Or is that someone you know?" I toyed with my earring. Tiny rumbles of anticipation spread through my stomach.

"I'm sure that she is... me."

I froze, letting go of my earring.

Not a demon. Not an entity.

The person who woke up in Betty's body wasn't Betty. She was legit.

'Sharon' was a walk-in spirit.

My stomach roiled. I'd heard of walk-ins, and even studied past cases, but never met one 'in the flesh'.

I sent a silent *'W.T.F.'* to the Goddess as I counted *Sharon* out of hypnosis. That piece of information was enough for today. The next step would be to find out who this Sharon Myles really was, and where she was from.

And why did she choose Betty?

SIX

ALEXANDRA

I discussed what I had gleaned from 'Betty' with Doc Holloway. I didn't share my methods when he asked, though. Just said I had told Betty that I believed her, and in doing so, coaxed the name "Sharon" from the patient. I didn't really have to lie to the good Doc, though. He already knew that I used hypnosis as my trusted method. Typically, I didn't share that piece of info with the medical community, however.

One risks being labeled a 'kook' when one uses out-of-the-box thinking.

I've been called a kook plenty in my life.

I try not to give people a reason to do so.

"She'd like to be called Sharon," I told the Doc. "I think, if you use that name, you'll have a calmer, more cooperative patient."

He merely chuckled and shook my hand. "Amazing work, Alexandra. Thank you for coming today. She is obviously delusional post-coma, but at least you calmed her down and that helps us immensely."

"No problem, Doc, happy to help." I smiled. "If I might add, I think it would be prudent to release Betty - I mean, Sharon - soon. She seems fine physically, so maybe getting back into the community would be the best thing for her memory?" Helping Sharon would be easier if I could see her privately, away from the prying eyes of the hospital ward.

"Well, yes, perhaps, but there's still some therapy involved to get her legs moving again. She's been bedridden for several months, so physical therapy is necessary." Doc nodded. "Let's see what Dr. Middleton's suggestions are first, shall we?" He stuffed his hands into his pockets. I guessed the good Doc had never dealt with this type of situation in his forty-year career, and was probably unsure of the path ahead.

"Thanks, Doc, if it's not too much to ask, can I follow up with... Sharon... this week? I'd like to meet Dr. Middleton too if that's ok."

"Of course, my dear, that should be fine. I appreciate your expertise and I'm really glad you came in today." Doc Holloway peered around his shoulder before dropping his head and lowering his voice. "Tell me, how is your mother doing? Have you seen her lately?"

I shook my head. "Same old, same old. She's barely responsive." I smiled. "I haven't been to see her for a couple of weeks now. Things at the shop were busy with autumn around the corner. The cold weather stock is coming in. My therapy practice has been quiet, however. Summers usually are. People are much happier when the sun is shining". I stopped and clamped my mouth shut.

I was babbling, because the subject of my mother turns me into a babbling weirdo.

Doc returned the smile. I appreciated his confidence and trusted him to keep the secrets surrounding my mother... well... secret. Saying goodbye to the Doc and staff, I headed down the corridor, stopping to give Jack Burke a hug. I'm pretty tall, almost as tall as Jack, which made the embrace quite easy. The foul odor of rotting fish, however, was a little too much. The stench filled my nostrils, and I held my breath, softly whispering a prayer to the goddess Eirene.

"Goddess Eirene, hear my prayer, embrace this man in your care, bring him peace of mind and soul, take his worries to your fold. So mote it be."

"Did you say something, Alex?" Jack broke our embrace, looking me in the eye.

"Try not to worry too much, Jack, and please, if you need someone to talk to, I'm here." Jack nodded but visibly relaxed. He looked down at his work boots, his hair was disheveled from hands running through it, and his flannel shirt was terribly rumpled and untucked from his jeans. I patted him on the arm before walking down the corridor toward the stairs.

I heard Doc Holloway talk to Jack, explaining that Betty would prefer to be called Sharon, and the staff on the ward were all instructed to do so to avoid any further distress on her part. At least until the specialist could make his own assessment and, hopefully, bring the real Betty back to herself.

I was happy to hear the good Doc had indeed listened to me.

Jack didn't take the news lightly, however, running his hands through his hair for the umpteenth time that day.

"What am I supposed to do, Doc? I can't call her by another name. She's my wife! She's my Betty!"

"I know this is difficult, Jack, but I'm going to need you to trust me for a while, at least until we have Dr. Middleton's assessment and figure out where to go from there," Doc put a hand on Jack's shoulder. "In the meantime, I think you may serve Betty better if you went home. Your being here seems to cause her a lot of anxiety right now."

Jack opened his mouth to protest, but Doc Holloway stood firm. "Just let us figure out a few things on our end, ok? I will keep you updated on her progress every damn day, I promise."

Defeated, Jack finally agreed with the good Doc and walked away. He paused for a moment, looking back toward Betty's room, then pushed past me and headed down the stairs.

CHAPTER
SEVEN

SHARON

The body I was currently living in still didn't feel like my own and had some serious defects. A little extra padding surrounded by loose flesh, for one. The pimply skin and loosey-goosey curls for another. Mammoth boobs that slid into my armpits when I lay on my back were definitely amusing. Nothing like being tickled by your own nipples.

The other thing - although there were likely many more I'd pick apart later - was near-sightedness.

I couldn't get a good look at Dr. Middleton when he walked into the room with Doc Holloway, but as he came closer, all of my senses came into focus, my sight being the first.

I gripped the gown at the place where my heart sat to calm the fluttering underneath the thin cotton. He drew me into his beautiful steel-blue eyes, set behind small wire-rimmed glasses. His shirt revealed a muscular body, despite his tall, lean frame.

Doc Holloway introduced us. "Bet... er... Sharon, this is Dr. John Middleton, from Lexington County Psychiatric Hospital. He's the doctor I mentioned to you this morning. He's here to do an assessment on you, is that okay?" he asked, ducking his head a little as if he expected me to throw sharp objects his way. I probably would have, if it wasn't for Alexandra convincing everyone to call me by 'my' name. Whether 'Sharon' was truly my name, I couldn't be completely sure, but I felt a hell of a lot more comfortable with it than I did the name 'Betty'.

The only Betty I knew was the pinup cartoon whose last name - Boop - made me think of... well... poop.

Blowing a curl off my forehead, I locked eyes with Dr. Middleton. He held out his hand for me to shake. I took it, noticing the delightful lemony fresh scent coming from his freshly washed hands. I knew all at once that I was a fan of cleanliness.

As I offered my hand for an embarrassingly limp handshake, Doc Holloway paused, eyeing the two of us before making his excuses and leaving so we could get acquainted. He rushed out the door, actually. I could swear he was visibly relieved, as was I, since I had decided that Doc Holloway was a goofy doofus.

"Hello Sharon, so nice to meet you." His voice felt like silk against my skin. "Dr. Holloway filled me in on your history here. You've been through quite an ordeal! Most of which you weren't even aware of." Still holding my hand, Dr. Middleton sat on the edge of the bed. I felt a giddiness rise from somewhere south of my stomach. Brushing another damn lock of bouncy curls from my brow, I heard myself titter;

"Yes, apparently! I hope you can help me, Doctor." The goddamned curl bounced back, right into my eye line of the handsome doc. I breathed out a huff before continuing; "The only thing that I'm sure of is that I'm not who they think I am." I absently waved my free hand toward the hospital hallway. "And, even worse, the 'Betty' they refer to me as - is married - with a child! I can't think of anything more disturbing!" I let go of the doctor's hand and clutched at my chest, which, thankfully, was quite generous. Score one for the body. I folded my arms in front of me, tucking them under the massive appendages, pushing them up over the sheets and into the doctor's view. He glanced at them quickly, then back to my eyes.

I gave the boobage a small victorious wiggle.

"Sounds distressing." He slowly shook his head, his eyes darting from my generous front back up to my eye line again.

"I just feel like that is not *me*. I'm not *Betty, married, with children*. I'm Sharon. But I don't know who that is, or how I came to be here." My eyes fell on his hands. His fingers were long and rather beautiful. His nails were trimmed and neat.

I liked that about him.

He was neat, clean, handsome, and smelled of lemons.

Not disheveled, gawky, and smelling like he bathed in a fish tank like Jack.

My eyes dropped a little further toward the lump in his jeans. I cocked my head at said lump and bit my lower lip.

"Sharon, I'm quite confident I can help you." He smiled. I liked the way he held his mouth, and for a moment, wondered what his lips tasted like.

I stifled a delighted shudder. "I hope so, doctor. The only person who's been helpful to me since waking up here is Alexandra Heale. She's a therapist in town. She helped me figure out my name so far." I smiled at the handsome doctor, noting a shadow of salt-and-pepper beard dappling his tanned complexion and the distinguished silver and grey threads running through his hair. His intoxicating eyes bore into me. I welcomed his warm look, despite the flash of heat that rode up my spine and flushed through my entire body, like an unexpected tsunami.

Great. Was I also menopausal?

I tried to imagine sitting on a bag of ice cubes, but the imaginary bag melted in seconds.

"I'm sure we can sort this incredible mystery out" Dr. Middleton smiled back. "Try not to worry. It's early yet. You've just woken up and things are bound to feel scattered and confusing." He stood up, leaving a slight rumple on the sheets where his very fine ass had been. "This week, we will see to your physical therapy and release, and set up meetings in the temporary office they've assigned me inside the hospital. We can meet every day. Would you like that, Sharon?" Dr. Middleton brushed a dark curl away from my face and another hot flash rode up and down my spine in jagged spikes.

I closed my eyes at his touch, sweat threatening to surface through my pores. "Yes," I breathed. "That would be amazing."

"Good. Then that's the plan. Hey, have you had your supper?" he asked.

I shook my head, no. I wasn't in the mood to eat earlier, but now, in the doctor's presence, I suddenly felt ravenous. My eyes flitted to his lips and perfect, straight teeth.

I hoped he felt ravenous, too.

"Then, allow me to see to your supper. If you don't mind, I'd like to join you. Perhaps get to know you a bit better?"

"Wonderful, thank you, Dr. Middleton." I replied, brushing more of the annoying curls off my face and straightening the hospital gown over my pendulous bosoms that had fallen to my waist without the aid of arms to hoist them up.

I suddenly wished I had a push-em-up bra.

Perhaps I could have Victoria Secret deliver?

Then there's the question of money, that I currently didn't have any, and how I would pay for what is likely a Triple H cup.

"Please, call me John." His eyes lit up behind his small glasses.

"Oh, thank you, John. Yes, supper would be a good idea. I'm suddenly starving!"

John excused himself, fetching the nurse to order dinner for two from the hospital cafeteria, then came back into the room, removed his sport coat, and hung it up. He settled into the chair next to my bed and loosened his tie, unbuttoning the top buttons of his shirt. I glimpsed swirly, dark grey chest hair on a muscled chest. I sighed. When he leaned forward, resting his elbows on his knees, I could see the outline of his carved shoulders and biceps pressing against the fabric of his dress shirt. My hand instinctively went up to my throat, and I swallowed what felt like a lump of lemons.

He was definitely the most handsome man I'd ever laid eyes on, at least in the eighteen hours since I'd been awake. Definitely more handsome than the man who claimed to be my husband. Jack... was that his name? I shuddered as I felt the extra generous layer of flesh on my neck. Then I looked down at my arms and wanted to sob again. I laid back against the pillows with a frustrated whomp.

"What's the matter, Sharon?" John asked.

"I'm not me," I breathed. "I don't recognize this body. It's terrifying." It really was.

"It's ok," he soothed, taking one of my hands in his. This shot rivulets of heat from my arm directly to my cheeks and pooled there. "Please don't worry about that now. You're absolutely lovely. The real you shines through. Pay no attention to anything else right now." John's voice comforted me. I looked into his beautiful blue eyes and smiled. He made me feel lighter, somehow, and more beautiful than I thought myself to be.

"Thank you, I appreciate that. I'm sure I can work with what I've got." I smiled, tucking my chin in and peering at him through curly dark bangs.

"I'm sure you will," John replied, stroking my hand. "Yes, I'm sure you will," he repeated as the supper trays arrived and we settled in for what I would later call our 'unofficial first date.'

CHAPTER
EIGHT

ALEXANDRA

J amming my long, wavy hair on top of my head and fastened the pile with a scrunchie, I settled onto the living room sofa, across from the fireplace in the house I grew up in. Not much in the house had changed since my mother's admission to the sanatorium years ago, including mom's massive collection of antique furnishings throughout the home.

The place literally looked like a museum curator furnished it.

Except for my witchy things, of course. I could take some liberties practicing my beliefs and traditions in my home, something I could never do when mom lived here.

Because my mother was as religious as they came.

A zealot, as they say.

So raising a natural-born witch was an issue for her.

For me, too, but, since I neatly sequestered mom in her long-time home at Lexington Psych, I could let my freak witch fly.

Not literally fly, of course, because then everyone in Castle Point would know - or remember, for those who had forgotten - that I'm a witch.

That would be bad.

Worse than just my mother knowing.

So, I kept the broom in the closet and instead, built an altar on the living room coffee table, facing North, of course, and adorned it with a black velvet alter cloth, feathers, candles, a small cauldron, my Mala beads, and a tarot deck.

The only other thing that had changed was the glass-walled greenhouse adjoining the kitchen. I turned it into an apothecary; a place for testing and creating potions, bath, and body products for the shop. The greenhouse windows were frosted, except for the ornate glass ceiling, which cranked opened to the sky above. No one could spy on me unless they wanted to risk life and limb climbing onto the roof. I kept the greenhouse padlocked from the kitchen side.

Beside the sofa, in front of a large bay window, was a matching chaise. On either side of the fireplace stood two floor-to-ceiling bookcases full of - you guessed it - antique books. Hidden among them was Cressy's grimoire - my grimoire now - as no one in my family handed one down to me.

Because no one in my family was a witch, so...

Adjoining the large living room is the equally large dining room, complete with an obscenely large crystal chandelier, ornate carved oak dining table, chairs, and matching china cabinet full of antique teacups, saucers, and a china set that had been in my family for generations.

Holding a notepad on my lap, I scribbled down what I knew of the Betty/Sharon case so far. Nibbling on the end of the pen between scribbles, I removed the spoon that had been stirring honey in my teacup on the side table and took a sip. Shivering, I pointed one finger at the fireplace, and instantly, a fire appeared, spreading warmth across the room.

My mom really hated when I did stuff like that, but I didn't care. Or at least, tried not to. If I didn't want to feel the paddle on my backside, I kept the magic to myself, honing my craft in my room. Or at Cressy's place, which I did when mom was at her bridge parties and bingo games.

Blackjack snuggled up on the cat bed in front of the hearth, keeping warm. "This one's a puzzler, Blackjack." The cat turned his head toward me and closed his eyes, disinterested. "I'm going to need help on this one." Blackjack mewed.

"*Surely you don't expect* me *to assist.*" I heard Blackjack's silky voice flow through my mind.

"Well, your help would be nice, yes, but I'm thinking humans would be more helpful, so you're off the hook - for now."

"*Goodie.*" Blackjack flipped onto his back and snuggled in for his umpteenth nap of the day.

Inspiration struck, and I suddenly knew what I had to do. Scribbling Sharon's full name, *'Sharon Myles'* on my notepad, I reached for my cell phone. Punching the name into Google, I quickly realized my mistake. Thousands of hits for a 'Sharon Myles' appeared.

Sighing, I retyped the name with 'deceased, State of Maine' behind it. This time, hundreds of hits appeared. Scrolling aimlessly through the pictures; I realized the futility of my efforts, as I did not know what this Sharon Myles actually looked like when she was alive.

Certainly nothing like Betty Burke.

"Of course." Chiding myself, I scribbled a note; *'Ask Sharon (under Hypnosis), where she's from'* then another note; *'Talk to Sheriff Blake'*. I ran my fingers up and down my forehead, attempting to push what-could-go-wrong thoughts from my mind.

I had one too many run-ins with the law, so asking for help from someone in uniform wasn't high on my list of good times. Besides, I had never been one of Blake's favorite people; I was sure of that.

He wasn't a favorite of mine, either.

The big, handsome football jock loved playing practical jokes on sad, gangly little 'weirdos' like me in high school.

My burgeoning abilities had gotten me into trouble more times than I cared to admit, but were difficult to keep in check where bullies like Blake were concerned.

One particularly nasty incident landed me in Juvie.

And an entire football team in the hospital.

If it weren't for Cressy and his mentoring, I would have ended up in Juvie way more often - or worse - the dungeon of Castle Dagon. And, if it weren't for his magical powers, the whole town would still remember the aforementioned cataclysmic event that landed me in the hands of the law.

Then I wouldn't have the reputation, and successful business I have today.

No, likely they'd have hung and burned me on the Castle Dagon pyre for being a witch.

For being...me.

Owing a lot to my mentor was the understatement of the century, but I took comfort knowing that I would have the chance to repay him in the afterlife.

My fingers automatically reached for the dangling vial of Cressy's ashes hanging from my ear.

For now, I kept him close.

I stretched, tossing the notepad on the couch beside me. Grabbing my now empty teacup, I wandered down the hallway to the kitchen, passing the stairs on the way. Eyeing the little door leading to a storage space under the stairs - now permanently nailed shut- I shuddered.

I had spent way too many hours in there as a child, against my will, sad and alone, my backside aching and outlined by whatever implement mom had handy.

Punishment for being 'a child of the devil.'

Punishment for being me.

When my mother went away, I nailed the little door shut, vowing never to enter any place of darkness again.

The hairs on the back of my neck told me I was about to break my vow.

CHAPTER
NINE

ALEXANDRA

Early the next morning, I went to the hospital before Dr. Holloway could do his rounds, or Dr. Middleton arrived at Sharon's bedside. Night nurses Nora and Penny were just switching shifts with the day staff when I arrived. After a quick word with Penny, I shuffled into Sharon's room and closed the door. Penny noted a DND on Sharon's room, giving us uninterrupted time.

"Hello, Alexandra. Lovely to see you today," Sharon chirped as I stepped into the room. My eyes widened. I had been expecting the same crabby Sharon I had left the day before, not this chipper, happy gal before me.

Was Betty back?

"Lovely to see you too, Sharon. You seem better today! How are you feeling?"

"Oh, just wonderful! Things seem so much brighter today." Sharon smiled. "The lovely Dr. Middleton spent the evening chatting with me last night. He's so great!"

Well, alright then.

I knew two things.

Sharon was still Sharon since she hadn't corrected me when I said Sharon's name. And this Doctor Middleton sounded like a super swell dude.

Maybe the spectacular doctor Middleton could figure out what the hell was going on with Betty/Sharon so I could go home and grab a nap.

But I had a feeling this entire case was a few levels below his pay grade.

Witchy-poo to the rescue.

I plastered my best smile. "Oh, I'm really pleased. I'm sure he will help you figure things out." I took a seat on the bed beside Sharon and patted her hand. "Any luck with remembering who you are?" I was ooey-gooey, gushing over this woman, trying to match her tone and expression. I needed her to be open and responsive if I was going to get any more answers from her. A calm Sharon was my way 'in' to figuring out who she really was and where she'd come from.

And what she did with Betty Burke.

"No, nothing yet. Dr. Middleton - John - he asked me to call him by his name - says my memories should come back with time." Sharon stated.

She seemed pretty sure of herself and her trust in Superstar 'John'.

"Oh, I'm sure he's right. Although... I think we may come up with some answers a little sooner than later if you're willing to try?"

Sharon fussed with her gown. "Yes, that would be amazing! What did you have in mind?"

"Remember yesterday when I asked you to just relax and let your name come to you?" Sharon nodded her head.

"Well, I'd like to try that again, only this time, we'll focus on where you're from. Could we do that?"

Sharon's eyes grew wider, then she glanced toward the closed door. "Um, I guess it's ok?"

"I'm sure Dr. Middleton wouldn't object if that's what you're wondering. If we come up with something, you could share it with him, or you can just keep this between us. Your decision." Although I would prefer Sharon to keep it to herself, I will face the potential backlash later for using 'alternative methods.'

Better to ask forgiveness than permission in this case.

"Ok, let's try." Sharon settled back into the pillows, ready for the next step. I closed the door, dimmed the lights, and pulled the curtains, blocking the early autumn sun.

I grabbed my notes from my bag and settled into the chair beside the bed. Then I took Sharon through the breathing exercises I had the day before. She was quick to settle.

Perfect.

"Ok Sharon, now I'm going to count from five down to one, and when I say 'one', you'll be completely relaxed. Five, four, three, two, one, and now." Sharon dropped into full hypnosis with the snap of my fingers. I glanced at my notes and started; "Sharon, I'd like you to remember the time in your life just before you woke up in this body, alright? Three, two one - now!" Snapping my fingers again, Sharon sucked in a breath. Her face screwed into a grimace and tears sprung from her eyes.

"Sharon, it's ok, you're ok, you're perfectly safe. Relax, just relax..." I soothed her back to a restful state. "What happened to you just then? Can you tell me?"

She wet her lips and spoke softly, haltingly. "I... don't

know… exactly. Everything is so… dark, and I just felt pain. So much pain." Her hands fluttered to her chest, and she gasped. "I don't want to be here!"

"It's ok Sharon, just relax, just let that go, there's no pain, you're safe. Can you move back in time further now, please, before the darkness? Go back to a time in your life that was happy. Can you do that?"

Sharon shifted, then smiled. A few moments later she said. "Okay. I'm there."

"Great, that's wonderful Sharon, you're doing great. Can you tell me what you see?"

"I'm at a lake… having a picnic. I think I'm with some-one… but I can't make out… who. I can just see… the lake, and… there's a picnic basket in front of me."

"That's amazing Sharon, you're doing really, really well. Stay there for a while longer and enjoy yourself." After a few minutes, I continued; "Do you know where you are?" Sharon lay still for a moment, then shook her head, no. "Do you see any signs posts at the lake or a newspaper on the blanket? Look all around you and tell me what you see."

Her eyes flickered and moved beneath her lids, her head moving from side to side. "I don't see any signs. Just… something in the water."

"What do you see in the water, Sharon? Can you tell me?" My heart beat out of my chest.

"It looks like… it's a… a giant turtle."

"A turtle? An actual turtle, like a sea turtle?" I needed better details if I was going to get any answers.

"No, it's not a real turtle, but… it's a bit of land… like a little island… shaped… like a turtle."

Well, that was plenty clear.

And may have to do, for now.

"Okay Sharon, that's really amazing. Great job. Just

relax now and see if you can go to another place. Maybe this time it's your home. Can you do that now?"

"I can't see anything. It's just kind of dark. Hazy. I'm tired." Sharon, still in a trance, exhaled.

"Ok Sharon, that's great. You did really well today. I'm going to count from one to five, and when I say five, you'll be fully awake, relaxed, and feeling great. Ready? One... two... three, coming back slowly... four... feeling your fingers and toes, and five, fully awake and refreshed." Sharon yawned and stretched. Her eyes fluttered open.

"How'd I do?" she asked.

"You did great, Sharon. Do you remember anything from this session?"

"No, not a thing. Did I come up with any answers?" Sharon looked hopeful, sitting up on the bed.

I paused, eying Sharon, willing my face to remain impassive.

Total hypnotic amnesia.

It didn't happen to many patients, only one in a large handful, but it *could* happen, and apparently, it had. Struggling to decide whether to tell Sharon what she had remembered, I decided against it. If I did, Sharon would tell Dr. Middleton. If Dr. Middleton didn't agree with my methods, which most doctors did not, then that might end any future sessions. That would also end any chances I had of finding out *why* Sharon's *spirit walked into* Betty Burke, and I couldn't take that chance, not yet.

"No, nothing today, but that's ok, I'm sure it will come with time."

Sharon frowned.

"Darn. Oh well, I'm sure you're right. Maybe Dr. Middleton - John - will pry it out of me." She smiled, shyly, peeking out from under curly bangs.

"I'm sure he's going to give it his best try. Maybe, for now, at least, we just keep this session between us? I'd hate for the good doctor to think I was stepping on his toes. After all, he's the doc!" Instincts told me to hold on to every piece of info I could find, for now.

A knock on the door made me jump. Dr. Middleton stepped into the room. I saw his aura enter before he did. It was shimmery and silver, with a touch of... red.

So strange. I did not know what that meant.

Speak of the devil and he enters?

Casanova returns to the body of the amazing Dr. John?

I suppressed a giggle.

"Well, hello ladies, I hope I'm not interrupting something?" Dr. Middleton's eyes narrowed when he saw me, so I returned the look. Just then, the hairs on my neck did a little dance, my witchy senses tingling. Dr. Middleton's aura suddenly lightened and became a happy shade of blue.

That was better, but still - something about the handsome Dr. M was a little weird.

Maybe Cressy would have some input.

I would have to summon him later if there was time.

"No interruption, John. This is Alexandra Heale. She's a therapist. She came to see me yesterday and was paying another visit." Smiling, Sharon straightened and brushed the curls away from her face, clearly excited to see the doctor again. I shot a glance in Sharon's direction. She shot one back at me, then winked.

Good, she'll keep our secret.

I noticed the exchange of glances between the doctor and Sharon and the shift in Sharon's aura. It was still muddy, but the undertone had changed to a blush-happy rose.

Sharon was smitten!

I couldn't really blame her, however. Dr. John was very good-looking, to be sure. Just over middle age - I guessed around 45 - fit and handsome. Older than the body Sharon was currently inhabiting, but neither of them seemed to notice, or care.

"Pleasure to meet you, Alexandra." Dr. Middleton extended his hand. I shook it then paused for a moment, hoping to get a read on his energy, but... nothing. I scribbled a mental note to ask Penny if she had any hits off the doctor when she met him yesterday.

"Pleasure to meet you too, Doctor." I smiled.

"Please, call me John." he smiled back. Sharon cleared her throat, so I pulled my hand away.

"I understand you're from the Lexington County Psychiatric Hospital. I thought I knew all the doctors there, but I don't recall seeing your name on the roster. Ever." I couldn't help it. Something about him made my insides cringe.

"Oh... Um... I'm not from Lexington, actually," John stammered. "I'm a coma specialist, originally from San Antonio, and was just assisting at Lexington when I got Dr. Holloway's call."

"Oh, I see. Well, that explains it then." I studied his features, trying to determine if he was hiding anything or not. Nothing seemed out of the ordinary.

I sighed.

Too much for one morning, and I had a missing spirit to find.

"Well, I better let you two get down to... business." I grabbed my bag and moved toward the door.

"Actually," Dr. Middleton said, "could I speak with you for a moment, Miss Heale?"

"Certainly." I waved at Sharon and followed John into the corridor, closing the door behind me.

"What can I help with?"

"You can stay away from my client if you wouldn't mind." Dr. Middleton's lips formed a thin line. He stood tall, crossing his arms in front of him.

Huh. Interesting.

Maybe my witchy sense was right after all.

"I'm sorry I can't do that." I shook my head and stood my ground.. Dr. Middleton's brows shot up. "I can assure you, I'm only here to support Betty - er - Sharon, Dr. Middleton. The Burkes are old friends, and I want to help in any way I can."

The Doc eyed me briefly.

"Fine. But just remember that I am the doctor in charge of her case. Don't interfere." He pushed past me, opened the door to Sharon's room, and closed it firmly behind him.

So, Doc M didn't like me on his turf.

I wasn't too happy with him on mine, so we were even.

I made another mental note to call Lexington County later and enquire about Dr. Middleton, maybe see if I could get a little more background information on him. I shook off the weird vibe emanating from Sharon's room. I walked to the nurse's station, hoping to see Penny and ask if she had any impressions from the doctor, but there was no sign of her copper-colored head. The day shift had taken over, and Penny would be home by now, likely sleeping.

I'll have to deal with all of that later. Right now, I need to go see Blake.

Scratch that. Large coffee. Then Blake.

CHAPTER
TEN

ALEXANDRA

After the session with Sharon, I stood in my favorite cafe, waiting for my complicated coffee order (caramel macchiato, double shot, extra almond foam, extra caramel - the way the Goddess intended). I pulled out my phone and did a few Google searches, looking for a lake or body of water called 'turtle island.' I had several hits. It seemed there were hundreds of lakes spanning near and far outside Dagon County - with small islands named after turtles, strangely enough - but none of which I could attach 'Death of Sharon Myles' to.

Grudgingly I admitted, my only other option was a visit to the Sheriff's department and talk to Deputy Sheriff Blake Sheraton.

I stopped outside the Castle Point Sheriff's Department and took a deep sip of my special coffee. Creamy almond foam hit my tongue first, followed by the dark, rich liquid of life. The cells of my body jolted awake. I took a deep breath and walked inside.

A wave of nausea washed over me, so I reached for the wall and breathed deeply. Memories from my teens slid through my mind. The teasing and taunting. Being called 'weirdo', 'gangly' or 'tarantula' - because of my long-hair and gangliness - real original - the 'sticks and stone's' situation gone horribly wrong. Then, feeling cold steel handcuffs on my wrists; being dragged into the Sheriff's office by a couple of burly officers, and accused of something that was out of my control. The topper on my poop cake was when they kicked me through the court system and straight into juvie.

It was a terrifying time.

Gathering strength, I walked to the bulletin board, stopping to flip through the 'wanted' and 'missing' posters. Nobody that I knew was 'wanted' or 'missing'.

That was a good thing.

Then I looked up at the framed pictures above the bulletin board. There were two photos in frames; one of the Mayor, Jeffrey Deibert, the second of the Sheriff, Gordon Roberts.

There was a third picture hanging above the two. A painting, framed with an antique, gold gilded frame. The Earl Dagon, Castle Point's founder and sole resident of Castle Dagon. The Earl died a few hundred years earlier, his castle now a museum.

A shrine to an evil asshole.

I shuddered. Knowing I'm an ancestor of the vile Earl made my skin crawl. I shook off the urge to head home and take a hot shower before approaching the reception desk.

Blakes's office was across the bullpen beside Sheriff Robert's. His door was slightly ajar, only his hands were visible. He was pouring a cup of coffee from the carafe on his desk and rifling through some papers. It had been a while since I'd seen or spoken to 'Blake the Great', someone that, until now, I crossed the street to avoid.

Unfortunately, or maybe fortunately, he was the only person in the Sheriff's department that I knew, and I really needed help from an authority with a database.

Taking a deep breath, I asked the hefty desk lieutenant if I could see Deputy Sheriff Sheraton. The lieutenant, barely glancing up from his desk, asked for my name and the nature of my visit.

"I'm here to report a murder. I think." I played with the tiny vial of ashes.

The lieutenant looked up, frowning.

"A murder? In Castle Point?" His generous jowls warbled at the question.

"No, not exactly. Look, I really just need to see Blake the Gre - er - Chief Deputy Sheraton. I can explain everything to him."

The lieutenant clasped his fingers across his generous belly, studying me for a moment. My toes tingled, so I shifted from one foot to another. Finally, he reached for the phone and punched Blake's extension. I watched Blake's hands pick up the earpiece.

"There's a Miss Alexandra Heale to see you, sir."

Blake hung up the phone and stepped out of his office. He looked across the bullpen, over desks full of tan-clan officers with shiny gold badges, and locked eyes with me.

A tickle of heat burned behind my eyes, then burst through my skull.

His features hadn't changed since his glory days as the Castle Point Quarterback Superstar. He was still annoyingly handsome, his dark, tousled hair worn slightly longer than the standard-issue haircuts of his deputies, and framed his chiseled features perfectly. It was clear by the solid V shape of his upper body he spent a lot of time in the protein isle at the grocery store.

His eyes went from open to hooded in an instant. He set his jaw and pulled himself up to his full height.

Crap.

He remembered me.

All at once, I felt very young and tiny.

I forced the younger 'me' - the 'weirdo', as Blake used to call me - back into hiding.

Nodding his head toward the desk lieutenant, he granted me entry into the bullpen. Keyboards clacked, phones rang. Several of the officers stopped what they were doing and looked up, smiling, as I walked by. I regretted adding the extra shot of espresso to my coffee. My nerves frayed in minute layers. My knees wobbled. I didn't trust my feet not to trip over the smallest piece of lint on the floor.

Blake filled the doorframe; a classic Blake the Great intimidation tactic. His eyes, still hooded, peered at me as I approached. His mouth set in a firm line. I could smell his cologne, 'Brut' if I could hazard a guess. The spicy lavender and amber fragrance wafted over me and I nearly tripped.

Keep it together, woman.

Remember, he's not a hot cop. He's an asshole who made your life miserable.

He motioned for me to step inside and closed the door behind me.

"Alexandra Heale. It's been a long time. You look great." I stopped short and looked him in the eyes, one eyebrow crooked.

A compliment? I mean, I know I didn't look like the geeky little 'weirdo' he teased as a kid, but...

"Thanks," I said, pursing my lips, biting back the urge to

spit out the childhood taunts that he spewed at me when he was just a young bully. I took a deep breath.

Mother Goddess, release the past, allow forgiveness, and make it last, I chanted over and over in my mind. Reaching for my earring, I took the seat offered.

"What can I help you with today?" he asked.

I paused at the question. Since I could barely walk toward the man, what made me think I could ask for his help now? I huffed out the breath I'd been holding.

Crazy is as crazy does.

He already thinks I'm feasting from the well of weirdness, so I may as well continue. My mouth went dry, then I blurted, "I think there's been a murder, well, a death at least, and I need help to figure out the where, and then I can figure out the why." Words came out in a hurried blast.

Blake's eyebrows shot up.

"You *think* there's been a murder? You don't know for sure? Do you at least know *who* was murdered?" He leaned forward in his chair. His biceps flexed, the short sleeves of his uniform tightening around them.

I shifted, uncrossing and crossing my legs.

Had he grown more biceps since last I saw him?

Mind you, I avoided him like vampires avoid sunlight, so maybe I just didn't notice.

Blake leaned closer, his biceps flexing.

My cheeks burned.

Yep - he definitely grew more... granite. I took a large swig of my coffee, swallowed, and tried to ignore the burn of extra-hot coffee down my throat. "Well... I'm assuming there's been a murder. And I have a name. I just can't really tell you how I know, or how I got the information. It's a client confidentiality type of thing." Words tumbled out of me.

Blake pressed on. "I thought that if a client murdered someone and told their therapist about it, the therapist is legally obligated to share that information with authorities?" Blake scratched the side of his head, ruffling his dark hair. I caught the scent of his shampoo and breathed deeply.

Dammit.

It wasn't just the lavender undertones of his cologne that reached my senses earlier. The unmistakable scent of lavender permeated the air.

He was using a shampoo from my shop!

The one I crafted personally!

I didn't even know he was a customer. I made a mental note to ask Teddy what else he bought later.

With lavender and mint tickling my brain, I blurted; "My client didn't murder anyone. She was murdered."

Shit.

"Excuse me?" Blake sat back in his chair, eyebrows practically raised to his hairline. "What the hell are you talking about?"

Realizing my mistake, I backpedaled frantically.

"What I meant to say is... my client *knows* of someone who *may* or *may not have* been murdered."

This was a disaster.

No way would he be willing to help me now.

I sat, my fingers flicking at my earring and waiting for the childhood taunts to escape Blake's soft, full lips.

Blake sat back, hands clasped, resting against his flat belly, contemplating me. The fabric pulled taut across his chest and I pulled at my earring again, a little too hard. I winced.

"Ok, I'll bite," he said, sitting up. "Who is the supposed murder victim?" He grabbed a notepad and pencil, already scribbling. I relaxed, ever so slightly, and took a sip of my coffee, careful not to take another scalding gulp.

"Sharon Myles. All I know is, she lives near a lake with a small island in the middle that looks a lot like a turtle. Turtle Island." *Mother Goddess, help me.*

Maybe I am nutso bananas.

I murmured a quick incantation; *'Goddess good, goddess great, please make this man cooperate. So mote it be.'*

Blake's hand paused briefly mid-scribble. He shot me a glance, then scribbled something onto the notepad. "And do you know *how* she was allegedly murdered?" He didn't look up from the pad.

"I'm not actually sure that she was. I just know she's dead." I wasn't about to share any of the Sharon/Betty details with Blake the Great, however. Why give him even more reason to think I'm wacko?

"Ok, so let me be sure I have this right. You know someone named Sharon Myles - from a place called or near a Turtle Island - is dead, you don't know how, but you have to find out, in order to help your client?"

That actually made sense, and Blake appeared to be genuinely interested.

Thank you, Goddess. "Yes, that's it exactly."

"Ok, give me a few minutes to run this through the database. Do you need a refill?" Blake nodded toward my coffee.

"No, I'm good, thanks, unless you have an espresso machine, almond milk, and caramel sauce?"

Blake shook his head. "None of the above, I'm afraid. We drink it strong and black here, the way God intended." He chuckled."The last guy who brought a fru-fru coffee into this office was assigned a permanent meter maid position - kidding!" He replied, seeing my horrified expression.

Blake left his office, the scent of his cologne and shampoo lingering. I took a deep breath and watched his ass as he walked toward the bullpen. I whistled under my breath. He had lost none of the football hero body, that was for damn sure.

Gained more of it, actually.

Too bad. Once an asshole, always an asshole, in my experience. Which, to be fair, wasn't much. It was just easier to keep men at broomstick length, so the affairs I had were few, and none of them great.

I could have created a potion for that, I supposed, but there were always more important things to take care of.

My love life was not one of them.

While Blake and his deputy sifted through the database, I took a better look around the office. High school football trophies, team pictures, and pictures of Blake with Mayor Deibert and Sheriff Roberts adorned the walls.

No pictures of a wife, family, or girlfriend, just football and work.

Interesting.

I had Blake pegged as the epitome of 'ladies' man' and figured that, by now, he'd be married to the prom queen, keeping her barefoot and pregnant, popping out enough little football stars to create an entire team. In school, he always seemed to have a cheerleader attached to him. I witnessed many catfights between cheerleaders over the jock, which I always thought was incredibly pathetic. How a gaggle of girls could get all up in each other's faces over an incredibly handsome bully was beyond me.

Rolling my eyes, I turned toward the bullpen. Blake and a lieutenant were crouched over a computer, pointing at the screen, talking, and taking notes. It was several more minutes before Blake came back into his office, shutting the door behind him. He threw his notepad on the desk and flopped into his seat.

"It's a good thing you came in for help today, Alexandra. Pretty sure you wouldn't have been able to figure this one out on your own."

Ahh, there he is.

That's the arrogant asshole I grew up knowing and hating.

Lips pursed, arms folded across my chest, I asked. "And why is that, exactly?" I mean, I can be pretty resourceful and Google the heck out of something like a rampant dog with the proverbial bone if I had the time.

Blake tossed the notepad in my direction. "You mentioned that this Sharon Myles is from Turtle Island, but that's wrong." I reached for my earring. "She's from Turtle Cove, in Connecticut. And she was murdered, apparently by her husband, Mitch Myles."

I stared blankly at the scribbles on the notepad. Mitch Myles, age twenty-eight, serving life in prison for the murder of his wife, Sharon. His address of residence for the past two years was the Seaside Sanatorium in Waterford, Connecticut.

Well, give me a pointy hat and call me a witch.

Sharon really existed.

And she had been murdered.

Nausea swirled through my belly. "He pled insanity?" I looked up.

Blake shook his head. "He didn't have to. When the authorities responded to the neighbor's 911 call, they found Mitch, blood all over his hands, holding a knife, hunched beside his wife's body. He was unresponsive, other than chanting that he killed his wife."

Stunned, I sat back in the chair. "Are there any news

articles with pictures?" If I could show the 'Sharon Myles' - who I was now certain beyond a doubt was a walk-in spirit - a picture of herself, maybe she could unravel her memories and find out more.

Blake tapped at the keyboard. "There is a news article about the murder and subsequent imprisonment of Mitch Myles, and a picture of the couple together. Looks like he stabbed Sharon multiple times, with the butcher knife the couple had received as a wedding present a few years before." Blake skimmed over the article and then turned the monitor toward me.

I leaned over - ignoring the urge to bury my nose in his hair and smell the lavender mint - and studied the picture of the couple. Sharon Myles was a very good-looking lady. Shoulder-length straight blonde hair, blue eyes, and a dazzling smile. In the photograph, Mitch Myles, a blonde-haired, blue-eyed match to his wife, gazed at Sharon with total devotion and love plastered on his face. They made a beautiful couple, and, in this picture from their wedding, looked incredibly happy.

The caption under the picture read, 'Mitch and Sharon Myles, high school sweethearts and prom king and queen.' They were likely the envy of all their friends. What provoked Mitch to murder his beloved? Or,, maybe the better question was, who?

Blake scrolled to a second picture of Sharon, alone. Her smile flaunted dazzling, perfectly straight teeth, and her blue eyes sparkled.

"The article says nothing about a history of instability or mental illness in Mitch or his family," I said.

Blake shrugged. "Doesn't mean it wasn't there. There are a ridiculous amount of cases just like this all over the country. The husband, wife, or one kid just snaps and goes on a rampage."

I nodded, but wasn't convinced. "Could you print those pictures for me? The article too, maybe?"

Blake obliged, handing the papers over.

"What are you going to do now for your client?"

I considered the question before answering.

"Book a flight to Waterford, Connecticut."

CHAPTER
ELEVEN

BLAKE

I sat for a long while after watching Alexandra leave my office.

I sat - because I couldn't exactly stand up.

Blood had basically rushed from all points in my body into my crotch the moment I locked eyes with her across the bullpen.

My mind and body were a little confused. I mean, I hadn't seen Alexandra Heale in years, except for a few times crossing the street, but something about her made my body react in ways it hadn't in a long time.

I knew she was a local therapist and owned the cute bath and body shop where I buy my shampoo. I also knew we had gone to school together, but I couldn't remember much about her. I guess we had little to do with each other back then.

Shame really, she's a damn gorgeous woman, so I'm sure she must have been a fine-looking teenager, too. I Googled images of our high-school annual. After a little searching through pages and pages of scanned images, I found her. The picture, a little dark and fuzzy, was definitely Alexandra. Same black hair, but pulled back, away from her face. No smile, her eyes dark. Beside the picture, where normally there was a "Most likely to..." there was nothing but blank space.

Weird.

Then, it hit me.

She was the Castle Point High resident 'weirdo'.

And I made her life shit-tastic.

I sat back hard in my chair. The blood that had previously hovered in my groin plunged to my stomach. I wanted to hurl. I knew I had been an asshole through high school, but to Alexandra, I was unspeakably awful.

Being the all-star football player every year wasn't exactly my doing. I had a lot of pressure to be a high achiever from my dad, a lawyer, and the richest man in Castle Point. If I didn't score, didn't win, didn't make the touchdown, or have perfect grades, then dad made my life a living hell.

So, I took out my frustrations on people who didn't deserve it.

Alexandra was one of them.

After my parent's murder, I shed my asshole skin. I became a cop because I wanted to protect people from bullies like me - and avenge my mom and dad. If there was one thing my dad and I agreed on, it was that we should hold lawbreakers accountable for their crimes, and the law is the backbone of our community.

I also made amends to the people I'd hurt. It took a while, but eventually, I apologized to a hell-of-a-lot of people for the bully I was and became the man I knew my father would have - mostly - liked.

Somehow, I'd missed making amends to Alexandra.

I knew I was awful to her, but I also don't really remember much about her. She was pretty quiet growing up, and not typically on my radar - unless I needed someone to... well, abuse, for lack of a better word. I winced, rubbing my forehead.

There was something else.

I wracked my brain, trying to put a pin on the memory, but it sped further away from me the harder I tried. What the hell was it? I closed my eyes, trying to conjure it from the dark corners of my mind, but all I could see was Alexandra, sitting across from me in my office. Her hair, flowing around her, the scent of her, fresh, with an undercurrent of roses? Her lips were incredibly full, even when she pursed them together. It made me want to reach out and stroke my thumb...

My eyes blew open, and I sat up straight.

The blood rushed to my groin again.

Stop, you idiot.

She wouldn't want anything to do with you, not after the way you treated her in high school.

But then again... *she* came to *me* for help.

Maybe I could help her find closure for her client if that's what this was all about.

Maybe I could make amends.

I have a few extra days off stored up, so... I could help!

Would she want me to help?

Probably not.

I clicked on the article I'd printed off for her, then clasped my hands behind my head and leaned back in my chair. I thought about Alexandra going to the sanatorium and meeting Mitch Myles on her own. A creepy, sick feeling raked my belly. I didn't like the idea of that, not at all. Mitch

Myles was, and likely still is, a very dangerous criminal, living in a sanatorium for the criminally insane.

And what about the sanatorium? I'd bet my highest-scoring football trophy that only psychiatrists, and perhaps a handful of family members, would be allowed visitation.

Alexandra was neither.

Neither was I, but... I have the law on my side.

I Googled Seaside Sanatorium and found a number. I should check - before I presume - that they wouldn't grant Alexandra access. *Yeah, good idea.* I dialed the number. A kind of jangled ringing greeted me on the other end. The ringing seemed to get louder the longer it rang. Nobody answered. I checked my watch. Mid-day and nobody is answering the phone? I hung up. Probably just busy.

I remembered that one of my deputies had a regular rotation to escort lawyers to Lexington Psych. It wasn't a hospital for the criminally insane, but they held a few crim-inals there - short-term - for court assessment. I stood up and poked my head out into the Bullpen.

"Hey, Paul. You head up to Lex Psych, right? Escorting legal for one prisoner there?"

Paul's head snapped up. "Yeah, boss. He's a crazy som'bitch and highly dangerous. Not my favorite gig, but... going there again this week. Why? You wanna come?" Paul chuckled, sliding his stetson back on his head.

"Nah, thanks. What's the protocol for visitation?"

"Ah, only his lawyer and doc are allowed to see him. Family too, but I hear they don't come 'round. Too scared of him, I'd guess." Paul took his hat off and tossed it on his desk, grabbed his coffee, he took a swig.

"Paperwork?"

"Yeah, I have to file with every visit. I got a package here, though, if you want it?"

"Yeah, that might help, thanks."

"Why you askin', boss? You heading to Lex Psych?"

"Ah, no, a little further south. Thanks." I closed my door and sat back in my chair, took another look at the article, and convinced myself that Alexandra Heale didn't stand a chance of seeing Mr. Myles at all.

Not without my help.

I picked up the phone and called Jimmy at our small local airport.

I needed to find out when the next flight to Waterford would be, and make sure I was on it.

CHAPTER
TWELVE

ALEXANDRA

I raced out of the Sheriff's department and turned toward the hospital, the articles and pictures of Sharon Myles in hand. The flushed heat through my body, provoked by my encounter with Blake, had finally run its course.

I wanted to punish my stupid blood supply and stupid hormones for wreaking stupid havoc on me.

Sacrilege, really, because I'd sworn to hate Blake Sheraton for all eternity.

Didn't my body know that?

I turned my thoughts from Blake to the pictures I held in my hand. After a few strides, I came to a dead stop. The pedestrian behind almost collided with me.

"Hey!"

"Sorry!" I stepped aside, needing to think. If I visited Sharon and show her the evidence so far, I would certainly shock the ever-living crap out of her.

Devastating her, even.

That is - if it didn't force her memories to the forefront. There was also the risk of running into Dr. Middleton and being evicted from the hospital. He would likely get his old-man knickers in a twist if he saw me.

The thought of Dr. Middleton's knickers made me giggle.

But, no. I couldn't interfere - not right now, anyway. Not while Sharon was under the hospital roof - it was too risky - and why upset Sharon until I knew more?

That settled it. I *have to* go see Mitch, and hopefully get more information on why he killed Sharon, so I have more to work with.

Turning toward my office, I rushed in, greeted by my receptionist, Maggy.

"I thought you said you weren't coming in today? I moved all of your appointments already!"

"I'm not really here. I just have a few calls to make. Thank you for moving my schedule. Could you also move the rest of the week? I have a feeling I'll be busy."

"Ok, sure. I'll start booking tentatively for next week, then. Let me know if anything changes!"

"Will do!" I waved, stepped into my office, and closed the door. Tossing my jacket onto the lounge, I sat at my desk and tapped on the keyboard, waking the computer. I did a search for Seaside Sanitarium and jotted down the number.

Taking a deep breath, I considered summoning Cressy before proceeding, but summoning the dead would take a little too much time, and - although I felt like I could use some help - I would be better off digging a little deeper on my own before disturbing Cressy's peace.

First, I had a couple of phone calls to make. One to Penny, then Lexington Psych, then the Sanatorium where

Mitch Myles currently lived. I selected Penny's number from the list of recent calls on my cell phone. After a couple of rings, a sleepy Penny picked up.

"...Ello?"

"Shit, sorry Pen, I forgot you'd still be asleep. You're on night shift this week."

"S'okay. What's up?"

"Well, first, I was wondering - when you met Dr. Middleton, did anything come up?"

"Um. Hmm. Well, to be honest, I kind of avoided touching him. It was a busy evening, and I didn't have the time or energy to get a reading, sorry."

"No, it's ok, I totally understand."

"Why? Did *you* get something weird from him? What's his aura like?" Penny perked up.

"Weird. At first. That's why I'm asking. I'm sure it's nothing. Chalk it up to my imagination going wild, as usual."

"Hmm. If I see him later today, I'll make a point of checking."

"Ok, great, let me know. Also, could you look after Blackjack for a couple of days? I..uh..have some digging to do in Sharon's case. I'll be away."

"Oh! Sure, of course. Did you find out who she is? Where are you going? Was I right? She's not Betty, is she?" Penny's excitement overtook her sleepiness. She wouldn't be going back to sleep after this call, for sure. I laughed.

"Yes, I think you're on to something. I found out a little more when I met with her today, but I can't go over that right now. I'm going to talk to someone who may know something more about Sharon Myles." After arranging Blackjack's care, we said goodbye.

My next call was to the Lexington County Sanatorium and connected with the receptionist.

"Hi Rachel, it's Alexandra Heale."

"Oh hi, Miss Heale. Did you want to talk to Dr. Joseph?" Rachel asked, referring to the doctor in charge of my mother, Belinda Heale.

"No, that's ok. I'm actually calling to ask about Dr. John Middleton. Apparently, he's on visitation from San Antonio. Do you know him?" I played with my earring.

"Yes, well, no. I mean, he's not one of our doctors. He was here briefly to consult on another case when he was called away. Did you need to speak to him? I don't know his whereabouts, but I do have his contact info if that helps?"

"Do you know what hospital he came from in San Antonio?"

"No, I'm afraid I don't. I just know Dr. James hired him to consult. He was barely here a day when he got called away. Do you want me to find out?"

"No, that's ok. If I need the info, I'll let you know. Thanks for your help." We said our goodbyes. A wave of guilt flooded my cheeks. I probably should have asked about my mother, but wasn't sure what the point would be. If there was any change in her condition, Dr. Joseph would have called me, and there hadn't been a change in twenty years, so the chance was nil to none.

The important thing was that Dr. Middleton was legit, so I could relax, a little, at least. Although he had a weird aura and was rude to me earlier, I could chalk that up to a doctor being protective of his patient and letting it go.

For now.

I picked up the phone once again. Punching in the number for the Seaside Sanatorium, I gathered my thoughts and scribbled some notes on a yellow legal pad. It took a few moments to make the connection before the phone rang. The ringtone was weird. More like a clanking than the typical 'ring-ring'. The clanking seemed to start out far away, then closer, until I had to move the phone away from my ear. When the receptionist finally answered, she also seemed distant. I tried to ignore the poor connection. "Hello. I'm a therapist from Castle Point, Maine. Could I speak with the doctor in charge of the inmate, Mitch Myles, please?" The receptionist didn't answer at first, but I could hear some kind of chattering on the other end. Pops and crackles broke through the line. She probably couldn't hear me. I raised my voice, thinking maybe the issue was on my end.

"I, uh, was wondering if I could visit Mr. Mitch Myles, in person?" I swallowed hard, gripping my legal pad.

The receptionist's voice seemed to rise, but the crackling and popping continued.

"..ine."

"Fine? It's ok? I'm sorry, but the connection is horrible."

I peered at the scribbles on the yellow legal pad and took a deep breath.

Dead silence greeted me from the other end. Then the crackling continued. The receptionist replied again.

"Ye...it's ...ine, Alexandra."

The line went dead. I stared at the phone for a minute, creases lining my forehead, and dialed again. The line clanged repeatedly in my ear, but no answer. I thought about the weird, choppy conversation. Most of it was cutting out except for my name. That was clear. And I'm sure I heard a "fine", didn't I? A tiny shiver shot up my spine.

My name.

Had I given the receptionist my name?

I wracked my brain for a bit, mulling over the conversation, but couldn't remember if I had or hadn't, so I let it go. The receptionist also said visitation was fine. At least, that's what it sounded like. I mean, I could probably come up with an excuse to see Mitch, regardless. I'm a credible therapist - that's got to be worth something. I cursed, regretting my decision *not* to spend another 100 G's and four years in school to become a psychiatrist.

I thought of Sharon, what she had told me under hypnosis, and Blake, what we found from his database, and I felt sure of my decision.

Because there was also someone else to consider; Betty Burke.

With Sharon currently possessing her body, where could Betty be? If I didn't find out what happened, what would that mean for her? Aside from being one of my best apothecary customers, Betty was well-loved throughout the entire community. Then there was her family to think about. Who would Alana and Jack come home to? Who would win first place at the county fair for her spectacular clam chowder?

Certainly not Sharon.

I called the local airport to book a flight from Castle Point to Waterford, Connecticut, and headed home to pack a bag, have a hot bath, and think.

CHAPTER
THIRTEEN

SHARON

"Gin. I win again!" I beamed. This was fun. Had I ever played gin before? I must have. I was pretty darn good.

"Oh gosh, yes, I guess you did." John smiled at me, gathering the playing cards and shuffling. "Another game?"

"Oh, sure, why not? I have no place to be." I smiled warmly at the handsome doctor, then stroked my stupid curly hair back, tucking it, as best I could, behind my ears. I frowned.

"What's the matter, Sharon?" John so sweetly asked.

"Oh, I'm just frustrated at this situation, I guess. I don't know how I came to be here, or who I am. I just know I don't feel like I'm *Betty Burke*. But what if that's who I am? I can't live with... this..." I waved a hand from the top of my head down the length of my body.

"Well, first, I think you look lovely." Dr. Middleton reached for my hand and I grasped it, dipping my head shyly. "And second, why not make a few changes? Become the person you *think* you are. There's no harm in that. In doing so, your memories may come back to you." John soothed me.

I loved that about him.

I lost myself in the deep pool of his gorgeous eyes. A flutter in my chest blended with heat through my belly, sending another Arizona heat wave through my entire body. "I guess you're right. What could it hurt?" I stroked the curly waves back with my right hand, my left lingered in John's. I turned his hand over and looked at the right ring finger. No ring. "You're not married?" A giddiness plunged through me.

"No. The right gal just hasn't come along, I guess," he winked. I flushed with all the pre-menopausal joys of womanhood. He held my hands in both of his. Feelings of comfort and ease washed over me and I smiled, batting my lashes - or what I had for lashes, which wasn't much. It appeared my eyebrows had claimed all the hair in the eye department. Nothing some good falsies and tweezers wouldn't fix.

"How long have you been a psychiatrist?"

"Oh, too long, I suppose. My entire career. Which has been a long one."

"You must love what you do."

"Yes, I suppose I do. Probably too much. That may be why I haven't been married. My work has fulfilled me. So far, that is." The corners of his mouth turned up, and I smiled again but refrained from batting the unavailable eyelashes. If I could guess, this is what it felt like to have a high-school crush. But I couldn't remember high school, much less having a crush. If the butterflies in my belly and the flush of my cheeks were a sign, then that's what I had. I wondered briefly if this was the way *'Betty'* felt about Jack Burke, knowing they were high school sweethearts.

I bowed my head.

Why couldn't I remember my life with him?

Why did the thought of *having* a life with him feel wrong?

I wasn't truly upset about it, though. I mean, the guy was Honky Tonk meets Bubba's cousin.

Pretty sure I didn't 'do' Honky Tonk.

"Hey, whatever you're thinking, just stop." John lifted my chin and looked into my eyes. Tears stung. "You have beautiful eyes, Sharon, and a beautiful smile. Now, show me your smile." I did. "Much better. Don't worry so much, everything will become clear in time. Just be patient." John patted my hand.

Just then, a pink puppy bitch nurse came into the room, carrying a lunch tray. I'd recently found out her name was Nora, but I never called her by that or any other name. Just referred to her - in my mind, at least - as PPBN.

Except for today, she wasn't wearing pink puppy scrubs, she was wearing blue scrubs with cartoon kittens.

Where'd she get her attire - Vet's-R-Us?

Fine. I'll call her *Nora*. Ugh. Her presence grated on me since the day she gleefully pulled the breathing tube from my throat.

"Well, I guess that's my cue. I'll leave you to eat your lunch. After your physical therapy session, I will see you later this afternoon." John slid his white doctor's coat on and turned for the door.

"Thank you, John. For this morning. I had a really nice time." I smiled, noting Nora's raised eyebrow and odd expression.

Mind your business, bitch.

Dr. Middleton merely smiled and waved as he left.

The afternoon's physical therapy session was painful, but I was determined not to throat-punch Teresa, my physical therapist. Her militant massaging and insistence on me to get up and walk was super annoying, but if I didn't play nice, I'd never get out of this place.

I lay on the bed while Teresa massaged and moved my legs. Then she helped me sit up and swing my legs over the side. Then she slipped her arms under my bra-less boobages, clasped her arms around me, and hoisted me up.

"Ready? Steady, ok. You're on your feet. Now, ground your feet on the floor. Good. I'm going to take one arm away. Ready?" Teresa's other arm held me tight as she slid one arm away.

I felt my legs buckling.

"Oh!" I cried. Teresa held me up.

"Plant your feet, that's it. Lock the knees. Hold tight. Good!"

I was standing.

"Oh!" I cried again, surprised and delighted. Teresa helped me to move, one leg in front of the other, just a few steps away from the bed, and back again.

"Ok, that's enough. Let's get you back on the bed. Great effort. We'll do more tomorrow." Teresa helped me settle back under the covers.

I was jubilant. Dr. Middleton - John - would be impressed by my effort today. Soon enough, I'll be walking, and when I could, I would walk straight out of this place, and into my new life.

Hopefully, with John by my side.

CHAPTER
FOURTEEN

ALEXANDRA

Holding my usual coffee order in one hand, an overnight bag in the other, I entered the small Castle Point airport and promptly froze.

Blake Sheraton was leaning against the front counter, chatting with the airport staff. I did a double-take, sure my eyes were deceiving me. He wasn't in uniform, just a tight-fitting blue t-shirt and an equally tight-fitting pair of Levi's. My gaze hovered over his very fine ass. Not that I'd seen a lot of asses in my time, but his took the proverbial cake. My eyes snapped up when I realized Blake had spotted me and was walking over.

"Hello, Alexandra. How are you today?" The way he said my name reminded me of the caramel sauce coating my morning coffee. Smooth and delicious. I took a quick sip and promptly choked on it, swallowing hard.

"Hello, Blake," I sputtered. "What are you doing here?" I pushed past him, not waiting for an answer, dropped my bag, and stepped toward the counter to retrieve my boarding pass, avoiding Blake's eyes. Lavender and mint tickled my nose as I slid my ID over the counter. I held my breath and waited for the scent to dissipate. Blake stepped beside me and the scent was back in full force.

"I'm coming with you to Waterford."

I froze, staring at the airport employee who was trying to hand over my boarding pass. I snatched it and turned toward Blake. "Excuse me? You're doing what, now?" Whatever gave 'Blake the Great' the idea that he could come with me? Tiny daggers pierced the back of my eyes as I tugged my earring. *Why was it so hot in here?*

I glanced up and noticed the large fan, not spinning. My index finger twitched, but I held back. Not like I could turn it on with an audience, especially not the Chief Deputy Sheriff of Mind-Your-Business in front of me.

"When you told me you were booking a flight, I did a little digging." He folded his arms in front of his Captain America chest. "They wouldn't grant access to see Mitch Myles unless you were a psychiatric doctor consulting on his case, which you aren't, or have his doctor's permission, which I'm guessing you don't." Blake gave me a full-wattage smile. It pissed me off.

I peered at him, trying to move my eye line above the radius of his chest and biceps.

He thinks he's so great. I smirked.

"Actually, I have permission, not that it's any of your business," I replied flatly, ticking one for the witch team on my imaginary scoreboard.

Blake peered at me, opened his mouth, closed it again. "Ahh, but it *is* my business - whether you have permission or not. If this visit has anything to do with murder or a resident of Dagon County, particularly Castle Point, well, there needs to be a law enforcement official there." Blake eyed me smugly, his eyes sparkling.

He had clearly prepared for battle.

Bravo.

I gave him a point, but what I really wanted to do was wipe the smug twist off his lips and poke his damn sparkly eyes.

Except that would be a shame. His lips and eyes were rather beautiful.

"We already know Mitch Myles committed murder. Hence the Sanatorium." I smiled, feeling triumphant. "My business with Mr. Myles is none of yours. There is information that I need from him for the benefit of my client." Point made. Tick one more for my side.

Blake held up a finger. "Yes, true. But we also know Mr. Myles is a known criminal, - a real psycho - from which you could use protection."

I let out a sigh.

Another tick for Team Blake.

He was a persistent bugger.

Blake stood a little taller. His pecs pushed against his t-shirt, the veins in his biceps pulsing. I peeled my eyes from his arms and rolled them to the ceiling.

Was he actually trying to be a knight in shining armor?

"They have guards there, you know. I hardly need you." Tick for me.

Blake was grinning.

"You need to have an official police escort, Alexandra. I have all the visitation documentation ready." A pile of papers appeared from nowhere. He waved them in front of me, which only wafted lavender mint my way. I tried to grab them, but he tucked them into his back pocket.

Why did he have to smell so good?

Lavender and mint are my favorites.

Sparks of heat pierced my skin from the inside out. All at once I found him annoying, sexy, frustrating, and kissable. Plus, he was gaining points on the scoreboard.

My head pounded. I rubbed my temples with my fingertips.

"Blake, what's really going on? Why do you really want to 'escort' me?" He paused, watching me rub my temples. Then his eyes softened.

"I'm curious. Plus, I think I could really be helpful. Besides, I already have my ticket." Blake smiled and showed me his boarding pass.

"Blake...er - Deputy Sheriff - I really don't need your help in this case, legal or otherwise." My head throbbed. I grabbed my earring, pulled too hard, and winced. I thought about the logistics of having Blake escort me to the sanatorium. What if I had to use my powers? I couldn't take the chance of exposing myself to the one person who could throw me into the dungeons of Castle Dagon and throw away the key. Good Goddess, things were going from tricky to impossible.

"Well, I disagree, and also, you're wrong. So, technically, you have no choice but for me to tag along." Blake grinned.

I set fire to the imaginary scoreboard and groaned.

"You're welcome, by the way." Blake leaned toward me and winked. I took a deep breath and leaned away from him.

He was ruining lavender and mint for me, dammit.

FIFTEEN

ALEXANDRA

Despite the relatively small, empty aircraft, Blake slid into the seat beside me and reached awkwardly for his seatbelt. His elbow bumped into my boob and I grunted.

"Hey!"

"Oops, sorry." Blake grinned and snapped his buckle together. Feeling exceptionally cramped next to Blake, I shifted toward the window. They needed a separate seat just for his shoulders. The roar of the twin-engine turbo-prop thankfully made it a little too noisy for talking, or so I thought. Blake didn't get that memo. With his voice only slightly elevated, he started a conversation. *Great.*

"I did a little more digging on our friend, Mr. Myles." *Our friend?* Oh, good Goddess. I didn't reply.

"He was Varsity, and Prom Queen and King."

"Yeah, I know. You and Mitch would have a lot in common."

"Except that he killed his wife. I would never think of

killing my wife."

"I didn't know you were married."

"I'm not, but still. I wonder how a man could turn on his love like that."

"*You never really know a man until you stand in his shoes and walk around in them.*"

"Huh?"

I rolled my eyes. That he didn't recognize a quote by Harper Lee didn't surprise me. I had to raise my voice to make my point heard.

"If you spent more time cracking books in high school than you did cracking heads..."

Blake leaned back. "Hey! May I remind you, I also made varsity - which you need near-perfect grades to do, you know. You weren't the only smart one in school, Miss Smarty-Pants, but you were definitely the weirdest."

I whipped my head around, my nose almost hitting his shoulder. I imagined throwing eye-daggers and hitting him right in the middle of his pupils. He leaned back, eyebrows high. I shifted in my seat, putting as much space between us as possible, and turned toward the window.

I said a silent prayer to the Goddess for patience, then silently chanted, *move, move, move.* As if hearing my thoughts, he unsnapped his buckle when the seatbelt sign turned off and moved him and his damn shoulders to another seat.

I took a deep breath and relaxed. The lavender and mint dissipated with the plane's air conditioning.

Much better.

Blake's head and part of his neck stuck up above the seat back, several seats away. He turned his head toward me. I whipped mine back to the window. We spent the rest of the trip in blissful silence.

The steward came by with a drink tray. I gladly accepted a cup of tea and sat back in my seat. Having Blake hovering around me would definitely make communicating with Mitch Myles difficult. Knowing Mitch was unresponsive, I planned on using my magic and ability to communicate behind the veil to see what was really going on.

I would either have to rely on old-fashioned verbal communication and therapeutic tactics or make some kind of excuse to be alone with Mitch. Maybe I would turn Blake into a warty toad for the duration of the visit.

I giggled.

He was already proving to be a toad, and had big warty bumps of muscle everywhere, so it wouldn't be a stretch.

Except I hate warty toads.

Even ones that smell like lavender and mint.

I shook my head a little and went back to sipping my tea. The landing was uneventful. As soon as the seatbelt sign turned off, I turned on my phone. Nothing eventful other than a text from Penny to tell me she didn't get a 'hit' from Dr. Middleton when she tried that morning. She got nothing at all, actually. Just a few dark shadows, which she thought was weird. I texted back a thank you for trying and rose to retrieve my overnight bag from the storage compartment above my seat.

Blake had to walk back to my seat to retrieve his. I sat back down while he did so, avoiding his eyes. "Look, I'm sorry I was rude earlier. I didn't mean it. You aren't weird. Maybe you were a little weird as a kid, but you certainly aren't now."

How mighty big of him.

I glanced up at the wall of muscle blocking me from moving into the aisle. If I'm going to be stuck with him today, I'd better be as civil as possible.

"Thanks. And I'm sorry if I offended you, too."

"Forgiven. Now, let's get out of this tin tube and get to the hotel."

Dammit. What?

"You booked a room?"

"Well, sure. I saw from your reservation that you planned to stay a couple of days, so I booked a room too."

"In the same hotel?" My voice rose to an unreasonable decibel. I cleared my throat.

"Of course. Makes sense that we go to the sanatorium together, so it makes sense that I stay at the same hotel."

"How do you know which hotel I booked?" Stupid question.

"How do you think?" Blake grinned. "I'm a cop, remember?"

"Isn't there some kind of rule against using your powers for evil?" I was ruffled. Get ahold of yourself, Alex.

Blake's smile widened. I wanted to knock out his perfect teeth.

"Ha. Even if I had powers, it's illegal to use them, Miss Heale, so I couldn't."

I scoffed.

"Sometimes 400-year-old laws were made to be broken."

"I suppose. But it's still a law, and in case you forgot, I'm a law-abiding kind of guy. Besides, if I had special powers, they would only be used for good. I promise."

"Yes, of course, I'm just being sassy." I conjured up a small smile. Careful, Alex.

Blake winked at me and stepped aside so I could step into the aisle. I felt his eyes on my back all the way to the tarmac.

Better not be on my ass.

CHAPTER
SIXTEEN

ALEXANDRA

We picked up the rental car and checked into the hotel (separate floors, thank Goddess). Taking a few minutes to freshen up, I met Blake in the lobby. He had changed into his uniform minus the stetson and gun belt - because where would that fit in your carry-on baggage - but added a Dagon County standard police-issue ball cap. I wondered if he felt naked without the gun, but his biceps were two loaded weapons, so that was something.

We drove to Seaside Sanatorium. I gasped when I saw the beautiful green acres of lawn and trees and the Sanatorium, a beautiful old brick building. Green ivy snaked around the brick. Next to the building, a round turret perched high above the sea below. A couple of orderlies and their patients roamed the grounds. The patients were handcuffed or chained. I shivered. To be captive for the rest of my life was the worst future I could imagine.

Trepidation crept through my veins. I was sitting next to a cop. Someone who had taken an oath to uphold the law - even if that law was an ancient one.

I shook it off and focused on the beauty of the dark brick building as we pulled up to the main door. A tingling, giddy feeling swept over me. There had to be some great hauntings in this place, no doubt. I briefly hoped I would meet a few, then thought better of it. It was a home for the criminally insane. Not a happy place. Any souls wandering these grounds would likely be in a lot of pain. My chest felt heavy with their grief.

We entered through the large wooden front door and stepped up to the reception desk. The inside of the building reflected the outside. Old but beautiful fixtures and furnishings adorned the reception area. A few steps away, double doors led to a stark white hallway. Blake presented his paperwork to the receptionist at the desk, who merely glanced at it without touching it. Out of nowhere, an orderly appeared, ready to show us to Mitch Myles's cell.

Damn, I could have definitely gotten through with either a glamor cast on my ID or some bogus paperwork in hand. Too bad the warty, great-smelling toad had to needle his way into my investigation. I tucked my hair behind my ears and ran my fingers over my earring, willing myself to make the best of a weird situation.

The Orderly led us down a white hallway, past several doors with small windows. We could hear inmates moaning, yelling, and screaming. A shudder ripped through me. I noted the absence of guards or other staff. The receptionist and a handful of white-clad orderlies are the only people around today, apparently. The Orderly unlocked the door and allowed us to step inside Mitch's small, dark cell.

I gasped.

Blake's sharp intake of breath echoed behind me. Nearly all the paint on the four walls was scratched off. A repetitive pattern of symbols covered every square inch, up as high as Mitch's arms could extend.

"Did Mr. Myles do all this?" I asked the Orderly, who merely nodded and left the room, closing the door behind him. We heard a distinct 'click'. I glanced at Blake, who tried the doorknob. They locked it from the outside. He peered through the small window into the hallway.

"Nobody's around. This place gives me the creeps."

I nodded and looked at Mitch. He had no aura, other than a dark cloud swirling above his head.

Inside the cloud was a swarm of... flies.

My heart slammed into my chest. I glanced at Blake, studying the drawings. He definitely didn't see what I saw, or surely he would have said something.

I looked at the cloud of flies again, knowing them all too well.

My mother had the same cloud hovering over her.

And if I wasn't able to help my mother escape a demon's grasp, how was I supposed to help Mitch? With a non-believing, law-abiding cop beside me, no less?

I moved closer to Mitch, sitting in a chair in the cell's corner. He was wearing a standard white jumpsuit, hands and ankles cuffed and chained to his chair. I studied his features. The bright blue eyes I'd seen in the pictures with Sharon were vacant and hollow, staring at nothing. His hair was shaggy and dull, the length nearly hiding his eyes. His skin was pale and sallow.

My heart broke for him. The entire situation was so surreal.

I walked slowly around the small space, studying the walls. Pulling my phone out of my suit pocket, turned the flash on and started snapping pictures of the walls and Mitch.

Blake slowly turned in circles, gawking at the etchings. "He must have spent hours doing this."

"Yes, for sure." I stopped and checked the pictures. They looked over-exposed. I turned off the flash and tried again. Too dark. I grabbed a notepad and pen from my bag and copied the etchings. They ran in repetitive lines around the room. I finished copying one line when I bumped into Mitch's chair. Laying my hand on his shoulder, I tried to pick up on a vibration or image, but nothing came. Penny would have more luck with the visions. I frowned, wishing I'd invited her to come with me.

"Is he ok with us being here?" Blake asked. I shrugged and spoke directly to Mitch.

"Hi, Mitch. I'm Alexandra and this is Blake." No response. The black cloud hovered, but I didn't see a shift in the speed of the flies. "We aren't here to upset you, I promise." Still, nothing.

Mitch just stared straight ahead.

"So, what's your plan?" Blake asked.

"Just try talking to him, I guess. You don't have to be here." I said hopefully. If I could be alone with Mitch, I could accomplish far more.

"Yes, I do. I'm not leaving you alone with a psychotic wife killer, Alex."

I rolled my eyes at him.

"Shush! He may seem listless, but he can still hear you. Don't upset him!"

Blake stood back and crossed his arms.

"Your show, doc."

I blew out a breath.

"Not a doctor," I whispered, "just a therapist with a ton of experience."

Blake motioned for me to start the interview. I stood in front of Mitch. Blake followed. I crouched down, reaching to take Mitch's hands, then thought better of it, laying my hands on my lap instead.

"Mitch. Mr. Myles, my name is Alexandra Heale. I'm from Castle Point, Maine. I'm here to talk to you about the reason you're here. Is it ok to ask you some questions?" No response. I glanced up at the black cloud of flies above his head.

Did the circling flies just speed up?

"Mr. Myles, can you tell me what happened to you before your wife's death? Do you remember?" Again, no response. This time I was certain the flies sped up.

"Looks like this is a waste of time," Blake mumbled. I frowned, wishing he wasn't here. This would be so much easier if I could use my magic to look behind the veil of Mitch Myles's mind. If I was going to achieve something today I'd have to try anyway. Open a few closed doors in front of Blake and take my chances.

I took a deep breath.

"Mr. Myles, I know you're in there. I know it wasn't you who killed your wife. I know you're under a spell - a Demon's Curse. Can you answer me?"

"What the...?" Blake stood up straight. "What are you talking about?" Ignoring him I persisted.

"Please, Mitch, I can help you. I just need you to look at me. Can you do that?" Slowly, Mitch raised his head, looked at me, then Blake.

His eyes were completely black.

Blake jumped back, his back slamming against the cell door.

"What the hell? Alex, what's going on?"

"Be quiet! Mitch, I know you're in there. Can you talk to me?" The volume of flies doubled, then doubled again, spread out and swarmed the room. I resisted the urge to swat them away, knowing Blake couldn't see what I saw.

Mitch sat back in his chair, the cuffs on his wrists pulled taut to the chains between his ankles. A slow, low growl came from Mitch's chest and rumbled up his throat. He opened his mouth wide, and hundreds of flies shot out.

This, Blake could see.

"What the fuck, Alex!" He ducked, swatting the flies away.

I wouldn't break from Mitch's black eyes. I screamed; *"Demon, I command thee, release this man, let him be!"*

Mitch closed his mouth, and the flies disappeared.

A low, deep laugh rumbled up his chest.

"You have no command over me, witch." The demon spoke through Mitch's body, but his mouth remained closed. I glanced back at Blake whose eyes were locked on Mitch.

"You have no right to this vessel, demon. I command you to release him!"

Blake came closer. "Alex, this is insane. We have to leave. Now."

"No." I turned back to Mitch. "Mitch Myles, you have the power to control the demon inside of you. You have to fight, Mitch. Fight back, *hard.*"

The demon laughed again. Chin down, black eyes looking through the blonde, dull locks, directly at me, then Blake.

With a roar, Mitch spread his arms, busting the handcuffs from the ankle chains, then pulling the handcuffs apart. He stood up, the chair clattering back, and ripped the chains from his waist and feet.

He was free.

Blake ran to the door and grabbed at the handle, but it wouldn't open. He banged on it, calling security, but nobody came.

"The demon cloaked the room, Blake. Nobody can hear you." I didn't take my eyes off Mitch.

"We have to do something, Alex!" Suddenly, Mitch rushed at Blake, grabbed him by the shoulders, and threw him across the room.

"Blake!" I yelled. Mitch stood over Blake, much smaller than the large, muscle-bound cop, but with the strength of everything evil inside him. Blake recovered quickly and scooted to the far wall. The demon moved toward him. Just as he was about to grab Blake again, I summoned all of my energy to form a bright, glowing ball of white light.

"Blake, duck!" I threw the energy ball as hard as I could toward Mitch. It hit him in the side, throwing him against the far wall. Blake scrambled toward me, his eyes huge.

We waited for a few moments, panting. Blake put his arm around my shoulders and I welcomed the weight of him. Mitch was passed out on the floor. The cloud of flies was gone, but, as Mitch stirred, the flies returned, gathering in a swirl above Mitch's head once again.

My heart dropped to my stomach.

The demon still had a hold of Mitch.

"Help me get him into a chair." We each took an arm and moved Mitch to his small, metal-framed bed. The springs squeaked as we laid him on the thin mattress. The cuffs were still on his arms, but the chains were scattered across the floor.

"What now?" Blake asked, his eyes huge.

"Cuff him to the bed." Blake grabbed his cuffs from his

belt. He cuffed Mitch's hands to the metal frame. Mitch, still passed out, didn't move.

"Not sure what good that'll do if he wakes up. He just busted through the last set." Blake ran his beefy hands across his brow, his hair plastered to his temples.

I said a silent prayer to the Goddess for protection and strength.

"I have to try tapping into his subconscious, Blake. Go behind the veil. If I don't, I'll never get answers."

And I'll have exposed myself to you as a witch for nothing.

"How do you tap into, or behind... whatever... the veil?" Blake asked quietly.

"I'll need a few minutes to go into a deep hypnotic trance, then I'll see if I can slip through his psyche without upsetting him."

"Hypnosis? That works?"

"Like nothing else. A close second in this situation would be clairvoyance, maybe."

"Clar-what?"

"Clairvoyance. Clear seeing or second sight."

"You have that too?" Blake's brow creased.

"Yes. But for today, this will work better."

"Huh. Interesting."

"Yes, it is."

Blake picked up the chair, moved it to the furthest corner, away from Mitch's bed, and held it for me. I sat, kicking off my shoes. I tucked my legs into a lotus position.

"Watch Mitch, okay? If he acts up, tell me - wake me up." Blake nodded, then leaned against the wall between Mitch and me, arms crossed against his chest.

Taking several breaths, I relaxed, deeper and deeper. The familiar darkness of space cocooned me. After a short time, I was floating in blackness; nowhere, nothing, and no one around me. I called out to Mitch in my mind. At first, there was no response, so I called again and again. Eventually, I saw a dark door surrounded by a thin stream of light. Approaching the door, I noticed intricate carvings in the wood. The same as the carvings on the walls in Mitch's room.

Flies swarmed around me in the darkness. Ignoring them, I reached for the door handle and turned. The door silently slid open.

Inside was the darker version of the same cell we were in, except the walls were oozing dark, gooey liquid. There was no furniture, just a chair facing one corner. Mitch sat, flies swarmed around him. I slowly approached.

"Mitch, can you hear me? It's Alexandra. If you can hear me, speak to me, please." Mitch slowly turned his head - all the way around to his back - facing me. He opened his eyes. They were black as night.

I kept my breathing steady, to stay in a trance.

"Please, talk to me, Mitch. I know you're in there." Then I heard a soft voice, like an echo, flowing through my mind.

"Help...me. Heeeeellp meeeeeee."

"Mitch, I am trying. I need to know who cursed you. Was it a demon? Can you give me a name?"

"Yeeessssss..... demonnnnn...."

"Okay, Mitch - what's the demon's name? Can you tell me?" There was a long, silent pause, then the echo flowed again.

"Nooooooo... I don't knowwww......"

"Mitch. If you can't tell me, can you show me what he did to you? Show me what happened two years ago?"

The room dissolved in front of me, everything except for Mitch, still facing backward in the chair.

A scene slid into view.

Mitch and Sharon Myles, were at home, making dinner. Laughing, enjoying each other's company. Everything seemed normal. Then, Mitch grew silent. His body stiffened, his back arching, a deep growl coming from somewhere deep inside. Sharon grabbed his shoulders, yelling at him, shaking him. He looks at her, his eyes black as night, and screams; "*YOU BELONG TO ME, AND WITH ME YOU WILL DIE.*" Sharon jumped back against the counter. She grabs a knife and points it at Mitch, yelling at him, terrified. He grabs her arm, takes the knife away from her,, and stabs her repeatedly.

The scene fades, leaving me alone in the dark with Mitch, still on the chair. He turned his head back to face the corner of the cell.

A hushed silence fell between us.

"Mitch, is there anything else? Can you please try?" I pleaded. "What did you see when the demon took over your body?" Mitch remained silent. "Mitch. I promise I will try to help you and Sharon. I'll do everything in my power to release you. But it may take some time. Please hang in there, Mitch. Hold on to who you really are." Mitch faded into the darkness.

I opened my eyes. The sunlight in the room had shifted. Blake was sitting on the floor, his back against the wall. Mitch was still laying on the bed, passed out.

"How long was I gone?"

"Couple hours at least. Did you find out anything?"

"Yeah. A demon possessed Mitch when he killed his wife."

Blake stood up and paced the floor, running his hands through his hair. "How do you know? What about when he attacked me? That was a demon, wasn't it?"

"Maybe, or the sentries surrounding him. They're all

around him, all the time." I waved at the black cloud of flies over Mitch's head, then remembered that Blake couldn't see what I saw. "You saw the flies coming from his mouth earlier? Those are them."

Blake shook his head.

"Gross. So, if he couldn't name the demon, how will you find out?"

"I really don't know, but there has to be a way."

Just then, we heard a soft click from the door. Blake shot to it, turning the knob. It turned. He opened the door and peered outside.

"Nobody's there." He scratched his head. The faint smell of lavender and mint, now mixed with sweat from a very anxious, rugged cop, wafted past me.

"Don't question it. Let's just get the hell out of here." I walked into the hall as Blake released a sleeping Mitch from the handcuffs.

The hall and reception area was empty. I didn't care about finding any staff members - I needed fresh air - and practically ran to the door. Once outside, I breathed deeply, willing my heart to slow its erratic beating. I turned and stared up at the brick building. There was so much negative energy attached to the building, I didn't know how the staff could handle being in it day in and day out.

I turned to Blake. His face was blank, but his eyes bore into me. He crossed his arms.

"So, you're a witch?"

I looked up at him, placing my hands on my hips. I levelled my gaze on his

"Yeah, I am. You gonna arrest me now?"

"Well... no. But..." He looked at me, his eyes calculating. "...you have some explaining to do."

CHAPTER
SEVENTEEN

BLAKE

I paced the hall outside Alexandra's hotel room door, processing what happened at the Sanatorium.

Alexandra's a freaking witch, for God's sake.

I thought her kind had long since been expunged from the earth. I mean, there are laws and everyone knows that. So many questions burst into my mind.

Were there more like her?

If so, who?

My biggest concern right now - as I wore the already thread-bare hall carpet down to a new low - was what I would do with...*her*.

I knew her reputation for helping people. Some of my friends were her clients. Plus, she had some awesome powers, and likely saved my life. If what she said was true, Mitch Myles was being controlled by a demon.

Demons I could understand, witches, however...

They were pure evil.

At least, that's what I grew up believing.

I halted when I heard Alexandra's door open. She stepped outside, closing the door behind her.

"Ready?" I asked. Duh, of course, she was, and she looked amazing. The worry lines I saw earlier had smoothed out, her hair was brushed to a glossy ebony. Her green eyes flashed and sparkled.

"Yes, let's get this over with." She turned and walked down the hall to the elevator.

We arrived at the diner in silence, me walking a little behind her. She smelled freshly showered, her rose perfume intoxicating. I stopped myself from imagining her under the steamy water, hair wet, soap suds dripping down...

I almost ran into her when she stopped at the diner door. The lone server shuttled us to a booth, handed out menus, and poured two glasses of iced water. I downed the glass in a few large gulps, then met Alexandra's gaze.

"Go ahead, Chief Deputy Sheraton. Ask me what you want to know." Alexandra leaned back, crossing her arms. I leaned forward, elbows on the table.

"How long have you been a witch?"

She paused for a moment, taking a sip of water before answering;

"My whole life. I was born with abilities."

"Did your parents know?"

"I never knew my dad, but my mom knew, yes, and she tried very hard to - let's just say - 'convert' me." She grimaced. I wanted to ask what she meant, but thought better of it.

"There are laws, Alex. She was trying to protect you."

"You call it protection. I call it abuse. But, ya. You're probably right."

"Where is she now?"

Alexandra looked down at the table, eyes dark.

"She's... gone."

"I'm sorry about that." The server refilled our water. I took a sip. "Did you ever think of relinquishing your powers? Your mom probably would have wanted you to. It's safer for you if you did."

"No, Blake. Giving up my powers is giving up who I am!" Tears glistened in the corners of her eyes. "For the love of the Goddess. It's the 21st century. Why we still abide by an old law created by some maniac 'Earl' is ludicrous." Alexandra leaned forward, her voice a harsh whisper. "Besides, I think you know by now that I can take care of myself."

"Yes, but nobody knows you're a witch, do they? I realize there hasn't been a hanging or burning in Castle Dagon for, like, well over fifty years, but the law is still in place." I took another gulp of water. "Are there others... like you?" I didn't mean for it to sound like she had some rare deformity, but that's kinda how it came out.

Alexandra glared at me.

"No comment."

So there was. Or there it wasn't.

It's possible she's the only one.

The Witch Hunters had been quiet for a long time, years even - because there were no witches to hunt. Clearly, that bit of information was incorrect.

"What do you plan to do about Mitch Myles?"

"I guess that depends on whether I'm going to be arrested when I get back to Castle Point." Alexandra stared at me. I could see the lines in her neck move as she swallowed. Her lips were pursed, but the natural fullness was still there.

I felt the sudden urge to run my thumb along her lips, but held back.

"Let's say we forget about laws, for now. What would you do with Mitch?"

She relaxed back in her seat. Just then, the server came to take our order. We looked over the menus quickly and ordered the specials. Once the server left, Alexandra continued;

"In order to expel the demon, I have to find him. If I can do that, then Mitch will be free."

"But how can you find the demon?"

Alexandra's eyes closed, and she took a deep breath. "First, I have to try talking with Mitch - again."

I scratched my head.

"But you just tried that, Alex! He's unresponsive and clearly unable to have a conversation. He's also capable of..." I rubbed the shoulder that connected hard with the wall when the demon threw me. It didn't matter that I was a good foot taller than Mitch Myles, and a hell of a lot stronger. Not when there was a demon controlling the puppet strings.

"Yes, that's true - but I have to try again. Maybe I could get more from him the second time."

I shuddered and studied Alex for a moment, eyes narrowed. "But... you tried that." I didn't mean to sound like a broken record, but I really didn't want to go back to that weird place.

"I know, Blake." Alex snipped, pulling at the earring in her ear. "But if I could go deeper into his psyche, hopefully I'll also be able to figure out who the demon is, so I can summon him."

"Summon him?" My voice squeaked. I cleared my throat.

"Yes, summon him. In order to expunge him from the earth, I need to summon him."

"Sounds complicated. And dangerous. How does it work?" I didn't like the idea of her being in danger but was curious about the summoning part.

"Yes, it's very dangerous. But I have to try. If I can find out who the demon is, then I..." Alexandra stopped and levelled my gaze. "I can fix this and release a couple of innocent souls."

I held her gaze, thoughtful. After several moments, I blinked, breaking the spell.

"So, how can I help?"

"You can start by not arresting me."

CHAPTER
EIGHTEEN

ALEXANDRA

We finished dinner in relative silence. The day spent with Mitch at the Sanatorium was long and exhausting. And what was there to say, really? I had exposed my abilities to Blake, as I feared I would, and now that the black cat was definitely out of the pointy hat, I felt the heavy anticipation of what came next.

Blake never said whether he would or wouldn't arrest me, which unnerved me to hell. Also, he still smelled and looked amazing - also unnerving.

I'd like him better if he were a warty toad.

Then the stupid butterflies that crashed around my stomach would calm down and I could live in peace, knowing a warty toad couldn't imprison me in a cell.

Finally, Blake spoke, breaking the silence between us.

"I really want to apologize for the way I treated you back in high school."

I froze, eyes wide. Blake dipped his head and played with his fork.

"You're apologizing? I... I... don't know what to say... thank you, that means a lot."

Blake shrugged. "I was a jerk back then. I'm not that guy anymore. I just wanted you to know that."

I couldn't help myself; I smiled.

"You were more than 'kind of' a jerk, Blake. You were pretty heartless. Not just to me, either." I watched his shoulders slump and his head dip further, reminding me of a sad puppy who'd been spanked with a rolled-up newspaper. "Hey, I'm sorry. I shouldn't have said anything. Obviously, you've changed or you wouldn't have apologized. Thank you, I really appreciate it."

Blake straightened up and smiled. The butterflies took flight once again.

"I actually thought you were kind of cute, despite the weirdness." He grinned.

"Really? I couldn't have known, coming from my vantage point inside a locker."

Blake laughed. "Damn. What kind of asshole would do that to such a cute little weirdo?"

"A pretty big one." We both laughed. I finally relaxed.

After dinner, Blake tried to pay the bill, but I wouldn't let him pay for me. He frowned when I shoved some bills toward the server. He probably wanted to be gallant and all that crap, but I didn't want to be indebted to him.

If he agreed not to arrest me, that was debt enough.

When we walked outside, he turned and started walking toward the hotel. I didn't. He stopped and turned back to me.

"Coming?"

"I think I'd rather take a walk." I nodded my head

toward the cliffs a short distance from the hotel, the sea sprays beckoning me.

"Mind if I join you?" Blake strode toward me, not giving me the option to refuse.

"Sure. Sounds great," I said through partially gritted teeth.

We walked slowly and in silence, the sun dropping quickly on the horizon. I breathed the salty sea air and felt the day slip off my shoulders, relaxed by the sound of crashing waves. It made me appreciate my house being on a rocky shore. I could open my bedroom window and fall asleep to the sound.

A heaviness settled in my chest.

If Blake arrested me, I'd lose my home. It had been both a prison and a safe haven for me since I was born.

I'd have to convince him to let me be, somehow.

Maybe seduce him.

Make him fall in love with me.

Would that be so bad?

"Tough day." Blake's voice jolted me back. He sighed and stretched his arms out. Stiffening, I expected to feel his arm around me but did not. I wasn't sure if I was disappointed or thankful.

"Yeah, it sure was," I agreed.

"Have you done that a lot? I mean, helping people like Mitch in how you did?"

"No, not a lot. Mostly my clients have pretty standard issues which are easily treatable using hypnosis."

"So, you don't really practice witchcraft?" His voice perked up.

"Not with my clients, no. Unless I think a certain spell might comfort them, and bring them some ease while they're going through whatever it is they're going through."

May as well be honest. Maybe he'd go easy on me when he arrested me later.

"Oh, well, that's something, I guess." Blake shoved his hands in the front pockets of his pants.

I glanced at him. "Witchcraft isn't what you think, Blake."

He quirked a brow. "How do you know what I think?"

"I grew up in Castle Point too, remember? I know the folklore, and it's wrong." My voice was firm, and a little louder the closer we got to the ocean, but I didn't care.

I was defensive.

"Care to enlighten me?"

"Not tonight, no."

We walked further, the silence a vast canyon between us. I couldn't leave it alone. The truth nipped at me to be told; "It's just that - "

Blake broke in. "- a witch killed my parents."

My stomach roiled. I stopped, gaping at him.

"I seriously doubt that, Blake."

He pursed his lips. "Well, that's the truth. In fact, I became a cop to find the witch who did it."

I moved briskly to the edge of the cliff, ready to hurl. Blake followed. I whipped around to face him.

"There's no way a witch was involved in the death of your parents, Blake. You must be mistaken." I suddenly felt very uneasy being this close to the edge of the cliff. I moved to a bench along the walkway and sat, gripping the seat.

Blake sat beside me, clasping his hands in front of him.

"Doubt all you want, Alex. There's a direct connection between my parent's death and a known witch. She disappeared right after they died."

"That means nothing. What proof do you have?"

Blake scratched his head. "Enough."

Tension dripped between us. My heart beat through my chest.

"Blake, I can't believe...."

He put up a hand, shaking his head. "Never mind that now, Alex. Look. I don't want to turn you in. Not right now, anyway. I think... the work you do is... amazing." He choked on his words, but I heard the sincerity behind them.

"Thank you, Blake. You don't know what this means."

"I think I do. If I hadn't experienced it for myself, I wouldn't believe it or be able to ignore the law, but I did, and I know you have a lot of work ahead of you, to help Mitch and your client..." He trailed off. "I'd like to help if I can."

"Thank you. I'm sure I'll be needing it." I sighed. "Won't you get in trouble though? With Sheriff Roberts, I mean. Once this is all over and you have to turn me in?" My voice was a mere whisper over the crashing waves.

Blake shifted beside me. "Let's just deal with one thing at a time. Can we agree on that?"

I nodded, letting the silence drop between us once again.

NINETEEN

BLAKE

Alexandra is a friggin' witch.

Alexandra's amazing.

Alexandra needs to be arrested for practicing witchcraft.

Alexandra needs to finish what she started, and I need to help her.

I got very little sleep. Fitful thoughts of Alexandra, and how beautiful she is, ran through my mind. But that just brought on a raging hard-on. Snapping back to cop mode and deciding to arrest her for witchcraft - partly to avenge my parents. Then, thinking how sexy she would look in a pair of handcuffs and back to a raging hard-on...

I did not rest easy, and the lines on my face and the bags under my eyes were the prizes. I took a long, hot shower before getting dressed and packing my bag. The plan was, we would head back to the Sanatorium, attempt another interview with the demon - or Mitch Myles - whoever showed up, and head back to Castle Point.

I thought about my promise to Alexandra not to arrest her and a huge guilt bomb exploded in my stomach.

I'm a cop.

Pretty proud of being one and staying true to my oaths - one of which is dealing with someone who broke the law.

Alexandra was that someone.

But Alexandra was also talented, smart, and amazing.

Not to mention forgiving.

And damn hot.

My standard-issue khakis got tight across my crotch. I sighed and ducked into the bathroom to splash cold water on my face, took another stab at erasing the dark circles under my eyes with my fingers, then gave up and left the room.

Alexandra met me in the hall. Her long, black hair floated in waves around her shoulders. Her eyes, darker today, with grey circles accentuating the green in them, told me she didn't get much sleep either, but she smiled when she saw me.

My heart jumped.

I hoped the circles under her eyes were because she couldn't stop thinking of me, but more than likely it was because she was terrified of being around me, the cop that could change her life in one instant. My brow instantly wrinkled at the thought of her avoiding me when we returned to Castle Point - or worse - running away from town for good. A frosty chill ran up my spine. I couldn't imagine not seeing her again, and that included sending her to prison. The damn pang of guilt shot through my belly, an intense, white-hot heat.

How could I keep finding the first witch in Castle Point in over fifty years from the Sheriff?

I mean, I'd be a friggin' hero.

To everyone but Alexandra.

My head throbbed.

"Ready?" Alexandra turned toward the stairs and we made our way to the car. I couldn't bring myself to talk about the day or evening before as we drove to the Sanatorium, feeling all at once like a big chicken. I didn't want to hear her say she didn't trust me, or she hated me, or even that she liked me. My stomach roiled, and I couldn't speak. We rode in silence. A silence I was grateful for.

When we turned down the Sanatorium's long drive, Alexandra gasped, then slammed on the brakes.

"What the f...?" I looked up, and couldn't believe what my eyes were telling me.

My jaw dropped to the floorboards.

"Blake..." Alexandra breathed beside me.

The Seaside Sanatorium was in total ruins.

Yesterday, it was a serene, beautiful place with green lawns, shrubs, and trees, now a barren brown, and that included copious amounts of ivy snaking around the building. The building itself, with its large wooden door, clean white trim, and sturdy brown bricks, was a crumbling mess.

"What the hell? Alex, drive to the front door." Alex slowly pulled ahead as we gawked at the formerly grandiose hospital. Windows were broken all over the place, and the front door askew on its hinges. Alex parked and turned off the ignition. We got out of the car and walked toward the front door.

"Blake, what happened?" Alex stood beside me. A shiver ran through her. "Do you think Mitch..."

"I don't know..." We stepped up the marble steps, shiny yesterday, now chipped and dull. The wooden front door was faded and covered in spider webs. I stepped inside, careful not to touch the door. I reached one hand out for Alexandra to take, which she did. We paused in the entry-way, brightly lit the day before, with pristine white walls and pieces of antique furniture in the waiting areas. Now the walls were chipped, peeling, full of cobwebs, and dirty with mold. Some parts of the ceiling had fallen in, bits of blue autumn sky filtering through the holes. Dust floated through the bright streaks of sun.

The furniture was strewn about, some on its side, other pieces missing altogether. The pieces that remained were dusty and torn. A mouse scampered from one couch and skittered across the floor. I instinctively reached for Alexandra, assuming she'd freak out seeing the mouse, but she stood, silently watching it disappear behind the reception desk.

Right.

She's a witch.

She probably used mice for making potions and crap.

I shuddered at the thought. Not for the sake of the mice, but for thinking that Alex could harm a tiny living being. Another question for another day. I shook my head and walked up to the reception desk, Alex still holding my hand. The desk was scratched and cracked from water dripping from the holey ceiling above.

"Blake..." Alex pulled her hand away and spun in a slow circle. "This destruction isn't fresh... It looks like..."

"... the place has been abandoned. For years," I finished. Alex looked at me, her eyes wide. "We are definitely not in Kansas anymore, Dorothy." A small side grin etched on her face, then disappeared.

"I think I'd be the witch in that movie, Blake, not Dorothy."

"Right." *But would she be the good witch or the bad?* "I

125

don't understand, Alexandra. We both saw the place yesterday. It was beautiful. Pristine." Alex was toying with her earring, glancing around.

"I don't understand either. Should we go down the hall? Check on Mitch Myles's room?" she asked.

"I can't imagine it looks like it did yesterday, but sure." We walked to the double hallway doors, one ripped off its rusty hinges, the other ready to fall. Careful to avoid the broken tiles, rusty gurney, and hospital carts scattered across the floor, we found Mitch's room. Alexandra pushed the door, cobwebs stretching and breaking apart as she did so. She brushed them away and stepped inside. I held the door open, not trusting that it wouldn't close and lock behind us. The walls looked the same as the walls throughout the rest of the building: grey, peeling, and old.

"The markings are gone." Alexandra breathed.

"What the hell, Alex?"

She spun in a slow circle, reaching into her pocket for her phone, and pressed on the photo album.

She sucked a harsh breath.

"The photos of the walls I took yesterday - of the etchings - they look just like the walls now!"

"Let me see."

She handed me the phone. My brain couldn't process what I was seeing. I saw the pictures the day before. A little dark, some a little over-exposed, but some markings were still visible. Now, it was just pictures of moldy, torn walls and furniture, including the bed that we had handcuffed Mitch to, now tossed on its side, the mattress ripped apart by small animals; the stuffing pulled out.

"The photo I took of Mitch! Is it still there?" Alex snatched her phone back and scrolled through the images. She jumped a little when she found the one of Mitch. "Oh my Goddess, Blake, look." She handed the phone back to me.

The image of Mitch was nothing but a ghostly streak of grey, with three dark patches, two where his eyes would have been, and one, a dark grey streak as his mouth stretched into a scream. My fingers fumbled with the phone. I grasped it before it could hit the floor and looked at the picture again before handing it back to Alex.

"Alexandra. What's going on?"

Alex eyed me, pulling at her earring before replying.

"It must have been a glamor."

"A glamor? What the hell is glamor?" How I longed for a Witch-to-English dictionary.

"It's a magical covering that changes the look of something."

I frowned, dying to ask for more information on that seemingly handy bit of magic, and whether or not she was capable of such a cool thing. "Who would have put it there?"

"I do not know, but I'm guessing the demon who possessed Mitch Myles."

"But, why?"

"I have absolutely no clue." Alex looked beyond my shoulder. Her eyes grew wide, then she bolted for the door. I followed, side-stepping debris as we walked outside. There was no temperature difference between the outside and the building. I shivered, despite the warmth of the sun shining high in the sky.

Alexandra stopped short of the car and spun around, facing me.

"Blake. The article... we saw it together... it said that Mitch was here... quick, Google the article!" Alex stood beside me as I pulled my phone from my pocket. I punched in the search terms I had used a couple of days before.

"Oh, my Goddess Blake." Alex whispered as I scrolled through the article. Everything was the same, news about the murder, the happy couple, the pictures - but there was one distinction.

Mitch Myles wasn't arrested and thrown into a sanatorium.

Mitch Myles took his own life.

With the same knife, he used to kill his wife.

"What? I don't understand." I stared blankly at Alex. Every hair on my body stiffened, a freezing chill running through me.

"The glamor must have extended to the article as well." Alex blinked repeatedly. "The article! I printed it out!" She turned and opened the car door. Reaching inside, she pulled some papers from her bag and stood beside me.

"It's the same article we printed. It says Mitch is in the Seaside Sanatorium." Her voice was harsh and raspy.

My chest felt excruciatingly tight.

Alex continued, her eyes scanning the article. "So, the glamor only goes so far. That's unreal. I've never heard or seen a glamor being used successfully over the Internet before." I could practically feel her body vibrating beside me. She tapped her finger to her cheek, thinking, "The call I made to the Sanatorium. It was so weird. The person who answered was distant, like we had a terrible connection, but... weirder. This explains it, I guess." She scrolled through her phone again. "The phone number I found for Seaside is gone from my searches. Incredible." I watched her beautiful features as she processed the information. Her eyes darted from her phone to the print-out to the building, to... nowhere.

"Was that call some kind of glamor too?" I wondered if now was a good time to ask how much she knew about glamor and if she could do them, but thought better of it.

Not the time.

As much as I really wanted to know what powers she possessed, I didn't want to piss her off, either.

"I don't know, Blake. I guess so. Or... a call from... some other place. Like, a world beyond this one..." She perked up, straightening and smiling a little.

"You seem kind of excited, Alex. I guess you're used to this stuff."

She eyed me, placing a hand on my arm. "Sorry, Blake. This must be terrifying for you."

I quirked a brow. I mean, I enjoyed a good paranormal movie now and then, but this... I straightened, determined to be the big man.

"Don't worry about me, Alex. But I have a question." She looked at me, her eyes urging me on. "What about the staff we talked to? And Mitch? Were they a glamor too?"

Alex shook her head. "No, Blake, those were actual spirits, in solid form. I should have recognized that when I saw them, but I didn't. They looked so real, so alive."

"Really? How do you know?"

"I can see spirits, Blake, and apparently, you were allowed to see them, too."

"Can you see them now?" I craned my neck around, looking up at the windows and door but nothing was there.

"Yes, I can."

"What? You can? Where?"

"Standing right behind you."

CHAPTER
TWENTY

SHARON

"Sharon, you're making excellent progress!" Dr. Middleton - John - watched as I stood on shaky legs with the help of my physical therapist, Teresa. John had a way of making me feel so good. Heat flushed my cheeks as tiny butterflies flitted through my belly. Walking was easy. Not tearing my hospital gown off in a fit of premenopausal fury was hard.

"Thank you, John. I really want to get out of here as soon as possible. No offense, Teresa."

"None taken! I'd like to see you on your way too." Teresa helped me back to bed. The therapy session was over. She excused herself and closed the door behind her. I felt a rush of warmth spread through my body again and pushed sweat-soaked covers off of me. This premenopausal nonsense was making me crazy.

"We should probably talk about what you plan on doing once you leave the hospital." John sat in the chair beside my bed.

"I've been thinking about that a lot. I'd like to get a small apartment, but I don't have any money." I pouted, smoothing the creases in my bedcovers.

"Well, yes, that's an issue. There's also the fact that, technically, you're a married woman. Would you be willing to live under the same roof as Jack Burke?"

I frowned. The thought of living with that tall, scrawny man left a bitter taste on my tongue.

I truly couldn't imagine hooking up with a guy who smelled like he'd just gone ten rounds with a school of tuna.

I shuttered. So gross.

"No. I don't know him. I haven't seen him since I woke up and don't want to. He's a total stranger to me, so I couldn't possibly live in his house." Tears welled, threatening to flow. Oh God, what if I have no choice? What if 'they', the hospital, Jack, or some other authority, *made* me live in his home? The idea of having to cook and clean and - worse - be a *mother* to his child... I shuddered again.

That would be a total nightmare.

"It's ok. I'm sure I can talk with Mr. Burke and make other arrangements. Don't worry about that now." I beamed and openly gazed at John.

My hero.

John returned the smile. "Have you had any dreams? Any memories?" I shook my head, no. Other than dreaming of John, that is. And what it would be like to kiss him and... stuff.

But I couldn't tell him that, could I?

"I haven't dreamt at all, actually. I'm pretty exhausted by the end of the day. With our sessions, then physical therapy..." I offered a small smile. I was trying as hard as possible to get on my feet. The quicker I could walk, the quicker I could leave and start my life.

"Ok, these things can take time. Has anyone else been to see you? Um... Miss Heale, perhaps?" John eyed me.

"No, I haven't seen Alexandra in a few days. I'm not sure where she is."

"That's fine. I just want you to take your time with things. Your memories will take some time. I want to ensure you are following my instructions, and not someone else's." John made his point clear, reaching for my hand and patting it, gently.

I pouted. "I really like Alexandra. You don't want me to see her?"

"No, no, that's not what I'm saying. I just want to make sure you aren't getting confused with different theories and practices regarding your memory." He held my hand in both of his.

"Oh, I see." Tears stung my eyes.

"What's wrong, Sharon?"

"Well, I have been thinking, what if I really am Betty Burke? I know I don't feel like I belong in this body, but what if I do? What if my memories come back and I figure out that I actually belong in this body, this town, and with Betty's husband? What do I do then?" Every fiber of my being wanted to run from that idea.

But, if that's the case, then who is Sharon Myles?

Why do I feel so certain that she is me?

A single tear spilled from each eye. John brushed a finger against my face, catching them. A pounding heat rushed to my cheeks.

"Goodness, so many questions for one afternoon. All the answers will come in time. In the meantime, it's important to follow your heart and the way it wants to lead you, no matter what the past dictates." John moved to sit beside me on the bed and took both my hands in his. I smiled. He smelled so damn good.

Like pipe tobacco and whisky. Rugged and manly.

I really liked that about him.

Wait. How did i know what pipe tobacco and whiskey smelled like?

John continued; "Sharon, I've been a coma specialist for a very long time, and I can tell you that some patients never recover their memories. They live full lives. Sometimes on their own, sometimes they fall back in love with the person they were married to. The important thing is to take things one day at a time, one minute at a time, and follow the path that's best suited to your current feelings. Do you think you can do that?" The warmth from John's hands swept through my body.

"Yes, I think I can do that, John. But, right this minute, I'm starving! Will you stay and have dinner with me?"

"Absolutely, it would be my pleasure." As if on cue, the door opened, and an orderly delivered dinner. Winking at John, I requested dinner for him as well, then dove into my meal.

TWENTY-ONE

JACK

I heard everything.

Standing outside Betty's hospital room door, I leaned against the wall, stupid tears tricklin' down my face. I regretted coming by today, after hearing everything Betty said. My chest felt all hollow and empty and stuff. She didn't sound one bit like she was wanting to come home to be with me and Alana.

The sorry sack of a doctor wasn't much help either, filling her head with ideas about 'following her feelings' n' such.

What a load of bull cucky.

I barely noticed the orderly delivering dinner. I needed to get out of there and make a plan to get my Betty back.

The bouquet of hand-picked daisies - Betty's favorite - was now limp and lifeless in my hands. Just a few minutes ago, they thrived with the life I was hoping to have with my wife.

It all seemed so futile now.

But, no. No, no, no, no, no.

She's my wife, and I'll be bringing her home, thank you very much.

I tossed the flowers in the trash and left.

TWENTY-TWO

ALEXANDRA

Poor Blake. I'd scared the living crap right out of him when I told him I saw the spirits of the dead sanatorium staff standing behind him. The way he jumped, like a black cat on a hot roof, almost knocking me over as he skidded away from the front steps.

I giggled.

Then I giggled some more.

Then I laughed so hard, I almost peed.

Now, on the nearly empty plane back to Castle Point, Blake - sitting across the aisle from me - turns to see what I'm laughing about. I slap my hand over my mouth and duck my head.

"Hilarious, Heale." He frowned, looking ahead at the handful of passengers seated near the front of the plane, thankfully far enough away not to hear us.

"Yes, I agree. It was *hilar*ious."

"Not." Blake scrunched his eyes, peering at me through slits.

"Oh, come on now, it wasn't like they'd hurt you. They're just harmless spirits!" He threw me a look that said he didn't care. "Aww, 'Blake the Great' afraid of a few specters?" I guffawed, then snapped my mouth shut when I saw the look on his face.

Oops. Crossed a line.

"Sorry, Blake. I'm just teasing. You have every right to be freaked out. It's been a weird couple of days."

"You got that right." He leaned his head against the headrest and blew out a long breath. "What's next, Alex?"

I pulled at my earring and chewed my lip. I thought about our seaside chat, and Blake's agreement - both delightful and heavy - to help me. I didn't want to think about my future right now, and what would happen after helping Sharon and Betty out of their predicaments. There was a lot more to think about right now.

"I'll have to check back in with my client."

Blake nodded slowly, the lines in his forehead crinkling.

"Can I ask you a question?"

I peered at him. "Shoot, Deputy."

He smirked.

"I'm confused. How has anything we found out about Mitch Myles going to help your client?"

Legit question. I pursed my lips. How much could I tell Blake? I still wasn't sure I could trust him with... well, anything, really. Then again, if I gave him more info, he might see how important it was to keep me out of prison.

I gathered my thoughts and looked at him. His beautiful brown eyes bore into me.

"My client is Sharon Myles."

I watched Blake's face as he frowned, his forehead creasing in fine lines.

"Sharon Myles? But... she's... dead." The words came slowly.

"Yes, I know. Her spirit has possessed the body of Betty Burke." Blake's eyes widened.

"Betty Burke? Like...Betty and Jack Burke? But she's still in a coma, isn't she?"

"Well, I'm not sure where Betty is, exactly. But I know Sharon Myles has possessed her somehow. If I can help Sharon figure out how she got into Betty's body, maybe I could find the demon responsible for killing her..."

Blake sat back in his seat and blew out a long breath. He ran his hands over his face, eyes, and into his hair. I could almost smell the smoke from his brain as he tried to work out everything I told him. That, along with everything we experienced the past two days...

"Unreal," he muttered, over and over.

"Blake..."

"Hmm?"

"You see why it's important for me to finish this, don't you?"

He pursed his lips before giving me a sideways glance, nodding his head.

"So, I can trust you? That you won't arrest me, I mean?"

He didn't say a word, only nodded again. "Promise you'll call me if you need help with anything." He held my gaze, his deep brown eyes piercing my green ones.

"I promise." That was something, at least. I relaxed back in my seat while the plane landed and taxied to the small terminal building.

We said goodbye before getting into my car. I could see him in my rearview mirror, watching me drive away. I tried to shake off the feeling in the pit of my stomach. A desire mixed with dread. Breakfast might help, but there wasn't any time. Right now, I wanted to see Sharon and show her the pictures of Sharon Myles. Maybe it would jog her memory. If that didn't, maybe showing her the pictures of Mitch Myles would.

Hopefully, Dr. Middleton wasn't around.

I parked and rushed inside with the file of pictures and articles stuffed in my handbag. Slipping past reception to the stairs, I walked carefully past Dr. Middleton's office, glancing quickly, but didn't see the doctor inside.

Dammit.

He might be upstairs with Sharon. I made a snap decision to try anyway and took the stairs two at a time. The day nurse waved at me without hanging up the phone. I turned to Sharon's room. Today was Penny's day off, so I'd stop by her place later to have a chat and pick up Blackjack.

Sharon's door was open, the TV blaring some early morning gossipy talk show. I peered inside the room. Dr. Middleton was nowhere to be seen. Relief flooded me as I stepped inside and closed the door behind me.

"Hi, Alexandra! So nice to see you!" Sharon clicked off the TV.

"Hi Sharon, how are you doing?" I stepped closer to the bed, my back to the door. I didn't want to get too comfortable in case I heard Dr. Middleton coming down the hall.

"Oh, pretty good! I'm going to be released soon!"

"That's amazing! So, physical therapy has been successful!"

"Well, yes, but I will need help. I'll have a cane for a few days or more, and attend physical therapy sessions, but otherwise, I'll be able to move on with my life!" Sharon's - or, perhaps I should say Betty's - brown curls bounced with Sharon's excitement.

"That's great. How are your sessions with Dr. Middleton? Have you had any memories?" Sharon's eyes grew a little dark, and she bowed her head.

"No, nothing yet. But John says that's normal. I just don't know..." she paused.

"Know what, Sharon. What's wrong?"

"Well, I decided I want to move out on my own. I want nothing to do with Jack Burke - I need to figure out who I am." Her words rushed out, cheeks flushed.

Poor Jack. He had such hope for Betty's return...

"Totally understandable, of course. Have you found a place yet?"

"No, not yet. Furnished apartments are a little hard to find, and I don't actually have any money."

An idea hit me like a neon sign flashing 'bar's open' above my head.

"Well, I have a big house and plenty of rooms. You are more than welcome to stay with me for the time being, if that interests you."

Sharon's eyes just about popped out of their sockets. She bounced up and down on the bed. "Oh my gosh, Alex! That's amazing! Yes! Oh gosh, yes, yes, yes!" I placed a hand on Sharon's and laughed.

"Great. That's settled then."

This was my opportunity to work with Sharon without the prying eyes and opinion of Dr. Middleton.

"Oh, but I can't pay you anything. I don't want to be a burden or a sponge." Sharon stopped mid-bounce.

"No, no, you could never be a burden. Blackjack and I would love the company."

"Who's Blackjack?" Sharon asked, smiling.

"He's my cat. He's a really sweet boy, most of the time. I'm sure you'll get along."

"Oh, I love cats! At least, I think I do. It's weird how

my thoughts and feelings go. Some things I know I hate, like tapioca pudding. But then the nurse or someone who knows Betty Burke is surprised when I don't eat mine because apparently, Betty would never pass up a pudding. It's confusing. Like, who am I, really?" Sharon leaned back, blowing a random 'Betty' curl from her face.

I had my opening.

"Well, that's actually something I wanted to talk to you about today. I think I may be able to help. Can I show you something?" I pulled the file from my bag.

"Oh, sure. What's that?" Pulling the photo of Sharon Myles from the folder, I handed it over, watching for any reaction. Sharon's breath caught. Her hand flew to her chest.

"I think I know this person! I feel like I've seen her before... she... she's so familiar... who is she?"

"That is Sharon Myles. We believe that this... is you." I watched Sharon's face, eyes growing wider, recognition lighting her up.

"Me! Yes! It's me! Oh my gosh, how did you figure it out?" Sharon was ecstatic. Then, something shifted. She held the picture in her lap, eyes growing darker. "Wait... if this is me... and I look like that, then what am I doing in this body?" Sharon looked up and locked eyes with me.

I swallowed hard.

Here we go.

"Well, it's possible that..." I paused, gathering my words "... the spirit of Sharon Myles - you - entered Betty Burke's body."

Sharon peered at me under heavy brows. "What do you mean?"

I reached for her hand and sat on the edge of the bed.

"Sharon Myles is... dead." I steeled myself for any kind of reaction.

"Dead? But... Oh, my God... how is this possible? How can I be dead? I'm right here!" Sharon burst into tears. I stroked her hand, trying to soothe her. If things weren't already confusing, they were about to get a lot worse.

"Well, you're right, in a way. You're definitely not dead - as you can see - you're living and breathing. But how you woke up in this body? That's what I have to find out."

Sharon was staring at the picture, tears streaming down her face. I already knew her next question before she asked it.

"How did I die?"

Yep, there it was. Truth time. I took a deep breath.

"Sharon Myles was murdered." I reached for a tissue and dabbed at Sharon's cheeks as tears poured down.

"Murdered. I was murdered?" Sharon's voice rasped as her breathing ramped up. She was hyperventilating.

"Just breath, nice and slow, slow it down, Sharon." I breathed with her, in, out, in, out slowly.

"How..." Sharon gulped air. "... how did I die?"

I eyed the oxygen mask hanging on the wall behind Sharon's bed and wished I knew how to operate the dang thing.

"Well..." I reached inside the folder for the picture of Sharon and Mitch Myles and the articles when the door opened and Dr. Middleton stepped inside. I stuffed the folder into my bag and slipped off the bed. Dr. Middleton eyed me and then noticed Sharon sniffling, wiping her eyes. She was still holding the picture of Sharon Myles.

"What have you done?" He was staring directly at me, his cheeks flaring. He walked over to Sharon and snatched the picture from her hands. "What the hell is this?" I pursed my lips and was about to speak when Sharon interjected;

"She told me that's me, Sharon Myles, and that I'm dead! That I was murdered!" Sharon burst into tears. John's brow furrowed as he stepped closer to Sharon's bed.

"Excuse me? What the hell are you talking about?" His voice rose.

Crap.

This wasn't going well.

"I found out who Sharon Myles is, and what happened to her. I was explaining it all to Sharon when you walked in." My words rushed out. I instantly felt small, my stomach roiling. This smacked of being confronted by my mother, and that never ended well.

Calm down, stand tall. You've got this.

"Miss Heale, could you step outside, please? We need to have a little chat." Dr. Middleton's tone was firm. I threw Sharon an apologetic look. Sharon just sniffled and wiped her eyes.

"I'll be back for you, Sharon. I'll get your room ready for when you check out of here." *Good job, Alex, just toss some fuel onto that flame.* The confused look Dr. Middleton gave me, and then Sharon, said I'd be hearing about that, too.

In the hallway, Dr. Middleton strode further away from Sharon's door and spun toward me. "Just what the hell do you think you're doing with my patient? What's this bull-shit about?" He held the picture of Sharon Myles to my face, spittle flying from his mouth, landing on my chest. I pulled back, grabbing a tissue from my bag and making exagger-ated spittle-swiping motions. I took a deep breath and pulled myself up to full height, looking him in the eye.

"Dr. Middleton, let me point something out to you. Since they have asked you to come here, you have made *zero* progress with Sharon." I held up a hand, fingers and thumb in the shape of an 'O' "I don't know what your methods are, nor do I care to learn, but they are completely ineffective. I have brought her closer to remembering who she is in only a couple of simple sessions."

"How dare you! She's not your patient, Miss Heale, she's mine. I told you to keep your nose out of it! Now, you upset her with this... this... crap?" He held the picture up to my face again and I snatched it, stuffing it in my bag. "You have no proof that this person is the same person laying in that hospital bed, crying her eyes out. You're feeding my patient false information and false hope."

I clenched my fists. For the first time in over twenty years, I felt the rising heat of my evil Dagon ancestral blood pour into my hands. The heat was a ticking time bomb, ready to unfurl and blow Dr. Middleton across the room.

I breathed, calming the temperate heat boiling in my veins and the shock to my system.

It had taken a stint at Juvie and years of learning to control my unwelcome legacy - I couldn't let it control me now. I had to get on top of this, and fast. I clenched and unclenched my fists, willing the heat in my veins to subside.

"Doctor, I told you before, and I'll tell you again. I will not stop helping Betty... or Sharon... find her memories. There are bigger things at work here, which you couldn't possibly understand." I stood firm and planted my now cool hands on my hips. Although I couldn't allow my dark powers to gain control, I was tempted to grab my wand from my bag and turn the Doctor into a toad.

That would be far more fun.

"Just what the hell does that mean? *'Bigger things at*

work'." He clenched his body from teeth to hands and bounced a little on his toes.

Dr. Do Nothing was hopping mad.

Turning him into a toad wasn't necessary. He already was one.

"Dr. Middleton, I work with people and situations that are - let's say - out of the ordinary. This definitely qualifies as that."

"Nonsense," he challenged. "Her behavior and lack of acceptance of her true identity are very common for someone straight out of a coma." He pointed a finger at me, "you don't know what you're doing, Miss Heale. And whatever you think you're doing, I want you to stop. Now." He folded his arms across his chest.

I mirrored him.

"I'll take it under advisement - but not from you. For now, you should know that I've invited Sharon to stay with me once she's checked out of the hospital."

Dr. Cranky Pants eyes narrowed, aiming hateful spikes in my direction.

"Well, won't that be convenient? You'll have all the opportunities you want to screw up the work I'm doing with my patient. Nice move, *Alexandra*."

"That's Miss Heale, thank you. And I can assure you, any work that Sharon and I accomplish together will be more than helpful. Good day, doctor." I spun on my heel and stomped down the hallway, feeling his eyes boring into my back.

On the other side of the door, I collapsed in a heap, leaning against the stair railing for support. I looked at the palms of my hands. I had taken every precaution to ensure my 'Dagon blood' would remain cold inside my veins. How it roused so easily was more than a little disconcerting. If I wasn't able to control it, then Dr. Middleton, the staff, Sharon and the entire wing of the hospital would've been in ruins.

I shuddered at the near disaster and wondered what it was about the doctor that pulled the heat from my inner being. Although I made some progress with Sharon today, I still had work to do. Exhaustion swept through my body as I jogged down the stairs.

No rest for the witches.

I had to summon Cressy.

CHAPTER
TWENTY-THREE

JOHN

Seething, I watched the hall door close behind Alexandra.

The bitch.

How dare she interfere?

Now that I found Sharon, I refuse to let anyone stand in the way of our future together.

That included the nosy Alexandra Heale.

Only question was, how could I stop her from interfering and ensure Sharon would remain in my favor?

First, I would have to undo what Alexandra had already done. I will treat Sharon as the Goddess I believe her to be. Win her over to my side completely so she wouldn't even want to get close to the truth.

To do that, however, I may have to take her away.

Forever.

TWENTY-FOUR

ALEXANDRA

B lack candles rolled in lavender and sage glowed from shiny brass stands on all four quadrants of the sacred circle in the middle of my living room - North, South, East, and West. A small iron stand holding a cauldron filled with sandalwood incense burned above a black candle in the middle of the circle.

Blackjack gave a delighted mew and rubbed against my leg, his tail curled around me in a warm embrace. I rolled my eyes. The only time I got any affection from my familiar was when I spell cast. I stood, surveying the circle.

Everything was in place.

"Are you summoning the Man?" Blackjack looked up at me, green eyes wide and reflecting the light of the candles.

"Yes, Blackjack. I need Cressy's help with the Sharon, Betty thing."

"Oh hooray. I miss that old codger." Blackjack practically twirled, his tail flicking every which way. He knew what

came next. Just a few more items to add to the cauldron, and I could summon my friend and mentor.

Scooping Blackjack up, I held him close to my heart, stroking his jet-black hair. He purred loudly as I added some witch's hair, copaiba resin, silver sage, and a small square of fabric cut from one of Cressy's many dapper, handmade satin suits to the small cauldron.

I kept every one of Cressy's suits hanging in the closet in my childhood bedroom. When I missed Cressy, I would slip in between them and breathe in the deep, aromatic scent of his cologne. I hated cutting into the fabric, so I used only small squares from inside the lining where it would do the least amount of damage to the flamboyant suits.

Blackjack jumped out of my arms and stalked the outer perimeter of the sacred circle, mewing, offering his help. The bright orange cauldron of flame flickered higher and higher with each item dropped in. I started the incantation Cressy had taught me years ago prior to his crossing to the other side. He said the spell would come in handy one day, but made me promise only to use it if his help was desperately needed. He was looking forward to a relaxing afterlife.

The memory made me smile. Thankfully, I rarely needed to summon Cressy and disturb his peace, but at the moment, I was feeling a little out of my league, so I felt justified. I repeated the spell three times.

"Heaven to Earth, hear my plea, bring back he who watches over me. Goddess and Gods of North, East, South, West, allow me to commune with my dear Cress."

Focusing on the caldron flame, my eyes glazed over. The flame rose higher and higher and then suddenly snuffed.

Tendrils of smoke curled around the inside of the circle until the soft apparition of my mentor appeared.

"*Cressy.*"

Waldo Cress's upper torso appeared, his lower portion forming the tendrils of smoke coming from the cauldron. In death, he was as flamboyant as he was in life. I smiled as my 'genie in a cauldron', wearing a satin smoking jacket, was fully formed. His dark grey hair was artfully slicked back, and a dapper, grey mustache lined his thin upper lip. His large, slightly uneven, yellowing teeth glowed in the candlelight as he smiled. He was incredibly tall, with long appendages. He held out his long arms. His long fingers, adorned with long, yellowing, sharply filed nails, reached for me.

"*Alexandra.* So lovely to see you, my dear girl."

I swept a portion of salt aside, stepped inside the circle, and felt the warmth of Cressy's embrace. I closed my eyes for several moments, soaking him in. At last, I pulled back and looked into his dark, knowing eyes. Blackjack mewed, bouncing around the outside of the circle, trying to get his attention. Cressy broke away from me and leaned down to pet him. Blackjack pushed into Cressy's hand, purring loudly.

"Cressy, I've missed you so much." Tears formed small pools in my eyes.

"To what do I owe this incredible pleasure?" Cressy smiled, his wispy long fingers holding me by the shoulders. "I see you still keep me close." He smiled as he gently tugged at my earring, the tiny vial with ashes inside. I smiled.

"I wear it every day."

"Sweet, silly girl." He smiled back, then his brow

furrowed, and he peered at me. "Why have you summoned me, Alexandra?"

I took a deep breath. "I need help, Cress. Something is going on that I don't know how to handle."

"I can't imagine there's anything in this world you cannot handle, my dear child." Cressy gave me a knowing wink, but I shook my head and explained the recent events, leaving nothing out. I told him about the glamor that must have been cast and the weird phone call with the Sanatorium. I showed him the articles, the blurred pictures of the Sanatorium's decay, and the drawing I made of the weird markings on the walls of Mitch's cell. I also told him about Blake, and my fear of what he would do with me after I solved Sharon's case.

Cressy regarded me thoughtfully. "It seems you are in a bit of a pickle, to be sure." His deep, resonant voice and polite speech were the same in spirit as he had been in life. Cressy's demeanor was a sweet gentleman persona over a powerful witch truth. I had never met or even known of anyone more powerful than Cressy had been. Hopefully, he could still pull some strings and help me from his new place of residence. "He doesn't remember what happened when you were a teen?"

I shook my head no. "He doesn't seem to. He apologized for being such a jerk to me, but other than that, he never mentioned it."

"So, the forgetting spell I cast over the town still holds."

"Yes, I guess, otherwise I would have to pack up and leave." Then the point Cressy was trying to make hit me. "Another forgetting spell?" Cressy nodded and smiled.

"Yes, sweet girl, you could easily cast a forgetting spell over Blake. We could do that now if you'd like."

Heat flushed my cheeks.

I felt so stupid.

Why didn't I think of that?

If I cast a forgetting spell over Blake, he'd forget everything that had happened the past few days.

He'd also forget all about me.

I chewed my lip and tugged at my earring. Cressy's hand pulled mine away, his other brushing against my lips. "You have feelings for the man in uniform." He winked.

Heat flushed my cheeks again.

"Maybe. Yes. I mean, No." I lifted my chin. "He thinks a witch killed his parents, Cress. Do you know anything about that?"

Cressy rubbed his chin. "Highly unlikely. Did he say how they died, or who he thinks is responsible?"

"No. We kind of ended it on an 'agree to disagree' silence." I shook my head. "What would you do, Cress? Cast the forgetting spell?" I looked into his deep eyes, pleading.

Cressy raised his crooked finger to his chin. "That's a good option, yes, but... I think I would reserve that for later. Right now, he may be an advantageous ally."

"What do you mean?"

"Well, he is 'the law', and really, if it weren't for him, you may not have found the information on Sharon and Mitch Myles on your own. Sometimes having the law on your side is a good thing."

"Oh great. But what if he turns me in? Then I'm not just in a pickle, I'm in the entire jar!"

Cressy chuckled.

"You will figure out a way, Alexandra, of that I am sure. *Be nice, play nice.* And, as they say, keep your friends close and your enemies closer. Remember that regarding this Blake fellow."

"Fair enough."

He kissed my forehead and looked at the drawings on the paper once again.

"The marks are intriguing. I have seen nothing like this since... goodness, literal ages." Cressy peered at the pictures, pressing a finger to his lips.

"And why the glamor, Cress? Who would have put it there? Why allow me to call the Sanatorium in the first place? Not to mention seeing Mitch, although I should have realized he was a spirit."

Cressy rubbed his chin.

"It's difficult to say. It's possible it was Mitch. If he somehow knew you were looking for answers, he could have led you there, but only given you as much information as he knew himself. And, as far as recognizing his spirit, a good glamor can easily mask even the most experienced witch."

That actually made sense.

Probably the most sense any of this made, so far.

How it was possible, I couldn't fathom.

"I still don't know what to do. How do I figure out who the demon is that possessed Mitch, and why did it kill Sharon? And why did she choose Betty Burke's body to walk into, and then what do I do about it?" I felt a little like the winey, scared eight-year-old that met Cressy almost thirty years ago.

Cressy guffawed lightly, and smiled.

"Oh, my dear girl, you can figure this all out on your own! You hardly needed to wake my slumber, although it is great to see you now."

I slumped.

"Please, Cress. Can you help me figure out who the demon is, at least? So I can find a spell to vanquish him?

Then maybe I can figure out the rest from there." I was on the verge of falling to my knees.

"Of course, my sweet. I think your first step is to have the markings interpreted. You may find the demon's name there."

"Who would do that? There are no witches in the underground who can interpret ancient dialects. None that I know of, anyway."

"There is one thing I can think of... although it's been several years since I laid my eyes on it. There is a book - and if my memory serves, very similar markings are in said book."

"Cressy, that's amazing! Who has the book?" I felt giddy. I wouldn't even have to expose myself as a witch to read a book.

"You will not like it. It's in Castle Dagon."

Dammit.

Not so simple.

"You're kidding me." The giddiness dropped to my toes.

"Sorry, my sweet. The curator of the museum in Castle Dagon would have kept it intact."

"Okay, I can deal with that, but it won't be easy. Mr. Fellows is a stickler about who can access the archives. But I'll try..."

I'm a therapist, doing research for a client.

Simple as that.

"Can you try to see who the demon is from where you are?" My well of hope stirred in my belly.

"Give me a few moments, and I'll see what I can do." Cressy swirled into a funnel of smoke and hovered in the center of the circle while Blackjack and I waited patiently. After several minutes, Cressy's form reappeared, his brow furrowed into deep lines. He pressed a long-nailed index finger against his lips.

"Alexandra, I..." he began, then stopped and pursed his thin lips.

"Cressy what, what did you find?" My breath caught.

"It's what I did and didn't find that's troubling. I could not locate the demon that had possessed Mitch Myles, I'm afraid. Something is blocking me." Cressy's furrowed brow revealed the concern we shared.

"What about Sharon Myles? Do you know why she's in Betty's body?"

"I couldn't get a simple answer on that, or any other information, but..."

"But what? Cressy, please..."

"I found Betty Burke."

"You *what*?" The breath left my body in a whoosh, gooseflesh pocking my entire body.

"Yes, indeed. *She's in the abyss, Alexandra.*"

"The abyss? What abyss? Where's the abyss?" I squeaked.

"She's trapped in limbo, neither in her body nor deceased. She's just... hovering."

"Oh no. No, no, no. What will happen to her?"

"If she isn't brought back from the abyss, she'll be trapped there for eternity. Her soul will never find peace."

"When? How long until she's trapped forever?" Pins and needles shot through my fingers and toes. I didn't want to know the answer. I could only picture Jack's sweet wife, Betty. He would be crushed if he never got her back, and I couldn't even explain why.

"Soon. You have little time, Alex. You've got to find the demon and banish it. You need its name. That will be the only way to release Sharon's spirit - and Betty's - I'm certain of that. Find it, summon it, and *say its name*."

I lowered my head, tears dripping from my eyes to the antique carpet below.

"But, *how*, Cressy? It's not like it's going to volunteer its name. I tried when I saw Mitch, but he couldn't say it. Is there another way?" I looked up at my mentor, my eyes brimming with tears and the weight of the task ahead.

"There has to be. And you are the best witch to find it, my sweet girl." Cressy held my hands in his ethereal ones. I felt the familiar warmth of his touch and a deep ache reverberated through my chest.

How did I end up here?

Banishing Imp's and non-threatening entities from my clients was a cakewalk compared to this.

This was real and incredibly difficult.

I felt like I was on the edge of Castle Point cliffs, peering down at the jagged, rocky shore below, about to fall into my own abyss.

"For now, I would start by gathering strength in numbers, my dear girl. Get some help, and fast."

"Cress, that's dangerous, you know that. If a gathering of witches was ever discovered... we could all be..." I couldn't finish my sentence. I didn't want to think beyond what Blake could do to me alone, never mind a coven.

"The risk is up to you, dear girl. Follow your senses. You'll do the right thing..." Cressy's apparition faded. He lifted his long, gnarly fingers to his lips and blew me a kiss. "I'm always with you..." He dissipated with the smoke from the cauldron as I reached for my precious earring.

All the candles extinguished with the last of the smokey vapors, leaving me and Blackjack in the dark.

I fell to my knees, sobs wracking my body. Blackjack

climbed up on my lap, licking the salty tears from my cheeks with his sandpaper tongue. How was I ever going to figure this out on my own?

Maybe Cress was right. I didn't have to.

"What's the plan, woman?" Blackjack's voice floated through my mind.

I thought of Betty Burke lost in the abyss and summoned the determination I needed.

"I have to help Betty, Blackjack." No matter the cost to my quiet life as a witch. I will risk my career and my life to help the Burkes. Now if only I could gather enough witches who will do the same. It was a lot to ask, but what choice did I have?

I wiped my eyes and reached for my phone to call Penny when it rang in my hand.

Blake.

I shuddered.

Had he been listening to my thoughts, or our conversation?

I dismissed the idea and answered the phone.

"Hello?" I tried to keep my tone light.

"Alexandra. It's Blake."

"What's up, Blake?" The dude held my future in his hands and I had to act like it was no big deal.

Insane.

"I just wanted to check in with you, see if you've had any progress with... you know." The last part of the sentence was barely a whisper.

Was he not alone?

Was I being paranoid?

"Why, you itchy to arrest a witch?" I sniped. "There must be some kind of exceptional trophy to add to your collection for that, I'd imagine." Goddess, I felt bitchy. Blake was the perfect person to unleash it on.

"Hey! I told you I don't want to arrest you. I'm calling to see if you need any help." Silence. "Also, to see if you'd like to have dinner with me tomorrow evening." I rolled my eyes.

This I did not need.

A part of me wanted to be in Blake's company, but the other part knew that a time bomb was ticking. As Cressy said, I may need Blake's help, so if I could stay in his good graces... maybe it was worth dinner.

After all, I had to eat, didn't I? I thought of seeing Blake again and suddenly felt ravenous, unsure whether the feeling was coming from my stomach or... lower.

"Ok."

"Ok? Really? Cool, that's cool." Blake's stammering warranted an eye roll. "Shall I pick you up?"

"No, that's ok. I'll meet you. Say eight o'clock at the Seaside Cafe?" I couldn't bear the thought of Blake stepping foot on my doorstep.

Too close for comfort.

"Ok, sounds great. See you then. And... Alex?"

"Yeah?"

"Don't worry, ok? You know what I mean..."

"Ok, Blake. Thanks." I pressed the end button and blew out a breath. I didn't know if I could trust Blake to keep my secret, but I'd have to... for now. Summoning a demon and getting Betty Burke back into her body was a bigger priority than my future.

I dialed Penny's number. Cathy, Penny's wife, answered.

"Hey, Cath, it's Alexandra. Is Penny home?"

"Oh hi, Alex! Yes, hang on a sec." Alex could hear Cathy

call Penny. After a bit of shuffling, Penny answered, breathless.

"Hey, Alex. I'm glad you called. I blasted the underground about helping Mrs. Twillinger with the payment of her fine and got a swell of donations. We should hit $10,000 within a couple more days."

"That's great, Pen." Tears welled up in my eyes once again as I choked on Penny's name.

"Alex, are you ok? What's wrong?"

"I need you."

TWENTY-FIVE

ALEXANDRA

Penny and I talked until late, and we agreed to meet at my place and summon the demon on the eve of the next full moon, a few days away. I was going to ask Penny if she could find more help, but decided against it. I felt bad enough about risking Penny's life by meeting. I didn't want others involved. If we weren't able to summon the demon, I would have to rethink my decision.

Before then, I had to bring Sharon home and try my best to get as much information from her as possible. That would mean more hypnosis sessions, preferably without Dr. Middleton's interference.

I headed to CPH early the next day. Penny was at the nurse's station. She greeted me, face stoic, our plans hidden behind small nods. "Is Dr. Middleton in with Sharon?" I asked, pausing at her door.

"No, he hasn't shown up yet today." Penny lowered her voice. "He's likely pissed that Doc Holloway signed Sharon's release forms, without consulting with him. I think Doc Holloway just wants her gone as fast as possible, and an end to the weirdness." Penny stifled a giggle. I agreed, happy to take Sharon off the good Doc's hands and free up a hospital bed.

I pushed the door open. Sharon was still in her hospital gown, sitting on the edge of the bed. She smiled when she saw me.

"Good morning, Alex!"

"Good morning Sharon. How are you feeling today? Ready to take on the world?" I tried to be positive and wondered if my tone sounded false. I couldn't help but think of poor Betty Burke; her spirit hovering in the abyss while Sharon roamed free in Betty's body. I had to agree with Penny. All the weirdness gave me a migraine.

"Yes, I'm excited to leave. Doc Holloway gave me the all-clear this morning. I haven't seen John yet though. I'm afraid he is a little upset with me for agreeing to live with you." Sharon dipped her head. A leopard print hair band held back her brown curls. I briefly wondered where she got it from.

Not important.

I wanted to be completely honest and transparent. If that meant that Sharon stopped seeing Dr. Middleton altogether, so be it.

I was tired of pussyfooting around.

"Sharon... I... well, as far as Dr. Middleton is concerned, he has asked me not to work with you. In fact, he asked me to stay as far away from you as possible and leave your therapy up to him."

"What? Does this mean I can't live with you? But why? You've been so helpful!" Sharon cried. "The only person to help me, really. Why wouldn't he let you help me?"

"No, no, you are still coming home with me, regardless

of what Dr. Middleton said. He wants me to mind my own business because he's the doc on your case. I'm not a psychiatrist, I'm a therapist, and, in his eyes, I'm not qualified to help you."

Sharon nibbled her bottom lip.

"Well, I think you're more than qualified. And I'd like to keep working with you, if that's possible?" She attempted to smile.

"Yes, I think it is, but if you want to keep working with Dr. Middleton, then we may have to keep it between us. For now, let's just focus on getting you settled in at my place, ok?"

"Yes... I mean, I'd like to keep seeing John - umm... Dr. Middleton, too." Sharon's sunny face fell.

A minor twinge of regret for putting Sharon in the middle of me and the Meddling Middleton spiked my temples, then quickly faded. With Sharon living at my house, away from his grasp, I would have the time and privacy to really dig into things.

The door pushed open. I was relieved to see Dr. Holloway walk in, which rapidly turned to dread when I saw he had Jack Burke in tow.

I watched Sharon's face. She merely stared at Jack, her lips pressed shut.

"Hello, Sharon. I found Mr. Burke in the hallway. He's brought you some of your things." Doc Holloway held the door open with his back, leaving his option to bolt on the ready.

"Hello Bet.... Uhhh... Sharon." Jack slowly approached the bed. He held out a bag of clothing, presumably, from Betty Burke's closet. Sharon took the bag from him and, without looking inside, set it beside her on the bed.

"Thanks," was all she could muster.

"I also brought you somethin' else. Somethin' that may help jog yer memory." Jack turned to the door and took two steps into the hall. He motioned toward someone and stepped back into the room. Behind him, a little girl entered.

Sharon took a sharp intake of breath.

Betty's daughter, Alana, approached Sharon.

"Mama?" Her big eyes pooled with tears. Sharon looked from the child to Jack to Doc Holloway, then to me.

"What the hell is this?" She spoke through gritted teeth.

"This is Alana, our daughter." Jack stepped behind the young girl, placing his hands on her shoulders.

"I don't have a daughter." Daggers flew from Sharon's eyes directly to Jack. Her face turned red.

"We have a daughter, Betty." Jack persisted.

"Don't call me that. *I'm not Betty*. I've told you that before. I don't remember you, I don't remember... *her*..." Sharon waved a hand toward Alana, pulled her legs onto the bed, and pivoted.

"Mama...?" Huge tears dripped down Alana's sweet little face. Her dark curly hair shook just as hard as her shoulders as she sobbed. "Please, Mama. Please come home. I've missed you so much. Daddy's not the same now. He's different and I don't like it. I need you to come home, Mama, please!" Alana flung herself onto the bed, reaching for Sharon, who remained immobile.

"*Leave*. Now." Sharon commanded. Jack reached for Alana as I reached for Jack. Doc Holloway just held the door, speechless, his eyes darting from one person to the next.

"Jack, I think it's best if we step outside." I held his arm and tried to coax him toward the door.

Just then, John appeared in the doorway holding a bag

163

with the insignia of a local dress shop printed on the side. He quickly surveyed the scene. "What the hell is going on here?" As he entered the room, Jack swung around to face him.

"*You.*" Jack stepped toward John, who dropped the bag.

Doc Holloway slid into the hallway, the door closing behind him.

I shook my head toward the escapee and reached for Alana, wrapping my arms around the crying child.

"Ok, guys. Everybody just take a breath." My demand fell on deaf ears.

Jack pulled himself up to his full height and puffed his chest at John who mirrored Jack's impression of a barnyard rooster.

"Stay out of this, Alexandra," Jack demanded. He clenched his fist and pulled his arm back, ready to strike John. "It's your fault my wife doesn't remember who we are. If you weren't such a shit doctor, we would have my Betty back by now. You useless piece of crap!" Jack yelled, throwing his fist forward and connecting with John's chin. His head flew back, then came slowly forward, his eyes glaring at Jack.

John grabbed his chin, working his jaw back and forth before reaching for Jack's throat. "You're the worthless piece of crap, Burke. You don't deserve Sharon!" He spewed before wrapping his hands around Jack's throat and squeezing.

Alana screamed. I peeled my eyes off the escalating fight to pull the child behind me. I could feel Alana's small body trembling, my own trembles a match to hers. I needed to stop the two idiots, and fast.

Sharon whipped her head around and stared at the men, mouth agape.

"Sharon, call security!" I yelled, trying to pry John's fingers from Jack's throat. Jack was pushing against John's chest, but he wouldn't budge, so he reached for John's throat instead. Both men were grunting and sweating, trying to catch their breath and choking at the same time.

Sharon didn't move.

She merely stared at John, her eyes glazed, her mouth in a small smile.

"SHARON! Call security!" I yelled louder. *For the Goddess's sakes, why wouldn't she move?*

Nothing.

I was about to yell at Sharon one more time when I saw how mesmerized she was by the two men fighting over her. The look of enjoyment on her face was baffling. I rolled my eyes, disgusted by the three 'adults' in the room.

I would have to separate the men myself, but had to act quickly and without being noticed.

I let go of the two testosterone laden idiots and reached for my bag. Pulling out my wand carefully, I checked no one saw me. Alana was hunched in the room's corner, her hands over her ears, eyes shut tight, tears streaming down her face. Sharon was still focused on John, and the guys... well, they were both red-faced and focused on each other.

I felt the wand pulsing in my hand. I flicked it one way, then the other. The two men flew back, away from each other. Jack landed on the floor by the bed, John against the door. Both men started gasping for air, coughing.

"John!" Sharon scrambled to get off the bed, her legs, still wobbly, nearly gave way beneath her. She clutched the night table, then the wall as she made her way over to John, kneeling beside him. She stroked his face. "Are you alright?" She pulled him closer, and he rested on her legs.

Jack rubbed his neck, taking deep, slow breaths as he

watched his wife care for another man. His brow furrowed deeply and his eyes turbulent. I slipped the wand back into my bag, unnoticed.

"I see how it is, *doctor,*" Jack's words came out in a raspy whisper. "I'll make sure your license is suspended for this, Middleton. You can't take a guy's wife and expec' to get away with it!"

"Jack, let's talk outside." I helped him up. He put an arm around my shoulders for support and walked to the door, forcing John to stand and help Sharon up so they could get out of the way.

Jack paused, looking longingly at Sharon.

"Goodbye, *Betty.* Don't you go expectin' any support from me, financial or otherwise! You've made your choice, now you can live with him." Spittle flew from Jack's mouth, his body shaking as I led him into the hall. Then I went back into the room and helped Alana to her feet and out the door, shielding the child from Sharon. I closed the door behind them. Alana ran into her father's arms.

"Jack. I don't know what you were thinking, but I understand. This is a lot for you and Alana to take."

"I just thought, maybe if she saw Alana she'd remember and would wanna come home with us." Tears streamed down Jack's face. Alana clutched her father and cried. I rubbed Alana's back and whispered a prayer to the Goddess to protect the child and erase the past hour from her heart. Alana's sobs softened to a whimper, then stopped.

"I'm so sorry, Jack, but if I can offer a bright side, I'm taking Sharon home with me. She agreed to stay with me for a while."

"Really, Alex? She's not going with...?" Jack took a ragged breath.

"No, not now, anyway. And I'm going to work with her,

ok? Against John's wishes. I'm going to help her, Jack. Help her remember." I said another prayer to the Goddess that I could keep my word.

Jack would never understand what was actually going on, and I hoped I wasn't giving the man false hope, but I couldn't let him go on living in grief. "Just give me some time, ok?" I asked. Jack nodded.

"Thank you, Alex. I'm sorry for... what happened in there?" Jack's shoulders slouched as he looked down at his daughter. "I'm sorry I put you in the middle of all of this, lil' girl." His daughter hugged him tighter.

"Can we go home, please, daddy?" Alana looked up at her father, then at Alex.

"Yes, let's go. Thanks again, Alex. Call me, please. Let me know how she is?" Jack's eyes pleaded.

"Yes, of course. Now, go buy Alana some ice cream." I smiled.

Jack nodded and turned to walk down the hall, holding Alana's hand. My heart ached for them.

It wasn't just one more reason to get Betty back - it was *the* reason.

I had to work fast.

Exhaustion clung to my bones as I turned toward Sharon's door and pushed it open.

TWENTY-SIX

JOHN

I helped Sharon back onto the bed, then sat on the edge and took her hand in mine. I stroked her fingers, marveling at the softness of her skin. I looked into Sharon's deep brown eyes. A gentle warmth flowed through me and I smiled.

"I'm so sorry, Sharon. I don't know what came over me. My protective instincts seem to surface where you're concerned." Sharon ducked her head and peered up at me. I adored the way she did that. A giddy feeling burned in my belly.

"It's ok, John. I understand. I'm sorry too. I wasn't expecting a visit from Jack, and certainly didn't expect him to pull a stunt like that. But I guess I don't really know him, so I shouldn't be surprised."

I stroked her hand again remembering the gift I brought her, grabbed the shopping bag and placed it on her lap. "For you. I wasn't sure what clothing you had, or if anything would even fit anymore, so I bought you something you could wear to Alexandra's. I hope that's ok."

"Oh, John! You're amazing!" Sharon reached for my hand again and squeezed.

My heart sped up. She made me feel like a schoolboy, in love for the first time.

Sharon opened the bag. "What did you... Oh, thank you! It's perfect!" Sharon pulled out a soft pair of lounge pants, a matching shirt, and complimenting sweater. She dug a little deeper into the bag and found a pair of comfortable shoes and a small bag of makeup. When she looked back in the bag, she blushed and pulled a bra with generous amounts of lacy fabric over the large cups, and several pairs of lacy underwear. She glanced at me, her face red, but smiling.

My heart skipped a beat or two as I briefly imagined her wearing the lacy bra and panty sets. A stirring in my groin meant I had to shift slightly away from her.

If there was ever a time to tell her how I really felt about her, now would be it.

I took a deep breath.

"Sharon, I wanted to talk to you..." Just then, that frigging bitch Alexandra stepped through the door. I let go of Sharon's hand and slid off the bed, standing beside her. Pursing my lips, I eyed Alexandra.

"Well, that was a complete shit show, wouldn't you agree, *doctor*?" Alexandra didn't hide her contempt.

The feeling was mutual.

"I'll admit it wasn't my shining star moment, but, in my defense, he started it." My voice grew quiet as I looked down, shuffling my feet.

"Well, no use crying over it. Look what John brought

me!" Sharon showed Alexandra the clothes, beaming. My heart leaped in my chest, watching her with excitement.

Alexandra's eyebrows rose as she looked from Sharon to me and back again. I sunk into the chair beside Sharon's bed and noticed that Sharon slipped the underwear back into the bag. Relieved, I let out a breath.

Alexandra sighed. "Lovely gesture. Did you see what Jack brought you?"

Sharon shook her head.

"Oh, I hadn't bothered to look, to be honest. I doubt whatever Jack brought me would be to my taste and probably far too big for me now."

Alexandra sighed again. "Do you need help to get dressed?"

"I can get dressed on my own. Be ready shortly."

Alexandra rubbed her brow and took a deep breath. "Ok, great, I'll make sure the discharge papers are complete so we can get you out of here." Alexandra nodded toward me, but I didn't bother to return the gesture.

I wished I could read her thoughts.

Not that I cared.

In my books, she was a charlatan, but Sharon seemed to like her, so I was careful to keep my opinion to myself. I wanted to continue seeing Sharon.

But not in a professional capacity.

Something I was about to tell her when Alex interrupted us.

Alone again, I slid back onto the bed, taking Sharon's hand again. "Sharon, there's something I wanted to say to you before Alex interrupted us."

"Oh? What was it?"

"I... well, I don't think that I can be your doctor anymore."

Sharon's eyes grew wide, and she pouted. "What? But why?"

She was the most adorable thing ever.

"Well I don't think you need me. You'll be moving in with Alex, and although I think her methods are questionable, I'm sure she'll be able to help you navigate any memories as they arise."

"But what if I still need you? Can I call you?"

"Well, that's the other reason I don't think I can be your doctor anymore." I took both of Sharon's hands in mine, stroking my thumbs across the top of her knuckles. I looked into her eyes. "Sharon... I... well, I seem to have developed feelings for you, which is completely unprofessional and could cost me my license."

Sharon didn't bother to hide her smile.

"Oh, I see... yes, losing your license would be an awful thing..." she whispered, breathless.

"Right, so I can't be your doctor anymore. Not if... if we want to continue seeing each other," I stammered, as I returned Sharon's smile. "Would you like that, Sharon?" She giggled. My heart skipped a beat.

"Yes, I'd like that very much, John." I brought her fingers up to my lips and placed a line of kisses across her knuckles.

I had her.

She belonged to me, and nobody could take her away from me.

Ever.

CHAPTER
TWENTY-SEVEN

ALEXANDRA

I waited patiently in the hallway while John and Sharon chatted. John appeared in the hallway and closed the door behind him.

"She's just getting dressed now, then you can take her home."

"Thanks. I will." This guy really grated on my nerves.

"You should know - you'll find out soon enough - I've removed myself from Sharon's case as her doctor."

I squinted at him.

"Really? Why?" John kept me waiting for an answer as he ran one hand through his hair, the other one planted firmly on one hip.

"Because I want to date her," he spat out, folding his arms across his chest.

Good Goddess, this man was a piece of frigging work.

I mirrored John's body language. Folding arms were better than flying fists, and I didn't exactly trust my ancestral powers where this guy was concerned.

"Is that so? And Sharon feels the same way?"

"Yes, she does. I told her that if any memories came up she needed to deal with, I'm sure she can handle it, with your help, in fact." He smirked.

Another strip of nerves grated off my spine.

"Oh, really? That's so big of you, considering you think I'm a charlatan." I hoped he didn't expect a big thank you from me.

Something was off about him. I just couldn't put a finger on it.

However, if intuition had an odor, this one would smell like rotten eggs on blue cheese.

What was his deal?

"I've never called you a charlatan, Miss Heale." John uncrossed his arms.

"True. Not to my face, anyway."

"I just question your...methods."

"Uh-huh. Well, question away, I really don't care. My success rate with my clients speaks for itself. I suppose this means you'll be over at my place all the time?"

"Possibly. Is that a problem?" John couldn't hide the grin spreading across his face. If my eyes could roll any further than the back of my head, they would.

"I suppose not, but I draw the line at sleepovers."

John chuckled.

"Don't worry about that, Miss Heale. I'm nothing if not a gentleman. Besides, Sharon is still healing, and I'd like to take time to get to know her better. Take it slow."

"If by slow you mean molasses in January, then okay." If I was successful in releasing Sharon to the spirit world where she belonged, and brought Betty back to her body from the abyss, then this relationship - and conversation - were practically moot.

Unless...

Blood ran cold through my veins.

Shit.

What if the repulsion I'd felt toward him was because *he's the demon who's after Sharon?*

I rubbed my brow furiously and studied John.

Oh Goddess, did I just agree to let a demon into my home and life?

Sharon walked out of the room, using only a cane, wearing the new outfit John had brought. Her hair was pinned up and back, away from her face, and she had applied some makeup. She smiled and stood beside John. He took her hand.

"Sharon, you look amazing!" John held her hand close to his chest.

I swallowed the vomit that threatened to paint his lab coat.

What had I done?

"Yes, you do, Sharon. Ready to go?" I stammered, grabbed Sharon's bag from the room, and briefly glanced at the empty hospital bed. The bag of clothes Jack had brought was still on the bed, untouched. I pictured Jack and Alana's sad faces as they left the hospital earlier.

The panic I felt when Cressy told me to *hurry or lose Betty forever* rose in the back of my throat. I turned back to see John and Sharon walking down the hall, John's arm bracing Sharon around the waist, supporting her. They looked into each other's eyes as they walked, smiling.

I was running out of time.

CHAPTER
TWENTY-EIGHT

ALEXANDRA

I parked in the driveway, opened the car door for Sharon, and grabbed her things.

"Your place looks pretty old." Sharon gawked at the grandiose white exterior of my Victorian-style home.

I tried my best to ignore her flat appreciation of what others called 'the nicest home in Castle Point.' "Yes, it's old," I replied, "almost 200 years now."

Sharon walked, with the steady assist of her cane, slowly down the hand-laid cobblestone path toward the porch. A short picket fence surrounded sizable gardens on either side of the path.

The gardens had been winterized weeks ago, and, other than some kale and a few winter squash, was mostly black earth and the occasional murder of crows, craving the rotten compost mixed within the dark earth.

In the summer, one garden was full of herbs used for cooking, creating and potion making. The other, an abundance of colorful vegetables for eating and sharing with friends.

"You live alone?" Sharon asked as we took two steps up the wraparound porch. The porch swing waved a greeting as it swayed in the cool autumn breeze.

"I do. Well, not alone. I have Blackjack." I smiled, opened the front door, and shuffled Sharon inside.

"Oh. More old stuff," she commented as she helped herself into the living room. She took a tour around, running a finger along the bookshelves and mantle before blowing dust off her fingertips. "You must really love antique furniture." Sharon picked up a throw pillow and swatted at it, releasing microscopic dust particles into the air before setting it down.

"My mother was a collector," I explained, "partly because a lot of the furnishings came with the house. She got hooked on garage sales and antique stores after that." I wasn't sure why I was trying to justify living among dead people's things to a woman who was... well, dead.

Blackjack sauntered in. When he saw Sharon, he froze, back arching, a growl resonating from deep inside his chest. I scooped him up, petting a purr out of him before he leaped from my arms and scooted from the living room into the adjoining dining room, the kitchen, and out the cat door into the backyard.

Sharon frowned. "I don't think your cat likes me."

"He just doesn't know you yet. He'll come around. Cranky old thing." I turned toward the kitchen, closed my eyes and connected with my familiar.

"Blackjack! Could you be any more rude?"

"Woman. What have you brought home now?" I smirked at my cat's apparent displeasure for our lovely new house guest.

"Someone who needs my help, you cranky bastard."

"She needs more than your help. She needs an Exorcist."

He wasn't wrong.

"Why do you think I brought her home?"

"Please tell me you will not be doing the exorcizing?"

"Ok, I won't tell you. Happy?"

"Hardly. I think I'll head over to the redhead's place for the duration of the creepy woman's visit."

"No, you won't, buster. I need you here to keep an eye on... things."

"Fine. But I want extra tuna every night until whatever she is, is gone."

"Deal. Come back now and make nice."

"If you insist. But you better come out here and look at your protection jars."

"Why, what happened?"

"You'll see." With that, Blackjack sauntered back into the kitchen, stopping to rub up against every corner and piece of furniture as he snail-paced his way toward Sharon.

"Quit stalling, or kiss the tuna deal goodbye."

Blackjack scooted the last few feet toward the chaise. He sat on the floor eying me.

"Huh. He must have changed his mind about me." Sharon reached down and stroked his head. Blackjack pulled back, glared at Sharon, and glanced at me. I narrowed my eyes at him. He twitched his tail and then leaned into Sharon's hand before jumping up onto the couch beside the chaise and settling in.

Sharon brushed her hands together, frowning. "Not a cuddler, huh?"

"Don't mind him. He's of the potato species and prefers couch over laps. Good boy, Blackjack." I smiled and could feel his contempt, but appreciated his performance.

I turned my attention to Sharon. "Your room is the only one downstairs, down the hall, next to the bathroom. I'll put your bag in there. There are fresh towels in the bathroom for you as well. Maybe tomorrow I can take you shopping for a few more things?"

"Oh, that won't be necessary. John has offered to take me, but thank you." I felt the hairs on the back of my neck prick up.

As much as I wanted Sharon to stay as far away from John as possible, I had to keep them both close. If John really was the demon that possessed Mitch and killed Sharon, I'd hopefully reveal that when I summoned him.

But first, I needed to find *his* name.

I forced a smile. "Oh, isn't that nice of John, and exciting for you? A fresh start and all..."

"Yes. I'm so happy to be out of that hospital. Most of the staff are complete idiots, with one or two exceptions. I appreciate you opening your home to me, Alex. Although, I don't plan on staying long."

A niggling wink of panic rose in my spine. I wondered where she thought she'd be going, and if I'd have enough time to do my digging. "Nonsense. Take all the time you need. It gets lonely around here, just me and Blackjack rattling around this old place." Blackjack had fallen asleep, satisfied he had fulfilled my wish to play nice with the weird lady.

"You've never married then? How long have you lived here?" Sharon glanced around the living room, a small smile on her lips.

"I grew up in this house, actually. And no, never married."

"Oh. Well, we can't all be lucky in love."

I shifted uncomfortably.

"Just haven't found the right guy, I guess."

"Right, I guess." Sharon nodded absently.

I sat in the small accent chair next to the fireplace and tried my best to shake off my mood. Sharon was a spoiled prom queen who clearly thought her poop deserved first prize. It did not thrill me to have her under my roof, but had no other option.

"Well, I do have a date tonight. Not that I have high expectations." I thought of Blake and silently wished that we were having a proper date.

A panty-melting, shirt-ripping good time.

Instead, I'd spend the evening sitting on porcupine quills, watching every word that came out of my mouth.

"Oh, that's nice." Sharon perked up. "Who is he? Is he cute?" Blakes's handsome features floated through my mind and settled into my butterfly-filled belly.

"He works in the Sheriff's department and yes, he's a very good-looking man. But, no expectations. It's just a dinner date at a local cafe." I smiled with some effort.

"A guy in uniform! Nothing hotter than that. Except maybe a guy in a white doctor's coat." Sharon smiled and checked her nails.

"Yes, well, to each their own, as they say." I smiled again. "Since I'll be gone for dinner, how about I order something for you? Then maybe you could take a long bath, if you can manage it, and just relax for the evening?"

"Sure. Thank you, Alex. I think I'll just rest here for a while, maybe take a nap while you get ready."

"Sure thing." I pulled the green and orange crocheted blanket - one my mother made years ago when green and orange anything was the color of choice - off the back of the couch and covered Sharon, tucking an extra throw pillow behind her head. She closed her eyes and swiftly matched Blackjack's gentle snores.

I crept into the kitchen and out the back door. I needed to check the protection jars around the perimeter of the yard, which, according to my sassy cat, needed attention.

A cool breeze off the ocean greeted me as I stood on the porch, looking over the backyard. The expanse of grass and trees, their leaves shifting to the jewel shades of fall, led to a rocky outcropping that looked over the ocean below. I walked past the arbor - where lawn furniture and a BBQ, tucked away for the winter, gathered dust - and approached the first jar's location at one corner of the un-fenced yard. There was a small pile of dirt, and the jar, broken on top of it, its contents spilled out.

What the actual hell?

I swiftly checked the other jars and found the same. All of them dug up, the jars broken, and their contents were everywhere. Who would do this? A shiver crept up my spine.

Was John here earlier?

Did he break the jars?

It would make sense if he was the demon, that he - or one of his minions if he had any - broke the protection, likely to gain easy access to Sharon. And if that were the case, then was there any point in making more, if he would just do it again?

I wished I had cameras installed, as Cressy had insisted many years ago, but my life had been pretty quiet and uneventful since he cast the forgetting spell over the community, so I refused the expense. I planned to double up the contents of fresh jars and attach a few extra sigils to the doors and windows, but that would have to wait until tomorrow.

Right now, I had a date with a tall man in a tight uniform.

CHAPTER
TWENTY-NINE

BLAKE

I settled into the booth at the far corner of the cafe, which had the best view of the bay. I sighed deeply, glancing around the nearly empty cafe as the server filled two water glasses and placed a couple of menus on the table. I glanced at my watch just as Alex strode through the door. My breath caught in my throat as she closed in on the table.

I hadn't forgotten how incredibly beautiful she was, but seeing her again...

I forced my jaw closed and offered a smile.

Alexandra slipped into the bench seat across from me and returned the smile. The scent - *her scent* - roses and...something earthy. Patchouli? Sandalwood? I tried to put a finger on it but realized I didn't even know one scent from the other. Whatever she wore was intoxicating and shot straight to my groin.

The server reappeared with her notepad in one hand and a pencil in the other.

"What can I get you?"

I nodded to Alexandra, who hadn't bothered to glance at the menu. "Just the Cobb salad, thanks."

"I'll have the loaded double cheeseburger, large fries, and a side of gravy." The server nodded and walked to the kitchen, scribbling their order on her pad.

"Big man, big appetite?" Alexandra sipped her water.

"I guess so. Didn't have time to eat today. I'm starving."

"And lemme guess. You have an aversion to green stuff?" Alex's mouth tweaked sideways.

"Greens fall into the fru-fru category, just like fancy coffees." I grinned and sucked back an ice cube from my water, chewing on it. Alexandra wrinkled her nose. I instantly stopped chewing the ice, wishing I could spit it across the room. Instead, I swallowed the rest of the cube whole.

"So, how have you been, Alex?" I smiled and ran my fingers through my hair. Alex leaned back, placed a hand on her stomach, and set her gaze on me.

"Since you saw me a couple of days ago? Ok, I guess. Escaped the noose so far, so that's a win."

I ignored her comment

"Any progress with helping... uh... Sharon?" I tapped a couple of fingers against my temple, willing the headache to dissipate. Alex took a deep breath and leaned back in her seat.

"Some, I suppose. But there's a long way to go."

I leaned forward, giving her my full attention.

"Interesting. What do you have to do?"

"Well, finding the demon who possessed Mitch Myles is the top, middle, and bottom of my list," Alexandra smirked and took a sip of her water.

"Have you figured out how you'll do that? Do you have... help?" my words rushed out before I could get a grip.

Alexandra pursed her lips and sat back, eyeing me.

"If you're asking me if there are other... people... like me in Castle Point, you'll never get an answer."

"I'm just interested, that's all." I attempted to sound casual and leaned back.

"*Why* are you so interested, Blake?"

"I just want to find out a little more about you. Maybe I can be helpful."

"Really? Haven't you learned enough about me already? Enough to hang me? Or do you need more?" she snapped, her cheeks flushed.

"Ouch, Alex. That's not what I'm doing here, honest." Alex studied my face as if trying to decide whether I was telling the truth. Meeting her eyes, I tried my best to look sincere.

It worked.

"Fine. Let's start again, shall we? No, I'm not any closer to finding the demon who possessed Mitch Myles, and no, I don't need any help. Let's just say I've got it covered and leave it at that, ok?"

It was my turn to study Alex. "Fine. But promise to come to me if you do?"

Alex hesitated before answering. "Sure," she answered, just as the server brought food to the table. We took our first few bites in silence.

"So," I took a huge bite of my burger, chewed, and swallowed before continuing. "What kind of...talents do you possess as a ... special person?"

I grinned.

She frowned.

Dammit.

"You make it sound like I'm some kind of weirdo."

I barked out a laugh and shook my head. "No, I don't think that at all." I winked.

Alex rolled her eyes. "Good. Because I'm not. And you don't want to know what I can do to people who think I am."

"Woah. Down, tiger. Relax." I raised my hand. "I recall you saying you've seen the inside of a locker a time or two. If you didn't fight back in high school, what makes you think I believe you would do so now?"

Alex met my eyes with her gorgeous deep green ones and they pierced my soul. My burger felt like a lump of lead in my guts.

Don't talk about the past. Check.

Time to backpedal.

"Honestly, Alex, I think your gifts are amazing." I dropped my voice to a low grovel and looked at her through hooded eyes before taking another bite of my burger.

"Thanks." Alex dropped her voice to a whisper. "So, by 'talents' I assume you mean magical abilities?"

I stopped eating, wiping my mouth. "Yes, I guess I do."

"Plenty."

I tried not to get too excited about the single bit of information she offered.

"Interesting."

Alex nodded, stabbing a few more green things on her plate.

"To say the least..."

"So, did you use your... abilities a lot? Like, at school and stuff?" I tried to sound casual, taking another bite of my burger before rushing her with more questions.

She stopped mid-chew and peered at me.

"No, never."

185

"I guess you knew the risks," I offered, my voice low.

"Yeah, I guess." She put her fork down and took a long drink of water.

I pressed on. "So, I'm curious. What 'plenty' of powers do you have, if you don't mind my asking?"

Alex studied me carefully, her fork partially loaded with another mouthful of green stuff. "Why do you think I'd tell you?" Corn and peas fell from her fork back into her salad.

I held up my hands. "Just... making conversation." I shrugged and took another large bite of fries smothered in gravy. "I want to get to know you better, that's all."

She gave up the veggie stabbing battle and put her fork down. "Well then, ask me about my apothecary business, or my cranky black cat, or my current knitting project, and you'll have yourself a real get-to-know-you conversation." A flush of red prickled Alex's face.

I chuckled. It looked like I would not get any closer to knowing the *real* Alex this evening, and what she could do. If what I'd been raised to believe was correct, then somewhere inside Alex the Witch was an evil streak that I had yet to uncover.

So far, she appeared to be a beautiful, kind person who truly cared about others. Until she dropped the 'good witch' facade and showed her true colors, I'd have to play along.

Besides, I kind of enjoyed getting her riled up. She was so friggin adorable when she was cranky. I thought of telling her that, then wised up fast. "Ok, ok. So. You have a black cat. That's a little on the nose for a witch, don't you think?" Alex merely shrugged."I already know a bit about your business. I bought my shampoo there."

"Yes, I know. I can smell it on you."

My eyebrows shot up. "Oh? I don't remember giving

you the opportunity to smell my hair." I grinned. "But I would if you'd let me."

Alex squirmed in her seat, her cheeks flushed.

Ha.

I wanted to stand up and take a victory lap around the restaurant.

"No, that's ok. I'm good." She picked up her fork and began stabbing at her plate viscously. The peas refused to cooperate.

"Hey lady, take it easy on the rabbit food." I chuckled as Alex victoriously brought a single pea to her lips and sucked it into her mouth, her lips forming a perfect, small 'O'.

I wondered how large the 'O' could go.

Then I swallowed.

Hard.

"What about you?" she asked, chewing and swallowing the pea before stabbing her plate for more.

"Are you asking whether I knit? No, unfortunately. Cross-stitch is more my thing. I'm working on a pillow now, in fact."

Alex stopped mid-jab and peered at me. "I can't tell if you're serious or not."

"Serious about cross-stitch? Most definitely. Can't get enough of it." I could tell Alexandra was fighting the smile spreading across her lips. She giggled.

Another win.

Another imaginary victory lap around the restaurant.

Smile lines faded from Alex's lips. "My mom used to cross-stitch. I still have her pillows. All over the damn house." She jabbed at another pea.

"You said your mom is gone. She's passed on?"

Alex eyed me thoughtfully, then nodded her head. "Unfortunately."

"Did she... was she... like you? Did you... uh.. inherit your gifts from her?"

"Oh, they're my *gifts* now, are they?" Alex avoided the question. "Sure would be nice if the lawmakers thought about it that way. Might not be so afraid of my life, if that were the case." She stopped when she saw my face.

I wasn't smiling, my eyes fixed on her. Alex reached for her earring and pulled at it. Tiny beads of perspiration dotted her temples. The scent of her perfume mixed haphazardly with the scent of... fear.

"You don't have to be afraid, Alex. I can protect you." I reached my hand across the table and grabbed Alex's free one. Her body softened, and she leaned against the backrest.

"I'd really like to believe that, Blake. You are literally holding my life in your hand right now." Alex glanced down at our hands. I held tighter. "The answer is no. I didn't inherit my abilities from my mother, and, like I told you before, I never knew my father. I just know I've had abilities for... a very, very long time." She glanced from our hands to me. I smiled at her but wouldn't let go. I was afraid to move, but was also aware of the clammy sweat forming in my palm. I hoped she didn't notice.

We spent the rest of the evening chatting about growing up in Castle Point. I could tell Alex was carefully tip-toeing around subjects that could lead to more questions about her abilities and where she got them. She dodged them by asking me about my family and my work. A lot of my questions about her went unanswered, but mostly, it felt like an actual date. We both relaxed and laughed more than I thought we would.

I held her hand through the rest of the evening, finally pulling away when the server approached the table.

"Sorry folks, the cafe is about to close," she said and placed the check on the table. I paid, and we walked out into the cool autumn air.

"Thanks for dinner, Blake, and...," she paused.

"And what, Alex?" I turned her body to face me. Shots of warmth traveled up my arms to my heart.

Alex looked up, her green eyes sparkling in the moonlight. "For making me feel... safe."

"You are safe, Alex," a warm heat ran down to my toes, pausing at my crotch.

"I'll call you tomorrow, maybe?" Alex moved toward her car.

"Sure." I said as she got into her car and drove away.

CHAPTER
THIRTY

ALEXANDRA

By the time I woke up, put on my robe and slippers, and shuffled to the kitchen for a cup of coffee, Sharon was gone. She left a note.

Alex - John picked me up for an early breakfast and a day of shopping! See you this evening.

P.S. Hope your date went well. - Sharon

Grateful for the minor miracle of avoiding post-date conversation with Sharon and dodging John, I poured a large cup of coffee, skipped frothing the milk, and instead poured two generous helpings of cream with one sugar and placed a spoon in the cup. With a snap of my fingers, the spoon stirred the coffee all by itself while I slid into a chair and thought about my date with Blake.

At first, I couldn't think. The lavender and mint, along with Blake's cologne, put my brain on hiatus. I debated whether to plug my nose before the questions started. I hated lying to him about my mother being dead, but I didn't need Blake to know *that* story. Not yet, and maybe never. I couldn't help but feel like I was in front of my inquisitor; the man who could seal my fate to the noose should he decide to.

I was thankful for Cressy's forgetting spell. Blake obviously couldn't remember the monumental 'incident' when we were teens, when I practically blew up the entire school in a fit of anger toward him and the cheerleading squad because they wouldn't stop teasing me for being 'weird.'

That was the first and last time my ancestral blood ran hard and fast through my veins, and out of my control. Cressy had to act quickly to cast a spell over the students and teachers, to make people forget I used my powers to throw desks, lockers, and 200-pound football players around. Instead, he had them believe I had done so with my strength.

As ridiculous as that seemed, it worked. I was hauled off to Juvie for the duration of the school year for causing so much damage. As an extra measure, Cress placed a forgetting spell on the entire town. Judging from Blake's questions - or maybe interrogation was a better word - the spell still held.

Cressy's advice filtered through me. *'Keep your friends close, but enemies closer. Play nice, be nice."* And pray to the Goddess that Blake ignores my beliefs - and his oath - until I get through this and either cut and run or cast a spell that would make him forget me. Forever.

A heavy, sick feeling crept deep into my heart.

I thought of his deep laughter, and how much I loved to hear it, but hated that I was trying to bring it out of him. The way his arms clasped me against him, I could barely hold myself up. His lips, and the kiss... A searing heat bolted through my limbs, into my hands.

The kiss is where things got crazy.

I didn't want to overthink it, but couldn't stop the overlapping images flashing through my mind the deeper Blake kissed me. Me and Blake making love, getting married, and holding our first child was overrun by thoughts of Blake hanging me from the noose in Castle Dagon.

I couldn't catch my breath.

And I couldn't afford to let Blake get to me.

Play nice, be nice. That's all I would do with Blake. Play nice and be nice. Keep him on my good side - but not my bedside - until this is all over.

Then, I could either make him forget me, or make him love me forever.

Easy as a coin toss.

Ya, right.

I thought about the broken protection jars around the yard. I hadn't considered Blake as the culprit, and never got a demon vibe from him, but since he held fast to the - highly incorrect - belief that witches were the source of all evil, then he was as good a choice as any.

I picked up Blackjack for a quick snuggle and a scratch. He lifted his head to meet my gaze and quirked a brow. *"If you're quite finished pining, you have work to do."*

"Yes, I know, lots to do today. I need to fix the protection jars and apply more sigils to the house - preferably before John and Sharon get back. Then this evening I have to take a trip to Castle Dagon to find a book. You wanna help me? Be the watchdog?" Blackjack leaped from my arms.

"If you insist on referring to me as my nemesis, then I must decline." He sat, turning his head toward me.

I giggled. "Ok, sorry. How about watch-cat? You're black and mysterious and very good at getting into places I can't and sniffing out danger. Might come in handy, having you there."

Blackjack looked at the ceiling, seeming to weigh his options of helping or holding down the couch. *"Fine. Don't forget the extra tuna deal we made, woman. You owe me for babysitting the weird lady last night."*

"Right. How could I forget? One tuna plate, coming up." I opened a can of tuna, dropping half of the contents in Blackjack's fancy bowl before removing the stirring spoon from my coffee cup and taking the mug onto the porch.

I finished my coffee and went inside to change. In the kitchen, I grabbed the padlock on the door to the greenhouse, then paused, eyeing Blackjack on the tree limb out back. He jumped off the limb and ran across the porch and through the cat door.

Pausing momentarily beside me, he nodded his head, and ran into the living room, up onto the chaise in the bay window, settling into his role as resident watch-cat. I removed the padlock key from my jeans pocket, unlocked the door, and stepped inside.

The air in the room was heavy with the scent of sage, rosemary, mint, and a mix of herbs and oils. All of the ingredients for creating magic hid in the drawers of an old apothecary cabinet. I pulled out several clean jars with lids, a black candle for sealing the jars, and the ingredients I would need to recreate the protection.

In each jar I placed:

3 sprigs of Rosemary,

3 sprigs of Basil,

2 sprigs of Fennel

2 sprigs of Dill

1 Bay Leaf

1 Fern leaf

1 pinch of salt

Sealing the jars, I lit the black candle and dripped wax along the edge of the lids. As I did so, I repeated the protection prayer:

"Goddess of the North, South, East, and West, come forth.
Place your blessings on these jars, so they may protect this
property, from the forces of evil and shelter all who dwell within.
So mote it be."

I took the jars outside and dug away from the previous holes, and a little deeper than before. Then I placed each of the jars in the four corners of the property, repeating the protection prayer with each one. I covered the jars with the dirt and patted them down, careful to add a few leaves to each of the areas, doing my best to disguise the new locations. I left the old holes dug up, the broken jars where they lay, to throw the jar digger off. Should he, she - or it - come back again?

Next, I worked on the sigils.

Using a small paintbrush and the same white paint I used on the entire house, I touched up the Algiz protection sigils hidden in the doorway woodwork. The Algiz, - a Y with an additional line in the center top of the Y - represented divine protection and sanctuary.

I decided to amp up the protection by adding Thurisaz Thor sigils as well - a straight line with a triangular point on the right side of the line - the sigil for protection, polarity, and regeneration.

I had just finished cleaning off my paintbrush in the kitchen sink when Sharon came in the front door. "Hello! Alex? Are you home?" Sharon's sing-song voice carried through the house. Blackjack scooted off the chaise and ran into the kitchen, stopping at my side.

"You fell asleep, didn't you? Nice watch cat you turned out to be. Lucky for you, I was finished," I chided him.

"I... may have closed my eyes for a hot second, only because I was bored out of my cat tree. Wait until you see what the woman did." Blackjack sauntered through the cat door and scurried up the tree limb.

What did he mean by that?

"I'm in the kitchen!" I called out, opening a drawer and throwing the paintbrush inside. I glanced at the door to the greenhouse, relieved I had remembered to lock it. I heard the thump-thump of Sharon and her trusty cane, making her way down the hall to the kitchen.

"Hi, Alex! How was your day?"

I turned to Sharon and gasped.

"Uhhh... wow! You look so... different!" I stood, mouth open, staring at the person who no longer looked like Betty Burke. The curly, brown hair, Betty's fun, bouncy signature, was now straight and dyed, bleach blonde. She held out her hands, previously short, clipped nails now inch-long French artificial nails. She brought her hands up to frame her face, makeup artfully applied.

I was gobsmacked. "Are... you wearing contact lenses?" I leaned forward, peering at Sharon's eyes.

Sharon giggled. "Yes, blue! Not prescription, just colored." She spun in a slow circle. "What do you think of my look?"

Sharon wore a new, snug-fitting dress that hugged her curvy figure and accentuated her generous cleavage. She must have bought a girdle, the kind that laces up in the back, or at the very least, a pair of Spanx. The previous rolls and loose skin were all tucked up and smooth against the fabric of the dress.

Other than the shape of her body and face, she looked more like the Sharon Myles of days gone by, and less like Betty Burke, from the days of now.

An icy chill gripped me as bile filled the back of my throat.

I swallowed hard.

I was one step closer to losing Betty forever.

I forced a smile. "You look amazing, Sharon. Really like... yourself."

"I *feel* more like myself, whoever that may be." Sharon smiled, smoothing her hands over her curvy hips. "Once I'm up to it, I want to jog. I think I used to love jogging."

"Where's John?" I peered behind Sharon into the living room.

"Oh, he went to his place to freshen up for dinner. He's taking me out to some fancy place on the hill overlooking the ocean. I have a ton of new clothes to put away and have to get ready for our date!" Sharon turned and thumped along to the front door, where John had dropped her parcels.

I followed.

"Wow, huh... need some help?" A sea of bags from some of the nicest shops in Castle Point were piled on the porch.

"Oh sure, that would be great."

"Sharon....?"

"Mhmmm?"

"Who paid for all of this?" Dumbfounded, I grabbed as many bags as I could with two hands.

"John did. He said I could pay him back once I'm settled and have a job. He's so sweet." Sharon smiled dreamily as she hobbled to her bedroom and opened the closet door.

I helped her unload the bags until I got to the ones from the "Beauty Beneath" lingerie store and stopped. "Uh, I think I'll let you sort this out on your own. I need to get ready, too."

"Oh! Do you have another date with the hot Sherriff? How did it go last night, by the way?" Sharon tittered.

"No, not tonight. Just things I need to take care of. I'll tell you all about my date later." I left Sharon and walked into the hall, closing the door behind me. Resting my back against the wall, I sighed.

The urgency of this entire situation fell on me like a ton of bricks. With Sharon's transformation, I felt like I'd taken five steps back for every one step forward.

I had to get to Castle Dagon, read the book and hopefully uncover the demon's name. Fast.

THIRTY-ONE

ALEXANDRA

As the autumn sun faded over the ocean view, its late evening beams burst into my peripheral between houses and trees as I walked to Castle Dagon, Blackjack in tow. The late afternoon air was cool but not intolerable, good enough to wear a simple black hoodie with my jeans and sneakers. My hair was pulled into a ponytail and hung, long and wavy, down the back of my sweatshirt.

The castle, towering high on the rocky cliffs, - the highest point in town - was far enough away, thankfully, that it wasn't visible from any part of my house or yard, but close enough to be a decent walk. I was grateful for the time to think.

For as much as he complained, Blackjack enjoyed a pleasant walk, darting in and out of bushes, avoiding annoying dogs, and taunting the ones behind secure fences.

When we arrived at the castle parking lot, I stopped and looked up. The sun was fading fast, but what remained lit up the ominous place from behind. Chills ran up and down my spine, and I shivered. Blackjack wrapped his tail around my ankle, comforting me until the shivers passed.

We slowly took the stone steps leading to the entrance.The museum would close soon, so several museum-goers were brushing past us on their way to the parking lot, commenting on the 'cute kitty' walking up the stairs. Blackjack, unamused, hissed and bolted, tucking into a nearby bush.

We stopped at the massive wooden entrance of the castle and studied the front of the building. I noted security cameras on the corners of the building. I pushed on the ornately carved front door with a depiction of the Demon 'Vine'. A bitter, metallic taste filled my mouth as I pushed open the large door and stepped in, Blackjack following closely.

Walking past the gilded paintings of Earl Dagon and his bride, Madeleine Bavent, I noticed a small group of people, presumably the last of the tour groups, shuffling around the massive inner vestibule of the castle. Blackjack crept, unnoticed, among the vases, plants and tables around the perimeter of the room. I tucked into the back of the group, and listened to the tour guide's yada-yada speech about Castle Dagon, and the DemonVine.

A history I knew all too well and loathed to be part of.

The animated tour guide and her overly enthusiastic attitude really grated on my nerves, but I needed to stay close and unassuming as I searched for security cameras and peered into open doors, looking for the book Cressy told me about.

Naturally, the guide's speech was completely in favor of the Earl Dagon and his establishment of our current laws.

The museum goers ogled the paintings and oohed and awed over the carved busts of the Earl.

I held my hand over my mouth, ready to hurl.

My skin threatened to crawl off my bones.

The cheerful tour guide finished her spiel. *"He then - thankfully outlawed the practice of witchcraft onto the growing village of Castle Point and beyond - to the entire world. A law that remains in place today! Isn't that great?"*

I wanted to wipe the sunny smile off the guide's face with an energy ball.

"Now, let's move to the castle courtyard and look at the pyre where the Evil Evelyn was burned, shall we?"

Bile rose high in my throat at the mention of the pyre and the giddiness of the crowd. I swallowed it down as I threw imaginary arrows at the guide. I shivered, pushing the image of Blake tying me to the pyre and setting it on fire from my mind. I couldn't let that happen. I hoped a forgetting spell would work on Blake, or I would have to escape Castle Point and leave my life behind.

A heaviness rested on the base of my belly.

Shaking the thoughts from my head, I moved away from the small tour group, as they walked through the great hall leading to the courtyard. Blackjack came out from the plant he hid behind and we slipped into the extensive library off of the grand hall, unnoticed.

The tall, circular room had a wall of curved windows on the far side looking out over the ocean, and floor-to-ceiling bookshelves holding ancient musty books around the interior. I paused for a moment to admire the large oak shelves and the iron railing running along the top, securing a tall ladder, steel wheels attached to the top and bottom, so it could move easily around the entire room.

The furniture was overstuffed leather, with wingback

chairs on both sides of a large rock fireplace in the center of the room. The fireplace was lit open from either side, the heat warming the entire room.

On the other side of the fireplace, in front of the curved windows, was a large oak desk with ornately carved legs. In front of the desk sat a pedestal and a glass cabinet, holding the largest book in the room.

That had to be it.

I hurried to the book. It lay open to a random page, but the language wasn't one I recognized. I grabbed the piece of paper with the drawings from the back pocket of my jeans. Several of the etchings from Mitch's cell were also in the book. Excited flutters rolled through my belly. Perhaps there were interpretations in the book as well.

Just as I was about to open the glass case, a voice came from the doorway and I jumped. Blackjack, who had been beside me, scurried under the desk.

"This room is off limits. How did you get in here?" I recognized the curator, Mr. Fellows, as he entered the library and shuffled toward me.

"Great watchdog skills you have there, Blackjack." I glanced down at my cat, peering at me from under the desk.

"The big man walks with light feet. Not my fault." He sniffed and settled back under the desk. I turned to the short, balding man with a deep-set scowl, whose head I could easily see over. Resisting the urge to bolt, I gave him my best smile and tried to conjure acting skills.

"Oh, hi Mr. Fellows. The door wasn't locked. I didn't know it was off limits."

"Oh, hello Alexandra." his scowl slipped away. "Well, it is. The door should have been locked, and you shouldn't assume you could just wander around. Where is your tour group? What are you doing here?"

"I was... um... just looking around and saw this book. Can you tell me what language this is?" Mr. Fellows, although a total crank-pot, was always eager to educate, not because he was a swell guy, no. Because he assumed everyone in the world was an uneducated fool. He scooped up his pince-nez glasses from the breast pocket of his jacket and snugged the wired-framed lenses onto the bridge of his nose, the chain from the glasses dangling down into the pocket where it was secured. He stared into the glass cabinet.

"The language is ancient, I'm afraid, and has never been translated." He slipped his glasses off his nose and tucked them back into his pocket.

"Would I be able to look at the book?"

"Why are you so interested?"

"Oh, I'm a history buff, that's all." I flashed my brightest smile. Mr. Fellows frowned.

"This book is ancient. It's kept under glass for a reason. The pages would fall apart from turning them." He shook his round head and grasped his hands behind him. "I'm afraid I'll have to ask you to leave, Alexandra. We are about to close the museum for the day." He extended one arm toward the door, ushering me out. I glanced back at Blackjack, peering from around the fireplace.

"Of course. Thank you for your time. I'll catch up to my group." I noticed Blackjack slip from the library and hide under a side table just before the door closed behind us. I smiled at Mr. Fellows, who grunted back, and watched me head toward the courtyard as he walked into a smaller room down the hall.

When I heard the door close, I doubled-back and dipped into the hallway leading to a staircase and into a wide hall. The hallway was lined with artwork, statues, and, predictably, full metal suits of armor. Blackjack raced from his hiding spot to join me.

"What's the plan, woman?"

"We need to lie low until the castle is closed. Then we'll go back to the library and get a better look at that book."

"What about security? There must be cameras everywhere." Blackjack had a point, but I shook my head.

"The only security cameras I saw are outside, around the perimeter of the building. Nothing inside."

"It's your jail time, lady. I'm just the watch 'dog' apparently." Blackjack sniffed and pointed his tail straight up in the air, passing me down the hall and into an empty bedroom.

"And not a great one at that." I followed my cat into the room and closed the door behind us.

We were in a dusty bedroom, not one on the tour, I guessed, or they would have kept it fresh and dust free. They set several pieces of furniture about the room, some covered with large sheets of cloth, most without. The room was chilly, dark, and smelled of old must and mothballs. My mother would have loved it, antique furniture being her 'thing'.

I brushed off an old settee on one side of the room and sat down, pulling my sweater around me to beat the chill. Blackjack jumped up onto my lap and settled down, tucking his feet beneath him. My eyes felt heavy, so I lay down on the settee, Blackjack snuggling beside my chest. I wrapped my arm around him, his purr lulling me into a deep sleep.

After some time, I heard a noise, the door creaking open. Someone was approaching. I peered into the darkness and tried to sit up, but couldn't move. My eyes were still tightly shut, my body heavy on the settee. Fear gripped my heart as the person - a man - approached me. Dim light from the rising moon streamed through the window and shed some light on the figure.

He wore black, pant legs to just below his knees, met white stockings and black shoes with large brass buckles on the top. Frills from his white shirt peeked out of his black jacket, and on his head, a pilgrim's hat. I tried again to roust myself fully awake, but couldn't move.

The man spoke, lips not moving, his voice breathing through my mind. *"There you are, my beloved. I've been waiting for your return."*

"Who are you?"

"Oh, my Evelyn, surely you remember me?" He snickered. *"We are inseparable, you and I, no matter what consequences arose, you will always be mine."* Blackness crept into my mind and the image of the man faded.

I awoke, startled. Gooseflesh overtook the clammy heat of my skin.

A bad dream.

I grabbed my phone from my back pocket and turned on the flashlight. The harsh white light lit up the room. The door was still closed, the bedroom undisturbed.

"Weird-ass dream," I muttered, waking Blackjack. I looked at the time on my phone and sat up quickly. We'd slept for hours! Blackjack stirred and meowed beside me.

"Shhh." I walked over to the door and peered out. There were no lights coming from the stairwell, so I tiptoed down the hall, Blackjack following close behind.

"Hopefully, the staff left the library door unlocked." I hurried to the library door and turned the doorknob. It opened, so we slipped inside. Blackjack was about to duck under the desk again when I stopped him. *"No sir. You're going to be a watch cat and stay by the door! Let me know if you hear footsteps."*

"Jeepers woman. Fine." Blackjack sniffed, farted, shook, and sat by the door, watching me with hooded eyes.

I approached the glass case holding the ancient book and tried to lift the lid. It wouldn't budge. Using my phone as a flashlight, I saw a lock on the side. I pointed my finger at the lock, setting my intention to unlock it, and focused on seeing the tumblers in my mind. I felt an intense heat flow from my finger to the lock and heard the tumblers turn. This time, the lid lifted with ease.

Carefully, I hoisted the enormous book from the case and placed it on the desk behind me. Holding my phone flashlight high above my head, I focused on it for a few moments, then let go. The phone stayed, hovering above me, shedding light over the book. Now hands-free, I could turn the pages, carefully pulling from the bottom corner of each.

The markings on every page were like the markings I saw on the walls of Mitch Myles' cell at the Sanatorium, but there were no interpretations. There weren't even any drawings or paintings to shed some light on what was written. I unfolded the paper I had drawn the markings on, smoothing out the creases. I could match up several of the weird squiggles and odd shapes, but with no transcription to interpret the language, I was no further ahead than I had been all week.

Blackjack startled me, rubbing against my leg.

"Time to move, woman, someone doth approach!" Blackjack the Over-Actor scuttled under the desk. As quickly and quietly as I could, I replaced the book, leaving it halfway open as I'd found it, and snapped the lock before slipping under the desk with Blackjack. We heard several footfalls of what sounded like a group of people getting closer to the library door, then bypassing.

I heaved a sigh of relief.

"Good job watch cat". I ruffled the hair on Blackjack's head as he gave me a sideways glance. *"Time to move."* Opening the door a crack, I peered into the grand hallway. Nobody in sight. I pulled my black hood up over my head and we slipped through the door, quietly closing it. We moved with soft footfalls toward the main entrance of the old castle and the large, ornately carved front door.

The door opened. Adrenaline coursing through me, I quickly retreated to a vestibule next to the courtyard and hid in the dark behind one of the large suits of armor, Blackjack zooming beside me. I cringed as I heard the footsteps come closer, then turn and head into the courtyard. Perspiration dripped down my back, my heart pounded. I waited for a few breaths before peering out from behind the armor's shield.

From this vantage point, I could see a group of tall, broad-shouldered people - presumably men - wearing long, dark cloaks in a circle around the pyre. They were chanting something I couldn't quite hear. I stepped away from the armor and moved closer to the courtyard entry, careful to stay in the shadows. *"Oh, my goddess, who are these people?"*

Blackjack followed close to my heels. *"I don't know..."*

Then it hit me.

Witch Hunters.

I was witnessing a sacred meeting of the Witch Hunters, a sect of men who had sworn to uphold the teachings of the Demon Vine, and enforce the Earl Dagon's 400-year-old law.

And I - a freaking witch - was practically in the middle of it.

Sweat sprung from my temples and along my collarbone under my hood.

I thought the group had disbanded after the witches formed the 'underground' over fifty years ago.

Clearly, I was wrong.

Assuming this was really them. But, of course, it had to be. What other group of hooded figures would meet around the courtyard pyre?

Certainly not the Rotary Club.

The men, heads bowed, - their faces shadowed by the hoods of the dark robes they wore - swayed in unison, chanting in a language I couldn't understand.

I glanced at the corridor wall across from where I stood. A large painting in a massive gold-gilded frame hung on the wall. I hadn't been to the castle in quite some time, so I couldn't remember seeing the painting before, but something about it pulled my attention away from the chanting men. I stood back and took a better look.

A woman with long, dark wavy hair seated on a settee similar to the one I napped on previously gazed off into the distance. The artist captured her expression and features perfectly. I stared at her face, then a flood of heat swept through my body.

The woman in the painting looked just like...me.

Barely glancing at the circle of men, I shot across the hall to get a closer look at the painting. Blackjack stared, wide-eyed, but stayed in the shadows. I read the placard on the wall beside the painting. *"Evelyn. Beloved mistress to the Earl Dagon, burned on the courtyard pyre, on the full Samhain moon, 1583."*

I shivered, nausea running amok, darkness at the edge of my vision.

I looked at the painting again.

The dream I had of Earl Dagon flushed through my mind. *Was he really there, in the room with me? And had he mistaken me for his Evelyn?* The resemblance was completely uncanny. The painting mesmerized me, and from where I stood, Evelyn's eyes seemed to look directly at me. I shuddered.

Blackjack hissed, startling me.

The chanting had stopped.

If I made any sound now, the group would surely hear it.

"Move it, woman!" My head snapped toward the circle of men. They slowly lifted their heads in unison. My heart leaped to my throat. If I didn't move my feet now, I'd definitely be seen. I bolted down the hallway into the grand corridor and toward the front door, Blackjack close behind.

The cameras!

I pulled the hood of my sweatshirt tighter over my head and opened the door. Blackjack bolted past me and we ran - as though Vine, Dagon, and all their minions were hot on our heels - down the stone staircase, through the parking lot, and into the black night.

CHAPTER
THIRTY-TWO

THE WITCH HUNTERS

"**D**ominic, Henry, see who's there!" The High Counsellor of the Witch Hunters gave the command. Two men, with hoods concealing their appearances, ran swiftly from the courtyard and toward the front door. The rest of us stood still, waiting for their return.

"Well?" The High Commander inquired as Dominic and Henry stood before them, huffing from the chase.

"We saw someone running across the street, but there was no way to tell who it was. The street is black, Commander and the intruder was wearing dark clothing."

"Check the video footage after our meeting then, see what you can find." The men nodded, acknowledging their orders, and took their places in the circle.

The High Commander addressed the group. "Does anyone have any witch sightings to report?"

I called out from the group.

"I do, Commander." A murmur arose from the men. No one had reported a sighting for over fifty years.

"Silence!" The High Commander ordered. He motioned toward me, "Come forward."

I moved into the center of the circle, slipped off my hood, and knelt before the Commander, head bowed.

The courtyard air stilled, the men silent.

"What say you, *Blake Sheraton*?"

A slick of sweat coated my brow.

"I may have a lead on... a witch."

"And just who may she be?"

"Sir, there is much to be determined as to her true status. I have had a brief interaction with her until now. If it pleases your Command, I would like more time to... assess her abilities before bringing my findings to your Worship's attention." The Commander considered my request and then nodded.

"Fine then, see what more you can uncover and report to me in our next session. If she does indeed have powers we can use, then we will proceed with the purification ritual and acquisition of those powers." Our High Commander, Sheriff Gordon Roberts, waved me off.

"Yes, High Commander."

I rose and stepped back into the circle.

THIRTY-THREE

ALEXANDRA

After a restless sleep, I awoke later than usual. Visions of Earl Dagon, the painting of Evelyn, and the mysterious meeting of the hooded men had me on edge. Even Blackjack couldn't settle, pacing around the house most of the night. I wished I hadn't stepped foot in the castle. I didn't need or want to know about the goings-on there after dark.

Besides, it was a futile excursion that could have ended a lot worse, and I was no further ahead in finding the Demon's name so I could vanquish him from Sharon's life. I would have to try another way and the only way I knew would be through Sharon, under hypnosis.

Hopefully, John hadn't poisoned Sharon against me, or this could also be a futile move.

I got dressed and made my way downstairs just as Sharon came in the front door. Her now-straight blonde hair pulled into a tight ponytail, her eyes sparkling through blue contact lenses. She was wearing a fitted pink jogging suit; a light sheen of sweat crossing her brow. "Good morning Alex! It's a beautiful day out there!" Sharon was annoyingly chipper. Blackjack peeled out of the living room and through the cat door the moment he heard Sharon's voice.

"Good morning, Sharon. You've been for a run? Legs doing ok?"

"Yes, everything seems in top shape. Well, getting there. I'm up to walking without the cane, at least. I'd like to lose a few more pounds - get a tummy tuck and a boob job as soon as I can afford it - and start working out at the gym." She smiled. "John is really pleased with my progress. He doesn't see any reason I can't find a job and apartment soon, although I'm not sure what I'd apply for. I'm not really sure what I'm qualified to do. John says that doesn't matter. He'd be happy to look after me until I find out."

We made our way into the kitchen to make coffee, my head pounding, listening to Sharon's chipper chat. I could forgo sugar in my coffee this morning. The gooey sweetness coming from Sharon as she yakked on about John was enough.

Too much, actually.

"Sounds like you and John are getting serious?" I tried desperately to un-furrow my brow, rubbing my temples.

The more time Sharon spent in Betty's body, getting closer to John, the more panicked I became.

"He's so sweet and kind and... yes, I'm very attracted to him," Sharon gushed.

I hardly knew what to say. Besides Sharon being so completely entranced by the man, what if I was right, thinking John was the demon? I opened my mouth to say something, then thought better of it.

Tread lightly, Heale. Don't spook the spirit.

I poured two coffees and changed the subject. "Sharon, I wanted to tell you something, but I didn't want to upset you."

"Oh? What's wrong?"

"Nothing is wrong, it's more... there are some details about who you really are that I've kept from you. I'd like to share them with you now if you feel strong enough to hear them?"

"Oh my, you've got me curious. Spill it!" Sharon swooped up her coffee cup and took a large gulp.

"Well, I told you I found Sharon Myles, and that she was murdered."

"Yes, I remember. You showed me a picture of myself and told me I had died! How could I ever forget that? Scared the bejesus out of me! Still doesn't explain how I ended up in this body, though." She clicked her long, fake nails on the counter.

"Yes, I'm still trying to work out how you woke up in Betty Burke's body."

"Any ideas?"

"Yes, well... kind of. See, there's a part about your past that I haven't shared with you yet. And I think we need to talk about it now."

"I'm all ears, girl. Spill!"

I took a deep breath. "Sharon Myles was married to a man named Mitch Myles. He's the one who killed her."

Sharon put her coffee cup down with enough force that a splash of coffee flipped out of the cup and landed on the counter. I automatically reached for a cloth to wipe it up, avoiding Sharon's eyes.

"My husband *murdered* me? Why?"

"Well, it's complicated." I trod lightly, keeping as much

as I could from Sharon until I felt confident that she would accept the truth.

"Why is it complicated? Did he get away with it or something?" Sharon's voice rose.

"No, he definitely did not. He committed suicide right after killing you."

No way on the Goddess's green earth was I about to tell her about the trip to Waterford, and meeting the ghost of her late husband.

Sharon's mouth dropped open.

"He did? Oh, my God." Her voice was a mere whisper, her eyes wide, unblinking.

"Yes, unfortunately. If he were alive, I could have maybe gotten some answers from him about the murder, which would have, perhaps, given me some insight into why you ended up... here."

Sharon slumped slightly, her new blue eyes growing dark, and took another sip of coffee. "So, what now?"

"Well, I have an idea..."

THIRTY-FOUR

SHARON

After I showered and changed into comfortable clothing, I joined Alexandra in the living room. Alex pulled the French doors leading to the living room and the heavy draperies closed, then lit some candles. The living room was dim, washed in candlelight, despite the bright autumn day outside.

It was weirdly eerie.

I didn't like eerie.

But I had agreed to undergo hypnosis, and hopefully, we would find out how I came to be in Betty's body. I wanted to know why I was here as much as Alexandra did, so I settled onto the settee in the living room's large bay window and pulled a blanket over my legs, ready to cooperate.

"Great, just relax, Sharon. Just like before, ready?"

I nodded and lay back against the settee pillows, although I doubted I could relax.

I was wrong.

After Alex counted me down, I was the most relaxed I'd ever felt, at least since waking up in the hospital. I felt relaxed, yet somehow alert, listening to Alexandra's instructions.

"Ok Sharon, you're doing great. I'd like you to take me back now, to your life before you woke up in Betty's body, can you do that?" I nodded slightly. "Good. Just allow yourself to float into that timeline, back to the time you were Sharon Myles, in Sharon's body, alright?" I nodded again. "Good, be there now." Alex snapped her fingers.

The moment she did, I left the present time. My mind slipped back into an empty, dark space, several years before I had come here, to this time, and found this body...

I immediately felt an ominous presence in the space with me. It wanted to touch me, to take me. I couldn't see what it was but felt myself running away from it, barely slipping from its grasp, and running. Always running.

Chills shimmered through me, making me uncomfortable. I shifted on the settee. Shaking, I whimpered.

"Tell me what's happening, Sharon." Alex asked; "What do you see?"

Tears formed at the edge of my eyes and slid down to my ears. My legs started shaking. I wanted to move, to run.

"He's... he's after me."

"Who's after you Sharon?"

I tried to focus on the darkness and see who was after me. There was nothing. Just a dark presence, and it terrified me.

"I'm not sure who, or what... but I need to hide."

"Where, Sharon? Where do you need to hide?"

"I... found a place. A woman. She's so beautiful, she's popular, smart, and rich, but... she's... depressed. She has everything, but nothing makes her happy. She wants to leave her life. "

After a few moments, Alex finally spoke.

"Sharon, did your spirit walk into Sharon Myles' body? Like you did Betty Burke's?"

I slowly nodded. "Yes. Sharon didn't want her life anymore. So, I... I... took over, so she could leave, and... I could hide..."

Now, I understood.

Betty Burke's wasn't the first body I'd walked into.

Sharon's wasn't either.

How many times had I run? How many bodies had I run into?

There was a gap of silence. I saw a cloudy circle of light poking through the dark. An image slowly appeared in its center, but it wasn't frightening. A man, one I knew very well, came into a hazy view.

My body began to tingle and vibrate, and a smile spread across my face.

"Sharon, what do you see now?" Alex asked.

"My... my... husband," I answered, shifting again, my body vibrating.

"Your husband? Do you mean Mitch Myles? Is that who Sharon?"

I looked again.

My heart rate sped up.

Mitch!

My husband, the love of my life.

My King.

And I was his Queen.

My heart leaped. Excited jitters tickled me.

Then memories flooded back. I remembered my life after I walked into Sharon's body. I still had her memories and could feel the feelings she had for Mitch. He was truly an amazing, sweet, kind man.

Why Sharon Myles would want to leave him, leave her life, I couldn't understand.

I was grateful to live an amazing, happy life with the most wonderful man in the world.

I could see us laughing. We had so much fun together all the time. Mitch was the most adoring man I'd ever met. He spoiled me rotten and gave me everything I could ever need, and more. He was my rock, my lover, and my friend.

My heart was full.

I could feel tears falling in a steady stream, pooling in my ears as I watched us together in our beautiful home. Laughing, talking, kissing, cooking and making love against the kitchen counter...

Then something shifted in his eyes.

Fear gripped my heart, and my breath came in shallow gulps.

"Sharon, what's going on? What do you see?"

"I see Mitch. We're cooking in our kitchen, and he... he... grabbed a knife." Terror ripped through my heart, shattering it to pieces.

"It's ok, Sharon, you're very safe. He can't hurt you. You just remember something that happened. You aren't really there, you're perfectly safe." Alexandra assured me.

I relaxed, then Alexandra took me deeper. "Sharon, I know Mitch hurt you, but can you see why? Can you look into Mitch's eyes and tell me what you see?"

"He has beautiful eyes. So blue... but they turned... so dark... completely black," I whispered.

"Ok, Sharon, you're doing great. Can you tell me who is behind the dark eyes?" Alexandra's voice was soft, reassuring.

My heart sped up a notch. It took several minutes for me to reply.

"It's not Mitch. It's... it's..."

"Who is it, Sharon? Who do you see behind Mitch's eyes?" Alexandra held her breath as I looked deeper into my husband's jet-black eyes.

Then, I saw *him*.

He was inside Mitch.

"I see him. *He's taken over Mitch's body.*" I breathed, my body quaking.

"Who, Sharon? Do you have a name? Who took over Mitch's body?" Alexandra's voice rose.

"*The One*. He found me. Again. Oh, no, he found me, he found me!" I cried uncontrollably.

"You're ok Sharon, you're safe. He doesn't know where you are, you're just remembering. I need you to tell me who *he* is. Who is '*The One*'?" I could tell Alex was trying to keep her voice calm, but her urgent words came in a rush.

An icy fear rushed through my body. I shivered.

"He's *the one who wants me*, has always wanted me, *will always want me*." Tears flowed down my face and into the pillows.

Alexandra's voice was insistent. "Tell me who wants you, Sharon."

Something shifted inside me. An ancient knowledge - an understanding - and a vision of my past life, all of my past lives came into view. My head rolled back and forth, back and forth, as if reading from an enormous book in front of me, my eyes still closed.

The answers came to me as clearly as words on a page.

"He's been after my soul for eternity, hunting me in every life I've ever had. He comes to me, presses his weight upon me, and takes me. He wants to mate with me, to impregnate me with his demon spawn. He will never give up. He's tried to possess my body and soul for thousands of years, and for thousands of years, I run. I run and I hide. I hide and I run, but I can never stay hidden for long. He finds me. '*I am his, and he is mine. I am his, and he is mine. I am his, and he is mine.*' This is what he tells me."

My head stopped rolling, my arms fell to the sides of the settee, and my torso arched. Something or someone wrapped its heavy arms around my midsection and lifted me off the settee, into the air. I rose, higher and higher, panting. Chills shot through me.

Alex raised her voice.

"*Who wants you, Sharon? Tell me his name! Please! I can't help you if I don't have his name!*" Alex pleaded, standing beside the settee, but not touching me while I continued to rise.

My legs and feet lifted off the settee, hanging in mid-air, my back arching my head dangling down.

Then, ever-so-slowly, my body spun to face Alex. I opened my eyes, but couldn't see. Something completely clouded them over, a milky white.

When I spoke, a voice, dark and resonant, the voice of a demon, rose from the bottom of my being and uttered a single word.

"*INCUBUS.*"

CHAPTER
THIRTY-FIVE

ALEXANDRA

Finally, a name.

Sharon's eyes closed, her breathing even. I reached for her, still floating, back arched, and pivoted her over the settee, then gently pulled her down until her body settled.

I counted her out of hypnosis, telling her she didn't need to recall what happened today. I hoped for full hypnotic amnesia, but whether that happened was out of my control.

Sharon laid back, her eyes fluttering, and breathed deeply then burst into tears.

"I remember. Everything." Her sobs turned to wails as tears poured from her eyes.

Dammit.

"I'm so sorry, Sharon. I know this was hard for you." I reached for her hand, but Sharon pulled away.

"My husband! He's *dead*." She sobbed, curling into the fetal position. "I loved him so much, Alex! After I... became

Sharon... he was *everything* to me. *Why did you make me remember?"* Sharon sobbed, her breath coming in ragged, throaty drags. "I was so happy being oblivious! Now, I remember our life together, and how happy we were. And... *he's gone."*

"Sharon, I'm so sorry, but we really needed to know. We needed to know what happened to Betty."

She sat up, her face red and screeched, "Did we? *Really?* Who cares about Betty Burke? I mean, *I'm alive.* Isn't that what matters? Isn't that enough? My husband is dead, but I have John, and we're building a future! Now *HE* is going to come for me. He always has, and he always will." Sharon slammed her face into the pillow and screamed, then sat up quickly, glaring at me.

Spittle flew from her mouth. "I thought I'd found a safe place to hide... *in Betty's body...* and you've ruined it! He's going to *know* that I *remembered* and he's going to come for me!" She launched off the settee and ran to her room, slamming the door.

I flopped onto the couch and sighed heavily, exhaustion and sorrow wracking my bones. I thought about everything Sharon said during the hypnosis session.

All the pieces were falling into place.

Sharon had done this before - who knew how many times - on the run from Incubus. She found Sharon Myles, a rich, depressed soul who wanted to leave the earth, so *'she'* took over. Then, after Betty Burke slipped into a coma after the accident, Sharon took over hers.

I felt faint, small dots flowing through my vision. I held my head in my hands, willing the dots away.

The demon, Incubus, was truly a vile creature. The most powerful demon I'd ever care to meet.

One I had to summon and destroy.

I did not know if I would be successful in summoning the demon to release his hold on Sharon and send him back to the underworld, but I had to try.

I still risked losing Betty Burkes' spirit to the abyss.

And, to top it off, Sharon didn't seem to care.

I supposed I shouldn't expect Sharon to think of anyone other than herself, really. Remembering her life with Mitch, and her past lives running from a lewd demon, topped the chart of acceptable reasons to be in the *all about me* camp.

I could give her that.

But only for a while.

Betty still mattered. Maybe not to Sharon, but she did to me, to Jack and to Alana.

That was more than enough reason to push on.

Blackjack came through the cat door and plodded his way over. He jumped up onto my lap, but my arms felt too heavy and thick to wrap around him.

"Made a mess of things, woman?" He licked his paw, barely glancing at me.

"Supportive familiar, as ever," I said, shifting beneath him. "But, as crappy as this has been for Sharon, I didn't actually make a mess of things. Yet."

"You're only getting started. Give it time." Blackjack eyed me, his whiskers twitching, as if trying to pull back into a smile.

"Gee, thanks."

I scooped Blackjack up and set him on the couch beside me. I got up and walked over to the large bookshelf beside the fireplace, pulling an ancient, large leather-bound grimoire off the lowest shelf. Blowing the dust off, I walked back to the couch.

The grimoire once belonged to Cressy and became mine upon Cressy's death. I shuffled through it until I found the section on demon history and lore. There were pages and pages of demon names I recognized and a lot I did not. I turned the pages until I found the one I was looking for, *Incubus*.

"*The Incubi demons dated back to Hebrew mythology, but their legends turned to folklore and finally, truth during the witch hysteria in Europe. Incubus was only attracted to young, beautiful women, mainly virgins. Victims of the Incubus would feel a heavy weight on top of them, paralyzing them while the demon performed perverse sexual acts with his ridiculously swollen member to create offspring. The children that resulted were half-human, half-beast, many of them with two mouths, two heads, extra fingers, or eyes. If the Incubus was unsuccessful at copulation with a female, he would continue to pursue her until successful.*"

Well, isn't that just super awesome?

I shuddered, feeling the need for a scalding hot shower.

Sharon had mentioned nothing about having children during any of her past lives. She must have escaped the Incubus for centuries, and he was obviously still in pursuit.

I closed the book with a thud and tossed it on the couch beside me, got up, and headed for the stairs.

Just then, Sharon's bedroom door opened. She came out holding a small suitcase. She paused when she saw me.

"You're leaving?" I asked.

Sharon sniffed. "Yes, John is coming to get me. He's renting a motel for me until I can find an apartment. I think that's the best. I'll come for the rest of my things in a day or two."

I shook my head. "I'm not sure how you're leaving is going to help your situation any, Sharon." I choked on my words, a little unsure of what to say next.

I took the plunge.

"Sharon, *what if John is actually Incubus*? Have you thought of that?"

Sharon eyed me, her hand clenched at her chest, then shook her head. "No, he just can't be. Please don't say that. John is wonderful. He's so sweet and kind to me, I think we're falling in... love...," her words dropped to a whisper. "Oh, my God. What if you're right?" she cried.

"I'm really sorry. Please don't feel you have to leave, Sharon. I honestly think staying here is a better idea."

Sharon wiped her eyes and shook her head once more. "NO! John is *not* Incubus. He can protect me!"

"Like Mitch protected you?"

The weight of my words rested on the thick air between us. Sharon looked at me like she'd just been slapped and the tears flowed again.

Her shaky voice rose. "John is good. He's pure. He can't be like Mitch was."

"How can you know for sure?"

Sharon wiped her eyes again and stared at me, the tears glistening in her blue contact lensed eyes. "I can't, I guess. But I need to go. I need to try."

"You don't, Sharon. You can stay here." I was grasping at reasons for her to stay. How could I convince Sharon that *I* was her best option for survival?

"Oh, but I do. *HE will find me. He always does.* Then you'll be in danger too." Sharon looked at me, her feet, shuffling. "I can't let that happen, Alex. You've been too kind to me. I can't put you in danger."

I sighed and extended my arms to give Sharon a warm hug. I didn't know what else to do. My heart splintered and ached for this woman, caught between two worlds, belonging to neither, but determined to find her place in this one.

I would have to be ok with letting her go, for now.

On the bright side - if I could find one - it would be easier for me to summon Incubus without Sharon in the house, and safer for Sharon.

"I understand, Sharon. You've been through a lot in the past few... centuries. It was clever of you to find a hiding place in Betty's body." I paused.

Something still irked me about the whole walk-in situation.

I had little to lose by bringing it up. "Sharon, have you given any thought to what will happen to Betty Burke now? She's still out 'there' somewhere."

A small part of me hoped to appeal to any sliver of good nature that Sharon possessed.

Sharon pursed her lips, pulling herself up and straightening her rumpled shirt.

"Not my problem."

She turned on her heel and opened the door. John's Porsche pulled into the driveway. Sharon looked back at me. "Bye, Alex." She left, closing the door behind her.

I stared at the closed door, jaw dropped.

I didn't want to scare her into running, but was baffled by Sharon not giving a care in the world about Betty. I felt like I was slowly sinking into quicksand. Whatever move I made, I might hurt or lose someone, including myself.

A slow burn rose from my belly. I had to sit down, gather my thoughts. I walked to the kitchen, poured a large glass of wine, and took a deep pull of the ruby relief.

My next steps would be to summon the demon - to vanquish him - and in doing so, hopefully, release Betty Burke from the abyss, and back into her body and her life.

Which would mean the end of Sharon's.

Again.

And, if I couldn't vanquish Incubus from his eternal cat-and-mouse game with Sharon, then Sharon would have to find another place to hide.

I took another gulp of wine, then another to chase it down.

"Not my problem..." I whispered, walking upstairs where a hot shower awaited.

THIRTY-SIX

JOHN

Sharon, a small wheel suitcase in tow, walked down the front path of Alexandra's home and slid into the passenger seat of my Porsche. My smile slid off my face when I saw her red-rimmed eyes.

"My darling, what's the matter?" I placed one hand on her leg and cupped her chin with the other.

Sharon sniffled. "Shitty day. I sort of had a fight with Alexandra."

I tried my hardest to hold back the small smile that threatened to touch my lips.

"Would you like to talk about it?"

Sharon sighed. "Sure, but let's go, ok?" She forced a smile and wiped her eyes.

I started the car and drove toward the motel, relieved Sharon's tears weren't about me, but the thought of seeing my love in such anguish sent tiny sparks of anger through my spine.

"Tell me what happened, Sharon."

I didn't drive straight to the hotel, so I could give her time to unload. Instead, I took her through the countryside, along beautiful lakes and rivers, falling leaves billowing behind us as we drove past near-naked trees.

Her words came in a rush. "Alex helped me remember a demon named Incubus possessed my husband, Mitch Myles, and through Mitch, murdered me. I found the perfect place to hide from the demon - inside Betty Burke's body. Now that I remembered who I was, it's likely that Incubus will find me again." She took a deep breath. "I hope you can accept what I'm telling you, and I hope you can help me." Sharon reached for my arm as I slowed the car and pulled over.

Silently, I weighed Sharon's words, and my anger grew.

"John, please say something. Do you think I'm crazy now? Because I'm not. I know without a doubt that everything I experienced under hypnosis is the truth." She took a deep breath.

She was so passionate, and I adored her for it.

I looked at Sharon, stone-faced, and took a deep breath.

"I believe you. But I'm mad. Mad at Alexandra Heale for putting you through this. I should have intervened when she invited you to stay with her. I could have stopped a lot of this from happening, and you'd be blissfully unaware. It's my fault and I'm sorry."

I leaned over and took Sharon's face in my hands, pulling her toward me, and kissed her deeply. I could feel Sharon's body relax and respond to my kiss.

She was mine, and I would never let her out of my sight again.

Damned Alexandra Heale.

The interfering bitch needed to be punished.

I pulled away, still holding Sharon's face in my hands.

Sharon, eyes still closed, sighed blissfully. Her eyes fluttered open. "Wow, that was amazing." She smiled softly.

I returned her smile with one of my own, still holding Sharon's face in both hands.

"Nobody can take you from me, Sharon. You're mine, and always will be." I punctuated my words by gripping Sharon's head a little tighter, then watched the smile slide from her face. "Did I say something wrong, darling?"

"N... no. It's just... Alexandra asked how I could be sure that *you're* not Incubus." She paused, searching my eyes before asking, her voice barely a whisper. "You're not, are you?"

I chuckled and released her face. "Of course not, darling." I started the car. "Let's get you to the motel."

THIRTY-SEVEN

JACK

I ducked down into the seat of m' old Ford as the stupid doctor's fancy pants Porsche rode by, with *my* wife in the passenger seat. Waitin' a few beats before starting my truck, I 'whipped 'round and followed Middleton's car to the motel.

I'd been tailing them since they left Alexandra's house, and I parked down the street from Alexandra's every day since my Betty moved in wit' her, except for the time I spent at home with Alana when she came home from school. Otha' than that, I hadn't been home or at work in days. I'd taken sick leave after the tussle at the hospital and was hungry for the opportunity to punch that old geezer Middleton's lights out - successfully this time, I assured myself, grinning at the thought.

My grin dissipated when I saw the doctor's Porche slide into a parking stall outside one of the motel's doors.

Bastard.

What the living heck that rat was doing with my Betty behind closed doors...

I wanted to retch my steak' n' eggs at the thought.

Suddenly sweating, I reached for the temperature knob of the old truck, but it was already in the off position, so I cracked a window and breathed in the cool, fall air. I watched as Middleton opened the passenger door and *my* Betty, or the blonde-haired, blue-eyed version of my Betty, got out.

I had to admit that the changes *this* Betty had made were certainly stunning. Not that I ever thought my Betty was anything less than gorgeous. I also noticed that this Betty had lost quite a lot of weight.

That was an ever loving tragedy.

Then I decided I could live with a thinner version of my Betty if I *had* to but would miss her lovely soft curves, beautiful big bouncy boobs and tight curls.

To be honest, I could live with anything, as long as she was back in my arms and my home, and from the embrace I just witnessed between this Betty and that rat bastard Middleton, the sooner the better.

If she wouldn't come home by request, then she would come home by force.

After all, she was mine, for all eternity and beyond.

I wouldn't take no for an answer.

THIRTY-EIGHT

BLAKE

Next in line for Sheriff, I spent many lonely evenings in the office, often doing the work of ten men. Whether the brownie points would do me any good come election time didn't matter. I had ethics and stood by them.

This evening, however, I wasn't processing reports. I was poring over security camera footage from Castle Dagon to see if I could find the intruder who interrupted the Witch Hunter meeting. I'd requested security cameras inside the Castle to the High Commander frequently but was always denied, and thankfully, we hadn't needed it.

Until now.

Scrolling ahead to the proper timeline, I spotted a hooded figure leaving the castle, and rolled the footage until the figure was out of sight. Then I loaded footage from the next available camera in the parking area and scrolled through to the matching timeline. There, I saw the figure again, dressed in a black hoodie. Whoever it was, was tall and lean, but it was too dark to make out whether it was a man or a woman.

I cut and blended the footage from all camera angles and ran it on a continuous loop, slowing the footage down as much as possible, peering closely at the screen. I stopped and zoomed in on the hooded figure. Based on the size and type of footwear, my best guess was a woman.

Then I spotted something else.

A black cat ran alongside the dark figure, then both disappeared into the night.

I sat back in my chair, screen frozen, footage zoomed in, then blew out a deep breath, clasped my hands, and placed them on the back of my head, leaning back further in my chair.

Was Alexandra at Castle Dagon that night, spying on our meeting?

And, if she was, did she recognize me under the cloak?

Asking her point-blank didn't seem a good option since I needed to keep her in my favor, not scare the bejesus out of her.

I thought of the last time we were together. The scent of her dove into my senses and I closed my eyes. I could feel my hands wrapped around her waist, her long hair tickling the back of my hands. I couldn't help but feel a pulsing through my body, the front of my standard-issue khakis growing tighter by the second. Thoughts of Alexandra's beautiful green eyes consumed me.

I was desperate to *know* her completely.

Perhaps I would do so while I tried to find out what powers she possessed.

Before taking her, *and* her powers.

A lump formed in my chest at the thought of stripping Alexandra of her powers and burning her on the pyre. Not that I'd ever seen the ritual performed, the last witch burned by the hunters was well over fifty years ago, before the witches went 'underground' - virtually disappearing from Dagon County - but I'd heard the stories from some elders. Those elders - most of whom had passed or were in the late stages of life and no longer used their powers - had gained immeasurable powers from the witches they sacrificed, a thought that sent a thrilling shiver through my spine.

Maybe I could get more information from Alex about the so-called 'underground' if it still existed.

Another thrill of excitement rushed through me.

If there is still an underground witch population in Castle Point, then there would be more witches to expose, and more powers to possess.

I could be a frigging *God*.

If only I could find them, strip them, and sacrifice them without other witches knowing. Could be tricky, but possible. My thoughts turned back to Alex and my khakis got tight again.

Maybe there would be a way around the sacrificial part.

Maybe there'd be a way to keep Alexandra for myself *and* possess her powers.

No, that would be impossible. I shook my head. She'd hate me for all eternity for taking what's rightfully hers by birth. Hardly the best way to begin a relationship.

And who knows what powers she possessed that could be mine? Maybe it would totally be worth the sacrifice. Enough to elevate me to a high degree within the Order. Keep the legacy my father passed down to me alive.

My chest tightened.

There was the ritual itself, however. It wasn't something I was actually looking forward to, but it was something we, the next generation of Witch Hunters, knew how to perform.

It was all in the book.

The sacred book of Witch Hunter knowledge and wisdom was under a glass case in Castle Dagon.

Was that what Alexandra was after?

I ran through the footage again, slowing it down, and zooming in. With the hoodie over her head, there was no way of knowing for sure, but how many people would prowl around with their black cat?

Also, how would she know about the book in the first place?

I recognized the writing on Mitch's cell walls. They had taught all Witch Hunters the ancient language as our first. My father was a sixth generation Witch Hunter and High Commander, and oversaw my education and establishment within the order.

Although *why* or *how* Mitch knew the language to write it in the first place, I had no clue. From what I knew, there were no interpretations of the ancient symbols for Alexandra to stumble on, which is a good thing. She won't ever be able to interpret the markings on Mitch's cell walls.

The ritual instructions for decimating the Witch Hunters. Forever.

I jumped as my cell phone rang. Glancing at the number, I hoped for a second that it was Alexandra.

It was not.

I quelled my disappointment and answered. "Blake Sheraton," I said gruffly.

"Sheriff Blake, this is Dr. John Middleton, of the

Lexington County Sanatorium." I sat up straighter. What would Sharon's doctor want from me?

"What can I do for you, Dr. Middleton?"

"You can place a restraining order against Alexandra Heale."

CHAPTER
THIRTY-NINE

ALEXANDRA

"A restraining order?" I shook my head at Blake, who was currently taking up precious space in my front doorway.

"Yes. Dr. Middleton called me yesterday evening, rather demanding, to be honest. He believes you are a danger to Betty Burke, or Sharon, as she claims to be now." Blake slowly spun his stetson in his hands, eyeing me. I shifted. The familiar minty lavender scent wafted toward me with every turn of the stetson. I willed my hands not to take the stetson and toss it into the yard.

Focus, Heale.

I focused.

Directly on the sinewy muscle of Blake's biceps as he spun his damn stetson over and over in his hands. I closed my eyes and took a deep breath, blowing it out in a huff. When I opened my eyes, Blake was staring at me, grinning. "What do you suggest I do?" I asked, placing my hands on my hips.

238

"First, I suggest you invite me in, so we can discuss this further." Blake ran a hand through his hair, and I held my breath, willing the scent of him to dissipate before it could reach me.

It didn't.

Instead, the aroma shot a wicked heat straight to my groin. I let out another deep breath and, holding the door wide open, waved him in.

Blake stood facing me, then leaned down to place a quick kiss on my lips. I tried to move my face, so he'd kiss my cheek instead, but my body wouldn't listen.

My tummy felt deliciously like melted chocolate, gooey and sweet. I led him down the hallway and into the kitchen, avoiding the living room, whose interior French doors I had closed just before opening the front door. The less opportunity Blake had to snoop into my witchy life, the better.

"Coffee?"

"Sounds perfect." I could feel Blake's eyes roving over my ass as we entered the sunny kitchen. I quickly closed the single door leading into the dining and living room before grabbing a couple of mugs and pouring coffee.

"Sugar? Cream? Oh, wait, no. You take it black."

"The way God intended, usually, yes." Blake smirked, pulling his bulk onto a kitchen island stool. "But today, why don't you make me one of your fru-fru coffees instead?"

"Ahh, living dangerously?" I worked making the macchiato. When I got to pouring the frothy milk, I had to giggle. Blake peered at me.

"Funny coffee?"

"I struggle to get the froth art just right. My attempt at a fancy heart design always ends up looking like male genitalia." *But, since most men's hearts live in their genitalia...*

"That so?" Blake grinned, peering at the mug I placed before him.

"Sorry dude. Looks like you got an enormous tree trunk to suck... I mean..sip." My cheeks burned, then burned again when I glanced at him and watched him lick his lips.

He hadn't even touched his coffee.

Just then, I was damn sure of his thoughts, and I didn't have half the psychic ability Penny did.

I turned away and shakily poured myself one, adding hot frothed milk and a generous dose of caramel sauce. I turned back to Blake and leaned against the sink, keeping an acre of kitchen island between us.

"Beautiful place you have. You've lived here all your life, right?" Blake slugged back a gulp of coffee, his eyes darting around the room as he licked the genitalia foam art off his lips. Blackjack slipped into the kitchen through the cat door and sauntered over to Blake, sniffed, and stood at the doorway leading to the living area.

"Ahh, this is your cranky fella?"

"Yep. That's Blackjack." I sipped my creamy coffee and cringed at the way-too-sweetness.

Blackjack meowed loudly, then tooted.

Blake's face crinkled. "Did your cat just fart?"

"Yeah, his ass is the gift that keeps giving." I opened the door enough for Blackjack to slip through.

"Hilarious, woman. You should apply to work at Comedy Central. I hear they're looking for new talent to heckle." He headed to the couch for his morning nap.

Blake spun the kitchen stool and stopped when he saw the lock on the greenhouse door. "What's behind that door?"

"None of your damn business, Sheraton."

"Oh, it's last names now, is it, Heale?"

I grinned again, then pursed my lips. Get ahold of yourself, for Goddess sake.

"Never mind that. What should I do about the restraining order?"

"Not much you can do really. Sharon - or Betty - signed off on it this morning, so just stay away from her, I guess."

"That makes helping her rather difficult." I took another sip of my coffee.

"And what progress have you made in those plans? Any luck finding the demon who possessed Mitch Myles?"

I opened my mouth, about to confess to sneaking into the Castle's library to read the book, but shut my mouth just as quickly.

"Black cat got your tongue?" Blake smiled.

"Ha ha, hilarious. I have made some progress, yes." I lifted my nose toward Blake with a smug smile.

"Legally? You haven't been doing anything that I'll be getting a report on later, have you? Or some video footage, perhaps?" Blake quirked a brow, watching my face.

I merely peered at him, trying to keep my cool.

Had he heard about my near escape from Castle Dagon?

"No, of course not." I sipped my coffee.

"Well, that's good. So, if John Middleton takes Sharon away from Castle Point, will that ruin your hopes of finding the demon who's after her?"

"Why? Did he say he's taking her away?"

"He didn't say it in so many words, but I would bet that's going to be his next move."

"Why would you bet on that? Did he tell you what Sharon remembered?"

"No, what did Sharon remember?"

I peered at Blake, coffee cup hovering in front of my lips,

calculating the ratio of information I felt safe enough to share.

"She remembered her life, lives actually, before finding herself in Betty Burke's body. And she remembered the demon who's been after her for thousands of years."

Blake leaned back and blew out a breath. "Wow, that's really something. How did she figure it out? Did you have to use magic?"

"No, just good old-fashioned hypnosis." I smirked.

"Oh. And she agreed to that?"

"Yes, of course. She wanted to understand why she came into this body just as badly as I do."

"Then why the restraining order?"

I shrugged. "Well, I don't really know, actually. I guess she thinks she's protecting me."

"Protecting you? From the Demon?" Blake's brows furrowed.

"Yeah, I suppose. She believes that, now that she remembers, it will alert him to her presence and he'll be after her...and anyone who stands in his way."

"And that would be you." Blake took the last swallow of his coffee and set his mug down.

"Yes, that would be me."

I poured more coffee into Blake's mug, minus the foamy genitalia. He stared at the black liquid for a moment before looking at me.

"What now? How do you 'summon' a demon? Magic?"

I peered at him across the island. "Yeah, Blake, that's kinda my jam."

He smiled. "But, how? Like, what do you do? Hold a seance? Abracadabra, some shit? What abilities do you have that would work for something like that?"

I cocked my head. "Curious little Witch Hunter, aren't ya?"

Blake fumbled with his cup. "What? No. Witch Hunter? Don't be ridiculous. I'm just asking."

I laughed.

Blake played with his mug and peered at me through hooded eyes. "Besides, I think the Witch Hunters disbanded, like, years ago."

"I certainly hope so, although it doesn't explain why we still have the stupid law against witchcraft."

Blake shrugged. "Some things die slowly..." He met my eyes, gulping his coffee down.

"Well, I don't plan on being one of them." I gathered the mugs and placed them in the sink.

"Can I help you with the summoning part? I could be the muscle!" Blake snapped his arms up into bicep curls, the fabric of his standard-issue shirt straining under the rocky hardness of his arms.

And now I have to change my pants.

"That's sweet of you to offer, but us witches like to do our summoning without the law breathing down our necks."

"We? You mean there's more than one of you? Who's going to help?" Blake set his arms down on the island and raised his eyebrows.

I could have slapped myself.

"No, no, just me. By 'we' I mean 'me'. I will do the summoning, just me, by myself, nooooobody else."

Dear Goddess, shut my mouth.

"Ah, ok. But you'll call me if you get into trouble?" Blake's eyes grew soft.

My heart fluttered lightly in my chest. "I promise. If the

big, bad demon comes after me, you'll be the first person on my speed dial."

He smirked. "Ohhhh, so I'm on your speed dial?"

I shook my head. "No, never mind, it's just... no."

"Well, you're definitely on mine."

I met his gaze and suddenly felt the need to look down and make sure I wasn't naked. "Good to know."

"I should probably get going. You promise you'll call me, right? Even before - or after - the deed is done?" Blake walked slowly down the hallway to the front door.

I followed, my eyes running top down along his muscular frame, pausing at his very fine ass. "So you can arrest me? Fat chance."

"Arrest you? No, so I know you're ok." He turned, and I almost slammed into him. He placed his stetson on his head and held both of my shoulders in his large, firm hands. I felt my feet hovering above the ground.

I glanced down.

Nope, still touching the floor.

I looked up and met his dark eyes.

"Call me, Alex."

I nodded my agreement. He let me go, leaned against the door for a solid second before opening it, slipping outside, and closing it behind him without saying a word.

FORTY

BLAKE

I rested against the closed door, adjusting my khakis to accommodate the swelling between my legs.

For the love of all things unholy.

That woman did something to me that I couldn't explain or justify. I thought of the council, my oath, and my expectations.

They were going to want a name soon.

Why did I open my mouth and admit I'd found a witch?

How could I get out of this now?

If I don't produce a witch, someone else on the council will start the hunt, and they'd find Alex because they wouldn't back down.

But that was justified, wasn't it?

I mean, witches were evil. They needed to be stopped.

Their powers needed to be in the Witch Hunter's hands, where they rightfully belonged.

Didn't they?

And what about my mom and dad? Although I have

never had a good lead on the witch who killed them, being with Alex would mean turning my back on finding my parents' killer.

Wouldn't it?

All the thinking put my badly behaving body parts in check. I set my stetson firmly on my head and walked to my car and drove off, tires squealing.

CHAPTER
FORTY-ONE

JOHN

"I feel terrible about it, John. Alex has been so kind to me, and believed me when no one else would!" Tears fell from Sharon's face. We had just arrived back at the motel after signing the restraining order against Alexandra.

I stroked her back. "My love, you said it yourself. It's the best thing for Alexandra. She will be safer the further the distance between you two."

We were sitting on the single King bed in our shared motel room. We had spent the night here, together, curled up after a rather passionate make-out session the night before, but I was careful to leave it at that. I knew I had her. I didn't need to push her into a sexual relationship.

Not yet.

That time would come, and soon.

I needed to ensure she was completely submissive and willing first.

Craving me.

A craving she'd never felt before, in this or any other lifetime.

"There is one thing that you may not have considered, my love, which I think we should consider now," I said.

Sharon dabbed her eyes and turned to face me. "What's that?"

"That Alex may be capable of conjuring the demon who's after you and banish him forever."

"You think she can do that? But that would be amazing!"

"No, my love, not necessarily."

Sharon's eyes grew wider "How do you mean?"

"If Alexandra can summon and banish the demon, that could disconnect the tie that you have with Incubus." I met her eyes to make sure she was truly listening, "but, in doing so, it could mean your spirit - the one animating this body - would disappear with the demon."

Sharon stared at me, her mouth agape. "You mean I would die? Again?"

"Yes, that's what I mean. And I would hate to lose you now, my love, just when I've found you and..." Sharon eyed me expectantly... "I've fallen for you."

She blushed. "I've fallen for you too, John. And I don't want to die! I don't want to leave this body! I worked too hard to find a place to hide, to live, and I'm not ready for it to be over!"

I gathered both her hands in mine. "Then I think we should leave."

"Leave? Castle Point? But where would we go?"

"Away. As far away as we can go." I kissed her fingers, and she smiled.

"Let's do it."

CHAPTER
FORTY-TWO

JACK

I watched my Betty and the piece of crap John leave the motel room, with their suitcases loaded into the Porsche, and sped off. I waited a bit before starting the truck to follow 'em. They'd gotten miles out of town, heading south on the narrow county road, when I realized that I'd been spotted.

The Porsche sped up.

I laid the pedal to the metal, but it was no match for the Porsche's ability to corner, and the distance between us grew until the Porsche was a shiny dot on the horizon.

I pulled my truck over and slammed on the brakes. I took a deep breath and bellowed. The sound of wailing coming from the truck sent birds into the air. A small doe 'n buck, nibbling grass in the nearby field, bolted. I slammed my hands against the steering wheel repeatedly until I had no feeling left in my palms.

They'd gone. The bastard took my Betty.

I wondered if Alexandra knew where they'd gone. Even

one bit of information was worth asking. I spun the steering wheel and did a U-turn, barely aware of the only other vehicle on the road coming my way. The driver slammed on the brakes and leaned hard on the horn. I didn't care.

My only concern was getting to Alex's and finding my wife.

CHAPTER

FORTY-THREE

BLAKE

I spotted Jack's old Ford hightailing it for the town, about thirty miles over the speed limit. He was barely aware of my flashing lights and siren, only pulling over when he heard my voice over the car's loudspeaker;

"Jack, slow down and pull over. NOW." Hearing his name, Jack slowed down, pulling the truck onto the shoulder. He jumped out of the truck when he saw me approaching.

"Whoa, Jack, stay in your vehicle, please." I held one hand out in front of me, the other resting on my service revolver in its holster. An automatic reaction. Jack froze, holding his hands high in the air.

"Blake, he took her! Help me get her back!" Tears sprung from Jack's eyes, and his face flushed.

"Who took whom?" I released my grip on the holster and walked up to Jack. "Is Alana ok? Who are you talking about? Betty?"

Jack nodded. "Yes, that sonofabitch Middleton took her

away. Help me, Blake, I wan 'er back! Set up roadblocks - an Amber Alert - anything!"

I studied Jack for a moment, watching him swipe tears and snot onto the arm of his flannel shirt.

I'd just left Alex's, our conversation fresh in my mind. A demon was after Sharon - who was actually someone who'd recently passed - and was stuck in Betty Burke's body. A headache welled in my temples. This was a lot to take in. Now, Jack tells me that Sharon's gone with John Middleton.

Was that demon Dr. Middleton?

If so, I better tell Alex.

"Jack, I want to help. I really do. But Betty's a big girl, capable of making her own decisions, and AMBER Alerts are for children, so..." Jack crumpled. My heart ached for the man. "I think the only thing you can do, is head home."

Jack opened his mouth to protest, then closed it again.

"I was just on my way over to Alex's place when you pulled me over! Maybe she knows where they went!"

I couldn't tell Jack about the restraining order Sharon had just placed on Alex, which also meant Sharon wouldn't be calling Alex to tell her their plans, but I wanted to give the poor guy some hope. "Jack, I'll check in with Alexandra. You head home, and take care of Alana. I'll call you if I hear anything."

Jack dug a toe into the ground before nodding.

My head told me there was nothing Alex could do about Sharon and John, but my gut disagreed.

I needed to let her know.

Besides, I thought as I shifted from one foot to another.

I needed to see her again.

FORTY-FOUR

BLAKE

J ack agreed to go home on the condition that I contact him the minute I knew anything. I promised, and watched him slowly drive away. I jumped into my squad car and screeched off to Alex's place. A giddiness welled up from somewhere deep inside me as I pulled onto Alex's street and parked in front of her house.

I jumped out of the vehicle, leaving my Stetson on the passenger seat, and took long, slow strides to her front door. The door opened before I could knock, but Alex wasn't on the other side of it.

"Back already? Forget something? Your tongue, perhaps?" Alex walked down the hallway toward me. I checked behind the door, but nobody was there.

"Cute trick."

"What trick?"

"Opening the door without touching it."

"Oh, what makes you think I did? Maybe the house saw

you coming and opened it for me," she folded her arms, tilting her head.

I noted the small magical talent, not assuming for a second that a little parlor trick was the only thing in her witchy repertoire, but would be a fun thing to have in mine, should I strip her of her powers.

The moment I thought about it, however, a sinking stone rested deeply in my belly. I looked at Alex, a light blush on her cheeks and long, jet-black hair resting around her shoulders, and the stone dissipated. I resisted the urge to grab her and bring my lips down on her, but only for a fraction of a second.

"Thanks, house." I kicked the door closed.

Alexandra stepped back and looked at me."Wait, why are you here? You just left."

I stood, my solid frame blocking out most of the front entry.

"I just saw Jack Burke."

"Oh? How is he?"

"He's a mess. Says Betty left. With Dr. Middleton."

Alexandra blinked her eyes rapidly. "Oh, Goddess." She stepped back.

"That's bad, right?" My brow furrowed as I searched Alexandra's face for the answer.

"That could be very bad, yes."

"Because you think Dr. Middleton is the demon, don't you?"

It was Alexandra's turn to study me, her eyes darting between mine like she was calculating how much information could she trust me with.

"Yes, I suspect as much, although the only actual evidence I have is his shitty attitude toward me and... his weird aura."

I cocked an eyebrow. "His weird... what now?"

This was a new word.

Alexandra shook her head. "Never mind, it's nothing. Call it a hunch. The biggest problem is if I'm not successful at... summoning and expelling the demon, then we are in danger of losing Betty Burke, forever."

I nodded, distracted by the way Alex bit her lower lip when deep in thought. "Right. Not good."

I shook my head and tried to focus. "So, what's the plan? I can't justify doing a credit card search to see where they end up. She's an adult, and I have to assume she hasn't left under duress." I followed Alexandra into the kitchen. The coffee mugs we'd just used were now washed and drying on the rack beside the sink. The girl liked to keep things tidy. I glanced at the kitchen door with the hasp lock firmly attached, leading into the greenhouse, curiosity creeping up my spine.

"No, I doubt she left under duress, unless..." Alexandra tapped her index finger on her forehead. God, she was cute when she was thinking.

"Unless what?"

"Unless he exposed himself to her as the demon. Then it's definitely under duress."

"But we can't know that for sure."

"No, we can't know that. There is a way to find them, though. Not exactly the legal way."

Alex looked at me, and I smiled. "A witchy way?"

Alexandra laughed. "Yeah, a witchy way. Although it's not really in *my* bag of tricks, I know it can be done."

"Can I help?" I tapped my fingers in front of me, like a kid waiting for a piece of candy to be unwrapped.

Alex laughed. "No, I doubt you can help me, but I know someone who can."

255

"Another witch?"

Alexandra snorts and slaps me on the shoulder.

"No comment."

FORTY-FIVE

ALEXANDRA

I dialed Penny's number before waving at Blake, watching his very fine ass walk toward his car.

"Hello? Alex? You still there?"

"Ya, sorry. Hey, I need your help with something."

"Ya? Ohhh, tell me more!"

"Well, where do I start?"

"How about what you've found out about Betty Burke and that whole situation?" I brought Penny up to speed, explaining the events of the past few days.

"Blake *knows* you're a witch? Alex, that's the worst possible news!"

"Really? You'd think the fact that a lewd demon has been hunting for a woman's spirit for the past thousand years would be worse news."

"Also bad. Very bad. But Blake? What if he arrests you for witchcraft? What then?" Penny's voice hit a pitch I'd never heard coming from my super-chill friend. "You end up on the pyre at Castle Dagon?"

"He's promised not to arrest me, and right now, I have no choice but to believe him. Besides, they have exposed no witches since the underground was formed...what, over fifty years ago now? I doubt they even follow that law anymore. Although..."

"Although what?"

"I saw a bunch of cloaked men in a weird meeting when I was in Castle Dagon. At first I thought it was a meeting of the Witch Hunters, but I didn't stick around to find out." I heard Penny suck in a breath. I rushed ahead. "I doubt they were Witch Hunters though. We haven't heard from them since the witches went underground. I can't imagine that sect is still a *thing*."

"Well, I doubt a bunch of mysterious cloaked men were meeting about Pickleball." I laughed, but when Penny didn't, it died in my throat. "Whatever it was, I think you should assume the worst and be prepared. The law hasn't changed, Alex, and until it does..."

I nodded my head in agreement, even though Penny couldn't see me. "Good point. So, that brings me to what I need your help with." I took a deep breath. "John and Sharon left Castle Point. We need to find them or..."

"Say no more, my Witch from another Bitch. Be right over."

Only a few minutes later, Penny knocked and let herself in.

"That was fast, Pen! Did you travel by broom?" We both giggled.

"Ahh, witchy jokes never get old." Penny flounced into the living room, then to the dining room table where I was laying out a large map of Dagon County. She leaned over the map, hands on the table, her wavy red hair spilling out around her shoulders.

"One location spell, coming up!" Penny reached into her canvas backpack and pulled out a small, purple velvet bag. She slid the contents - a rose quartz pendulum - into her hand.

I busied myself lighting candles around the dining room and closing the heavy draperies, blocking the late morning sun.

"Do you have pictures of John and Sharon?" Pen asked.

I produced the picture I had of Sharon from her previous life, and one I printed off of Dr. Middleton's Alumni page. "I have one of Betty, but since Sharon is currently occupying her body, I thought the location spell might work better with a picture of Sharon, from her old life."

"Ah, bravo, smarty pants." Penny placed the pictures at the edge of the map closest to her. "Ok, let's get started."

Penny held her pendulum over the two pictures and closed her eyes. I hovered my hands over the map, lending my energy.

The two of us repeated the location spell.

"Goddesses of the North, East, South, and West, hear our plea, grant our request. Help us locate those lost to us now, and help us fulfill our sacred vow, to protect those who are in danger, help us find them now, not never."

The pendulum swirled in a small circle at first, then gained some momentum and swirled wider and wider. It changed direction and swung back and forth in longer and longer swings, pulling Penny's hand in a certain direction.

Penny moved her hand holding the pendulum over the map, starting at Castle Point and moving in the direction that Blake said they were heading when Jack last saw them.

The Pendulum abruptly turned and shortened its swing, as if traveling down the same road as John and Sharon. Penny continued to move her hand in the direction the pendulum took her.

Blackjack appeared out of nowhere and jumped up on the table. He sat, his head rolling back and forth, following the direction of the pendulum swings, then raised a paw, ready to swipe. "Don't you dare touch it, kitty, or I'll have to cast a spell to bind your adorable puddy tat feet!" Penny scolded. Blackjack pulled his paw back and licked it as if that was his plan the entire time.

The swings got tighter and tighter. Penny moved her hand a little until she was over a focal point, where the pendulum came to an abrupt halt, vibrating over a small town only two hours away.

"Got it!" Penny cried. To be sure, she lowered the pendulum toward the map, watching as the vibration of the crystal came to an absolute standstill. "Yes, we definitely have it!" I leaned over and peered at the name of the city.

"Ellsworth! They stayed on Route 1 the entire way. Great job, Penny!"

"Don't crack open the bubbly yet." Penny's copper curls bounced as she shook her head. "Ellsworth is huge. It's a needle in the haystack scenario. We have to figure out where they may *be*."

I slumped. "You're right. Dammit." I thought about it for a moment, then snapped my fingers. "Ouija board?"

"I thought you'd never get it." Penny chuckled. "Pendulum's great for direction and location, but would take forever to scour through lists of hotels with. Grab your board, witch!"

I opened the large armoire in the living room. Inside, I kept extra candles, a large container of salt, more crystals, and herbs for easy access when I was working on my altar. I grabbed the Ouija board. Yet another thing Cressy left me - and my mother would have promptly burned if I hadn't kept it hidden in my mattress - and brought it over to the table.

Penny cleared away the map, moved Blackjack and the candles to the edge of the table, and sat opposite me. We lay the antique wooden board - with the letters, numbers, yes, no, and ask again, carved into the oiled wood - between us on the table. I placed the ornate brass planchette on the board, the pointer directed toward the letters.

Penny shook her hands out with gusto, blew on her fingers, vigorously rubbed her hands together, shook them out again, and gently placed the tips of her fingers on the planchette. I giggled at my friend's enthusiasm before placing my own fingertips on the other side of the planchette.

We repeated the location spell we used earlier, and waited for the Goddess to communicate through the antique board.

"Nothing's happening" Penny cocked her head to one side.

"I remember Cressy telling me that sometimes it takes a while. The Planchette's pretty heavy."

Penny nodded her head. "Makes sense, I guess." We waited, our fingers lightly touching the planchette.

"Let's close our eyes and really focus. Help the Goddess along," I offered.

Penny closed her eyes, took a deep breath, let it out, and tilted her head up. I smiled, crinkling my nose, as Penny's breath blasted me in the face, and closed my eyes.

We focused our attention on pictures of Sharon and

John in our minds. Finally, a couple of minutes later, the planchette moved.

"Woo-hoo! Here we go!" Penny opened her eyes but kept her fingers on the planchette, willing her energy to help the Goddess. I did the same.

The planchette picked up speed, but was slow enough for us to make out the word "H-o-l-i-d-a-y-I-n-n." We both cackled.

"How incredibly romantic of him to take her to a hotel chain," Penny said with a laugh, holding her belly.

I nodded my head. "Too funny. But, the question is, which Holiday Inn? There *have* to be a few in Ellsworth." I scratched my head.

"Mm-Kay, now what?" Pen asked.

"We google all the Holiday Inn locations and try to get a bead on the right one?"

"Sounds like another solid plan. You're just full of good ideas today, aren't you?"

Penny pulled her phone out of the back pocket of her jeans and started punching at the keys. "Looks like there's only three! Shouldn't be difficult!" She named the three locations and tucked her phone back into her pocket. We placed our fingers on the planchette once again.

This time, I asked the Goddess to give us a yes or no answer for each of the three places. The planchette moved toward the 'no' on the board when I asked about the first two places.

"Third time's the charm?" Penny asked.

"Let's hope so." We concentrated on the planchette and asked. This time, the planchette moved to the 'yes'.

Penny threw her arms in the air and cheered. "Ding, ding, ding, ding! We have a winner, folks and fairies!"

I laughed so hard, tears dripped from my eyes.

I PUT the map and Ouija board away while Penny went into the kitchen to make us tea.

I walked into the kitchen. "I should probably call Blake and let him know I found Sharon and John."

"Yeah, you should probably call the super hot Deputy Sheriff dude and tell him exactly how you used your witchy ways to locate people who technically aren't missing." Penny anchored her hands on her generous hips and shook her head at me.

I giggled. "I told you, he already knows I'm a witch and has promised not to turn me in. So far, he's been good on his promise. I'm pretty sure the demon scared the life out of him when he threw Blake against the wall at the Sanatorium." I pulled out my phone and pushed on Blake's name from the recent calls.

Penny scowled. "I'm pretty sure you have major hot Sherriff bicep blinders attached to your head, missy." I groaned and flicked a hand at her to hush her up.

Blake answered on the first ring.

"Speed-dial, am I right?" he teased.

"Ha ha."

"Did you and Penny have any luck finding our missing participants in the summoning play?"

I froze. Blood rushed to my ears.

"Penny?" I glanced at Penny. Her jaw dropped and her freckles disappeared into the white areas of her face. "Who are you talking about, Blake?" Total silence followed my question. "Blake?"

"Uh... I saw nurse Penny heading to your place as I was leaving this morning. I just assumed she was the help you called in."

I quickly hit the mute button on the phone. "Penny, did you see Blake's squad car on your way to my place this morning?" Penny shook her head no.

"Dear Goddess, does he know I'm here? Does he know I'm a witch?"

I shook my head. "He says he saw you on your way here and just assumed." Penny started breathing hard, her hands went to her knees, then she flopped down onto the kitchen floor. I heard Blake repeat my name. I hit the unmute button.

"Sorry, I'm here. No, Penny was just... coming over to see Sharon. Penny was her nurse at the hospital and wanted to check up on her. But since Sharon's not here..."

"Ahh, I see. My mistake," Blake said slowly. "It's just that you mentioned you knew someone who could help you find Sharon and John. I just assumed it was Penny..."

"Oh, well, no. It wasn't. It isn't. In fact, turns out I didn't need any help. I figured it out all by myself." I peered over the island and saw Penny lying flat out on the kitchen floor, still white as a sheet, staring at the ceiling.

"Oh, that's cool. How'd you do that?"

I rolled my eyes at his question. "A smart witch never reveals her methods, Blake."

I heard a forced guffaw from the other end of the phone.

"Oh. Well, that's great that you figured it out. So where are they?"

I gave him the name of the Holiday Inn the Ouija board spelled out.

"Got it. Ok, so, what do you need me to do?"

CHAPTER
FORTY-SIX

BLAKE,

S till sitting in my squad car, watching Alex's house, I listened intently to Alex's instructions. I took notes in my notepad, but all I really wanted was to gouge the pen into my own eyes.

How could I be so stupid and let it slip about seeing Penny? I needed Alex to trust me if I was going to find out more about her, and about Penny too.

"Ok, let me see if I have this straight. You need me to head to this Holiday Inn, find out which room John and Sharon are in, and stay with them while you summon the demon? How do you figure I do that, exactly? What am I supposed to say when they ask why I've showed up at their hotel, likely interrupting their happy time?" I rubbed my temples. I heard Alexandra snicker and felt a sharp pain run through my head and chest.

I loved the sound of her laughter.

And I was desperate to stay on Alex's good side, partly

because I needed more information from her, but also, I just loved helping her.

Being with her, around her, or anywhere near her, regardless of the crazy goose-chasing wild and weird task she was giving me, felt right.

"Hey, might I remind you that you offered to help me, Blake? No take-backsies."

A small smile crossed my lips. "Oh, I remember. I also remember being thrown against a wall by the demon you think may or may not be inhabiting John Middleton. Talk about being thrown to the lions. What happens when you summon him, exactly?"

"If the demon is living inside John, then you shouldn't be in any danger when I summon him. John will just wake up and seem a little dazed and confused, but the demon won't be there. It'll be here, with me."

I hated that idea. Not my role in this messed up play, but Alexandra's.

"Then wouldn't it make more sense for *me* to be there with *you*? You know, to protect you?" Again, I heard Alexandra's low laugh and closed my eyes. I wished I was with her right now.

"I'm the witch, remember? I think I can protect myself. I need you there, because, after I summon the demon, I'll summon Sharon's spirit next. I need both of them here in order to break the connection between them and send them both to the other-worlds."

My head pounded. I knew more about the 'other worlds' than I could admit to Alex right now, but the thought of her doing this alone worried me.

"Right, ok, makes sense, I guess."

"I need you there, Blake. To be with Betty's body especially. Hopefully, when I summon Sharon, Betty's spirit will slip back into her body, and she'll need to see a familiar face if she - no, scratch that - *when* she wakes up."

"Ahh, that also makes sense. She'd be pretty terrified to wake up in a hotel room next to Dr. Middleton." I nodded my head as if she could see me. "Oh my God, I just thought of something."

"What?"

"What if... you know... she and the doc are... you know... *doing it* when you summon them? Then Betty could wake up with a stranger on top of her!" I shuddered, thinking how horrified Betty would be if she woke up to...

I couldn't even finish the thought.

"Blake, I won't start the process until I know you're there, in the hotel room with them, so...."

I blew out the breath I'd been holding. "Oh. Good plan."

"Blake?"

"Ya?" There was a long pause.

"It's a good thing you're cute."

CHAPTER
FORTY-SEVEN

ALEXANDRA

I hung up the phone and walked over to Penny, still flat out on the kitchen floor.

"That's it. I'm going to be arrested for witchcraft, locked up, key tossed into the bay. Or worse." Penny's voice was barely a whisper.

I couldn't help it. I giggled. "I think you'll be ok, Pen. I threw him off your scent." I moved to help Penny up off the floor. She let me, shaking out her copper mane and brushing off her jeans.

"I'm not so convinced, Alex. And right now, I just want to go home to my wife and say goodbye."

"Penny! You're being overdramatic." I moved to hug my friend, but Penny pushed me away. She's, not once, ever done that. My heart thudded in my chest.

"Am I, though? I know it wasn't exactly your fault that Blake found out you're a witch, but he's *the law*, Alex. And he's great at his job. I know you like him, that's obvious, but can you really trust him to keep your secret?" Penny rasped, on the verge of tears.

I bit my lip and stared at the floor. Could I really trust Blake? I hadn't thought of Plan B...running away. I was too caught up in finding the demon. Blake promised to let me do that, but what about after?

I thought I should let Penny off the hook and try summoning the demon myself. A cool breeze tickled the back of my neck and Cressy's voice whispered through my mind. *"Strength in numbers, girl. There is strength in numbers..."* The voice vanished.

Right. I needed Penny.

I just had to convince her that everything would be ok.

"You have a point, Pen. Why don't you see if you can get any psychic visions from me? See if you can see anything in my future - about Blake?" I held my hands out to Penny, who just stared at them.

"I guess. I mean, I haven't gotten a hit off you yet, and we hug a lot, so, I'm not sure..."

I moved my hands closer to Penny. "Worth a shot, ya?"

Penny wiped her hands on her jeans, shook them, then took my hands in hers. She immediately closed her eyes and breathed deeply. Within a couple of seconds, she let go of my hands and stepped back, her eyes open wide.

"What? What did you see?"

Penny shook her head. "Nothing."

"But that's good, right? There's nothing *to* see?"

Penny shook her head again. "It either means I can't access the answers right now or...there is no future to see."

I slumped, then reached for the vial earring.

"I'm sure the information just isn't accessible to you now, that's all." I tried to smile.

269

Penny shrugged. "What do you want to do now? About Blake, I mean."

"I have to trust him, for now. I'll figure out what to do after we summon and expel the demon from Sharon's life." I paused, almost afraid to ask. "You'll still help me with that, won't you? Blake has agreed to go to Ellsworth and watch John and Sharon while we do the summoning, so he won't even be around to be nosy."

Penny took a deep breath, blowing it out hard. "Of course, I'll still help you. I wouldn't let you attempt something this crazy alone. I'll be back in a few hours before the moon is full, and we can do this together." Penny reached for me, hugging me close.

It was my turn to sigh.

FORTY-EIGHT

BLAKE

I tucked my notepad into my shirt pocket, started my squad car, and slowly drove towards Alex's house. I would have to pass it on my way out of town. I chided myself again for mentioning anything about Penny being at Alex's house. How could I be so stupid?

Alex had told me that Penny was just there to visit Sharon, but I knew that had to be a lie.

When I'd left Alex earlier, she was about to do some voodoo magic stuff to figure out where John and Sharon had gone. Penny arrived right after that. So, either Penny was also a witch, or, at the very least, she knows Alex is one.

I saw Alex's front door open and stopped the car, two houses away, partially hidden by neighboring hedges. I watched Penny give Alex a hug, got into her car, and sped down the street in the opposite direction from me.

I'd been holding my breath the entire time.

I debated whether to follow Penny or maybe see if I could find out more about her and her brand of magic.

That would have to wait.

Right now, I had to clear up a few things at the office and head to Ellsworth, find John and Sharon, and stick to Alex's plan.

FORTY-NINE

ALEXANDRA

After Penny left, I took a glass of wine, a plate of chicken salad, and Cressy's ancient grimoire out to the table on the back porch and read the page about the Incubus. The next part of the text was about how to summon the demon and the second part, how to expel it.

The summoning spell, I noted, was meant to stroke the ego of the demon, which would hopefully convince him to be in our presence. The second part of the spell was the complete opposite.

I only hoped it would work.

The full moon peeked out from behind random, thick clouds. I shared my chicken salad dinner with Blackjack - the chicken part, anyway - Blackjack was pretty particular about where he got his greens, the backyard grass being his preference. He also preferred to bring those greens up again on my antique living room carpet, much to my disgust.

After dinner, I took my wineglass and sat on the back

steps to enjoy the moonlight sparkling on the wet grass and trees from a recent rain. I sipped my wine slowly.

Blackjack lay beside me on the step, tail flicking, as he peered up at the bright moon. His silky thoughts floated through my mind. *"Nice night for a summoning."*

"Agreed. The only night, really."

"I'd like to help but, without opposable thumbs, I'm not that handy in this department. I can pace the protective circle though. I've gotten rather good at it over the years." Blackjack turned his head toward me and I smiled down at him.

"We've actually had some pretty fun times together, haven't we?"

"Fun for you, *perhaps..."* He flicked his tail at me as I stroked his fur. It glistened under the light of the glowing moon.

"Fun for you too, brat." I smiled and took another sip of wine, finishing the glass.

Penny appeared on the porch, startling me and Blackjack. "Whatcha doing out here? We have a demon to summon!" She clapped her hands together. "Chop chop, missy!"

Blackjack bolted, skittering off the porch, tail high in the air, through the cat door, and into the house.

"Weirdo," Penny called after him.

I chuckled. "Ok, I think I'm ready." We went inside. "Did you let Cathy know what we're doing?"

Penny shook her head. "I told her you needed my help, but as far as what it's about...our relationship operates on a very successful 'need to know basis'. And, since she's not a witch, there's not much about my alter-ego that she needs to know." Penny flopped on the couch. "Besides, I couldn't tell her what I don't really know myself. She scooped up

Blackjack, forcing a cuddle. Blackjack resisted, then settled onto her lap and purred loudly.

"So, ready to do this?" Penny asked with a wink. I nodded.

"Yes. Although I was second-guessing whether to include you, then Cressy reminded me that two witches are better than one. I can't think of anyone I'd rather conjure a lewd demon with than you!" We both giggle.

"You know me so well." Penny said, lounging on the pillows. "Besides, I told you there was no way I'd let you do this alone. Maybe it's time to revisit forming a coven?"

I pursed my lips. "Perhaps. But until I know I'm not in danger of being arrested by Blake, I say we keep this between us for now. Agreed?"

"Agreed."

I snagged Blackjack off Penny's lap and placed the grimoire there instead, showing her the page about the Incubus.

Penny read the pages, shaking her head. "For the love of a goddess, this Incubus is a real piece of work. I mean, talk about the worst date ever. This guy could really do some damage to a gal." Penny shuddered.

Putting myself in Sharon's shoes, running from Incubus was horrifying. Bile rose in the back of my throat, a chill running through my spine. I couldn't think of that now. I needed to get this over with as quickly as possible.

WE WORKED SILENTLY, first rolling up and moving the antique carpet in the living room, then creating the salt circle in the center of the wood floor beneath. We lit the tall pillar candles around the room, and set up large black candles around the circle, at the five points of the pentagram. Then we doused ourselves with protective oils of Angelica and Cedarwood.

Blackjack watched with interest from the sofa, legs tucked beneath him. He meowed every so often, giving direction, which I took.

"Think that's about it?" I asked Penny, who was holding Cressy's grimoire, her finger sliding down the page.

"Seems to be. We have the candles, sage, incense, salt... hmmm we're missing holy water."

I smacked my forehead. "Good Goddess, Penny, you're so smart. Not exactly sure how we'd vanquish a demon without it." I went to the armoire and pulled out a glass vial.

Penny closed the grimoire, placing it on the sofa. She pointing at herself with her thumbs. "All brains and a booty right here." she wiggled her bottom. We both giggled. "Who blessed the water for you? Father O'Reilly?" She asked, holding the vial up to the candlelight, and inspecting it as if she expected to see tiny crosses floating in the holy liquid.

"Yes, every time my mother made me attend mass as a kid, I filled vials from the font and snuck them out of the church."

Penny handed me the vial, making the sign of the cross in front of me. "Doing God's good work, I see, Witch!" Penny cackled. "Go forth in your witchery and prosper!" She held up one hand, separating the middle and ring fingers while holding up the edge of one eyebrow with the other.

I laughed, thankful for her. The task before us was scary, yet somehow, she had us laughing. "That may be your best impression of Spock ever."

My cell phone buzzed.

Blake.

Heat crept into my cheeks as I glanced at Penny.

She held her nose to make a nasal operator voice. "Hottie Sheriff, line 1 for you, Miss Heale."

I rolled my eyes and hit the green button. "Hello? Blake?"

"Hi, Alex." The sound of his voice sent a shiver down my spine and I straightened, glancing again at Penny.

"Did you find the hotel?"

"Sure did. It's a pretty nice place, actually. Just have to find their room. I'll text you a thumbs up when I'm inside." We disconnected.

"Ok, Penny. Let's get started."

CHAPTER
FIFTY

BLAKE

I went to the hotel reception desk and presented my badge. Although I was still in uniform, so the badge was hardly necessary.

"Can I help you, sir?" The hotel clerk, a pimply-faced young man who looked to be in his early twenties, nervously folded his hands at the front desk. I read his name tag.

"Charlie, I'm looking for these two people." I took out my cell phone and showed him the pictures of Betty Burke and John Middleton.

Charlie nodded his head, eyes wide as he looked at the pictures. "She doesn't look too familiar, but this gentleman checked in just a few hours ago, yes."

"Thanks, Charlie. I'm going to need a room number..."

"Oh, umm, we really aren't supposed to give out people's room numbers, sir. I actually shouldn't have told you as much as I have already..." His Adam's apple bobbed up and down.

I leaned closer to the desk. "Oh, I think you can make an exception in this case."

Charlie gulped and gave me the room number.

I thanked him and strode to the elevator. Their room was only on the second floor, so I ditched the wait and pushed open the door to the stairwell. Taking steps two, sometimes three at a time, I reached the second floor easily. I briefly thought it strange that I didn't hear the stairwell door close behind me, but shrugged it off and opened the door to the second floor. I followed the signs on the walls until I found room 220 and knocked. John Middleton opened the door.

"Sherriff? What are you doing here...?"

I held the door open with one hand and called into the room. "Is everyone decent? We need to talk."

John stepped back, and Sharon joined him. I pushed the door open wider and stepped inside. Just as I was about to close the door behind me, Jack Burke forced his way in.

"Jack! What the hell? What's going on here?" Sharon squealed. John was about to speak when Jack lunged for him, pushing me out of the way with the strength of a man three times Jack's size.

"What the..." I stumbled sideways, then recovered, but not before Jack had his hands around John's throat.

"She's *MINE*, you son of a bitch. How dare you try to take 'er away from me." Jack's face was almost as red as John's.

Sharon screamed.

The two roosters went at each other like they were fighting over the newest egg layer in the coop. "Jack! Let go!" I put one hand on Jack's chest and the other on John's and pushed. Jack finally let go.

John fell backward, gasped, and clutched at his throat.

Sharon rushed to his side.

I pushed Jack up against the door, my forearm on his throat. He coughed, grasping my arm.

"Stop, Jack! Settle down and I'll let go, ya? Get a hold of yourself!" Jack's eyes bulged. He looked at me, then gave a small nod.

I let go.

Jack slid to the floor.

Blood rushed to my hands, ready to smack Jack for being such an idiot. "You followed me all the way here?"

I glanced at John and Sharon. He seemed to be okay, breathing normally, still sitting on the floor with Sharon cradling him in her arms.

"Ya," Jack croaked. "Some cop you are. Didn't even notice you were being followed the whole time. I'd been watching you all day since you told me to go home this morning. I knew you'd go see Alex, and she'd know how to find Betty, so I stuck 'round." His lips curled as she stared at the couple.

I repressed the urge to put my foot through his chest. "Jack, what about Alana? Who's with her?" I asked.

Jack waved a dismissive hand. "Oh, just relax. I called Betty's mom. She was waiting at our house by the time Alana came home from school. She's fine."

I placed my hands on my hips and pulled myself to full height. "Why are you here, Jack?"

I towered over Jack, still sitting on the floor, and used my intimidating bulk to keep him in place.

"Why do you think? To get my Betty back from that asshole who took 'er from me!" Jack's eyes were wild.

"*I'm not Betty*, Jack, you stupid, gangly idiot! You need to leave. Now!" Sharon screamed, her blonde hair clinging to her tear-soaked cheeks.

John hoisted himself up to standing, then promptly sat on the edge of the bed.

"Sharon is a free woman. It's up to her to decide who she wants to be with, and she chooses *me!*" he spat. Sharon sat beside him, draping an arm around his shoulders and eying Jack defiantly. "Get the hell out of here, Burke, you have no right to Sharon, she doesn't belong with you, *she belongs to me!*" Spittle flew from John's mouth, landing on Jack's jeans.

Jack looked from John to Sharon, then he stood up, made an over-emphasized sweeping motion with his hands, brushed the spittle off his jeans, and leaned forward.

I placed one hand on Jack's shoulder, holding him back when he spoke in a low, growly drawl.

"I'm not going anywhere. Not without *my Betty.*"

CHAPTER
FIFTY-ONE

ALEXANDRA

We stood back and inspected the setup. Everything was in place.

My cell phone buzzed.

"It's a text from Blake. Jack Burke showed up at the hotel room! Blakes dealing with it."

Penny shook her head. "Good Goddess, what next?"

"Let's get this going. I can imagine John and Jack are at each other's throats. The quicker we can summon the demon, the quicker everyone can get on with their lives."

Thoughts of Blake arresting me after everything was over floated through my mind. I pushed them aside.

We stood on either side of the salt circle, Blackjack pacing the perimeter. Glancing at Penny, we closed our eyes. Breathing deeply, we started the summoning spell from Cressy's grimoire.

"Goddess of the north, south, east, and west, please be with me on my quest.
I summon thee demon, Incubus, to our sacred space, so we may commune if it pleases your Grace.
With great respect and humility, we will be, in making this request of thee."

We repeated the incantation, repeatedly, but nothing was happening.

Blackjack's loud mewing broke our concentration.

Penny shook her head. "It's not working!" Penny shook her head.

Penny bent over the grimoire and checked the book for clues. She shook her head. "We're doing everything right. I don't get it."

I paced back and forth across the living room when I heard Blackjack's velvet voice floating through my head. *"Call the man. He'll know what to do."*

I stopped and stared at him.

"That's brilliant, Blackjack!"

"What? What did the cool cat say?" Penny scooped Blackjack up and gave him a squeeze.

"He suggested we call Cressy and get his help."

"Oh, that really is brilliant. Good job kitty." Penny ruffled Blackjack's head. He jumped from her arms and shook, glaring at Penny, then at me.

"He really hates it when you do that." I giggled.

Penny cackled. "I know. That's why I do it." "So, how do we call Cressy?"

I opened the grimoire to the page with the incantation to summon my mentor. Penny read the verse, whispering it to herself, before taking her place on the outside of the circle once more.

"Ready?"
"Ready."

"Heaven to Earth, hear our plea, bring back he who watches over me.
Goddess and Gods of North, East, South, and West Allow us to commune with our dear Cress."

The swirl of black and grey mist appeared quicker than it had the last time I summoned him. I guessed it was because there were two witches performing the incantation, and, as Cressy had mentioned, two were better than one.

Cressy's apparition fully formed in the circle. He smiled. Blackjack stood up on his hind legs, pawing at Cressy, delightfully mewing.

"Ladies! Such a pleasure to see you both. Penny, you've certainly grown into a beautiful witch since I last laid eyes on you. What can I do for you two?" He held his hands together in front of him, his long, yellowing nails clicking when they connected.

"Cressy, we've made a lot of progress since I summoned you last…" I explained the past few days. "… but we can't seem to summon the demon on our own."

He smoothed his pin-striped mustache with his fingers. "I see. That is a pickle, indeed. The summoning incantation should have worked. This must be one hell of a powerful demon to resist your casting."

I gently gripped my earring. "That's what I thought. Any ideas?"

"Well, I'm happy to see that you listened to my advice and got some help, although I was hoping for more. A full coven would do the trick."

Penny wrinkled her nose, peering at me. "See? I told you, we need to form a coven together, Alex!"

"Right, ya, but we don't have time for that right now. We need to do this tonight. We can't wait for another full moon and give Sharon and John the chance to disappear. Any other ideas, Cress?"

"Just one. Instead of summoning the demon first, try summoning Sharon Myles." Penny and I looked at each other.

"You mean, as bait?" Penny asked, then blew out a breath.

Cressy clasped his hands together and nodded. "That is precisely what I mean."

I tapped two fingers against my lips. "I had planned on summoning Sharon after the demon, then separating the two, but ok. What if he appears on his own, and takes Sharon with him? That's kind of something I wanted to avoid."

"Ahh, yes. Good point. You'll have to be ready with the separation spell. That should do the trick, I suspect." Cressy nodded his head, satisfied with his input.

I flipped through the grimoire until I came to the page. "Found it. Cressy, do you think you could stick around? We could really use your help with this one."

"I thought you'd never ask." Cressy's apparition walked to the inner edge of the circle. I brushed some of the salt away, creating a space for Cressy to walk through, so he could join us on the outside. Penny spread fresh salt on the opening, closing the circle again.

Outside the circle, Cressy's apparition seemed fully formed. He opened his arms to envelop me in a hug, which I gladly took. I could smell his after-shave, the spicy scent filling my senses as I breathed him in. "Ok, let's get going," he said.

The three of us stood on three corners of the pentagram, just outside the candles marking the lines, and started the incantation.

As we finished, thunder rumbled from somewhere in the distance, then loomed closer, until a sudden flash of lightning and a subsequent boom crashed over the roof of the house. Me, Penny, and Cressy all jumped, staring at the ceiling. Another boom shook the house, shaking the crystal chandelier over the dining room table.

Cressy stared at the ceiling. "Looks like a storm is brewing, ladies."

"Looks like it's brewing inside too," I said, pointing toward the protective circle.

A swirl of black and grey clouds appeared inside.

FIFTY-TWO

BLAKE

I was trying to negotiate a truce between the two hotheads in the hotel room when Sharon's body slumped forward and fell onto the floor. Jack rushed to her side as John knelt to scoop her up.

"Betty! Betty!" Jack tried to pry the body from John's grasp.

"Sharon! Sharon! Talk to me!" John held her firmly, but she slipped from his grasp as Jack pulled at her arm.

I knelt down to assist. "Check her breathing," I barked at John.

John pressed two fingers to her neck. "Her pulse is strong. She must have fainted. It's your fault, Burke! If you hadn't shown up...." John's face was reddening as he shouted at Jack.

"My fault? If you hadn't tried to take 'er from me in the first place, we wouldn't be here right now!"

I placed my hands on both of their chests. "Back off, guys. Separate corners. Now!" The two men let go of...

Betty, or Sharon - I was as confused as they were - and moved away from each other, then knelt on opposite sides of Sharon's.. or Betty's... body.

They both started stroking her hair and arms.

I rolled my eyes, stood up, and grabbed my cell phone, pushing Alex's number.

Alex picked up before the ring.

"She fainted."

"She's here."

CHAPTER
FIFTY-THREE

ALEXANDRA

S haron's spirit slowly filled the inside of the salt circle. Another flash of lightning and a clap of thunder, louder this time, struck overhead. Penny, Cressy, and I all ducked as if to avoid the lightning from striking us down inside the house. The distinct rapid-fire sound of rain on the metal roof preceded another flash of light.

"Blake. Stay on the line." I tapped the speaker on the phone and placed it on a small side table. Me, Penny, and Cressy watched Sharon appear before us. She looked exactly like Sharon Myles from the pictures.

Blonde, tall, lithe, and beautiful.

A Homecoming Queen.

Sharon blinked her eyes rapidly, then glanced around the room, her brow furrowing when she saw me and my crew.

"What the hell's going on? How did I get here?"

I was about to tell her when she looked down at her

own body and saw the truth. "No, no, no no no no. What did you do?" She looked directly at me, pointing a ghostly finger.

"Sharon, I'm so sorry. This was the only way."

"Oh, my God, no. How could you? I want to *live*! I don't want to be dead again. Please, put me back!" Ghostly tears pooled in her eyes and spilled over.

"I can't do that, Sharon, not until I've expelled the demon trying to hurt you," I explained.

Sharon merely shook her head. "It can't be done, Alex. He'll find me. He always does. I'm not sticking around to find out what happens." She moved to the outside of the circle, attempting to bolt, then flew back when she hit the edge.

"Quick, Alex, we have to bind her before she figures out how to escape," Cressy urged. I sprang into action. Pointing a finger directly at Sharon's spirit, I focused on my intention. A stream of silver blue light flowed from my finger, toward Sharon, wrapping around her body.

Sharon tried to move out of the way, but the blue light wrapped around her too fast and lassoed her, binding her arms, hands, and body in place. "Let me go! Alex, this isn't fair! Let me go, now!"

"Start the incantation, now!" I whipped my finger into a circle, tying off the bonds, the last bit sealing her mouth shut. We started the summoning process once again. Tears streamed down Sharon's cheeks as she tried helplessly to wriggle out of the bonds.

Each tear that fell was a sucker punch to my gut, intensified by the rain pelting against the windows and roof.

Lightning flashes lit up the room, followed by roaring thunder.

We repeated the incantation three times.

This time, I saw wisps of black smoke appear - and hundreds of flies.

An ominous form took shape.

"Blake? Can you hear me?" I yelled, my eyes peeled on the dark figure inside the circle.

"Yes," came from the speaker on my phone.

"Has John collapsed?" I asked.

"No, but Jack has..."

CHAPTER
FIFTY-FOUR

ALEXANDRA

"What?" A freezing chill burst within me as the shadowy image of Jack Burke appeared.

"Jack?" Penny and I said simultaneously, then looked at each other, eyes wide. I shook my head, mouth agape.

"You're the demon?" Penny croaked. She shrank back.

"No, it can't be. You're *Jack,* you're... not John Middleton..." I reached for my earring with shaky fingers.

Jack's spirit reached out to me. His eyes were enormous, his expression a shocked surprise. *"Alex... help me! He's got me! Help me, please!"* The fear I saw in Jack's eyes matched the fear tearing through my heart. My palms and temples dripped with the heat of the room's energy, and the effort of the conjuring.

"Jack! Why are you here? Where's Incubus?" Jack opened his mouth to speak, but no words came.

His shape shifted.

292

"Alex, look." Cressy raised a hand at the image of Jack, pointing a crooked finger toward him.

The room took on a hushed silence that lasted only a millisecond as Jack's image dissipated, the demon's body taking shape.

Incubus.

Another boom of lightning flashed overhead, the storm raging. Rain pelted the windows harder and faster, as if trying to get inside.

A strong wind kicked up inside the living room, spinning like a small tornado, its center being the demon. The wind picked up objects from around the room, pictures off of the mantle, and books from the shelves, scattering them around.

Blackjack meowed loudly from under the couch. The tornado of wind pulled at him while he dug his nails into the hardwood floor, clutching fervently I reached for him, dragging him out from under the sofa, and held him tightly to my chest, my black locks whipping my face as I did so. I ducked and dodged moving objects flying around the room.

"Holy Mother Goddess, protect us!" Penny yelled harshly, her curly copper locks nearly straight as the wind pulled. She planted her feet, steadying herself, and batted the oncoming objects out of her way as she stared at the demon rising before us.

The tornado picked up speed as Incubus's body fully formed into a solid beast.

He stretched up, farther and farther, to his full height and width - a massive demon - his head just touching the living room ceiling. His heavily muscled body was covered in black skin. His head was round, with jagged horns protruding from either side of his skull. Large, pointed ears jutted out from behind his horns. His hair, wavy and black, ran uninterrupted from the top of his head to the beard on his face, tracing down his body in long whips. One solid eyebrow perched above two black eyes and a large, defined nose.

The tornado dissipated leaving the now fully solid Incubu standing within the circle.

The storm outside calmed too, the thunder and lightning heading in a southern direction, but the rain still pelted the windows and smattered cantankerously on the roof.

My feet rooted to the floor like a statue set in concrete, staring up at the beast. I could barely breathe. Cold sweat punctuated every pore of my body. Penny stepped back, her skin ashen. Even Cressy stood back, wide eyes staring. Blackjack jumped from my arms and skittered under the sofa, hissing. Sharon screamed beneath the bond of silver-blue light.

Incubus eyed our gathering from his place inside the circle. His body was so large, he barely left room for Sharon's spirit, still floating beside him.

He turned his focus to Sharon.

His voice, deeply resonant, boomed through the living room, shaking the crystal chandelier hanging over the dining table. "There you are, precious." Penny covered her ears and shrunk back. Sharon craned her neck to one side, trying to avoid his eyes. She tried to scream again. He placed an enormous finger on her lips, over the silver blue cords. "You did a good job of hiding in the mortal's body, my precious, and I almost had you when I took the weakling. It is upsetting that you went with another. I was about to kill them both and snatch you back, but it seems these witches interfered just in time. Now, here you are, prepared to follow me into the realms forever."

"No!" I screamed.

What had we done? All of our work to summon Sharon and bait the demon, just for him to escape with her now?

I felt the white-hot heat and acrid taste of bile rising in my throat. Incubus ignored me and focused on Sharon, whimpering beside him.

"It's all right, my precious, we are together again. No need to be sad." He laid his hand across her ghostly chest, the expanse of his hand nearly covering her entire front, and slid his fingers down, over her breasts, then to her belly, then further, to her core. "Ahh, my precious. You are ripe and ready for my seed. And I will have you, as I have before. This time, you will produce my heir."

Sharon's face twisted with fear. She tried to scream, but the silver-blue bindings held true. Incubus looked at the magical bonds holding Sharon in place and laughed. A blast of hot, putrid air pushed the three of us back another step.

I held my nose.

Penny retched.

Incubus scooped a finger under the top ring of the silver-blue bond and pulled down hard. The bond dissipated, freeing Sharon.

I jumped. "Quickly! Say the separation spell!"

Incubus whipped his head around. He narrowed his great, black eyes, holding Sharon in place with one large hand, and gathering an energy ball in the palm of his other. A sharp smell of sulfur burned my nose and eyes as the ball grew bigger.

"Hurry! Say the spell!" I yelled.

The three of us practically screamed as we chanted the separation spell, certain it would somehow make it more powerful, the louder we yelled.

"Goddess good, goddess right, remove this spirit from the demon's sight.
Never to be together again, strip this spirit from the demon's domain."

The energy ball forming in the demon's hand dissipated with a wisp of yellow smoke just as quickly as it had formed.

Incubus paused, his massive brow furrowing.

He looked down at the space beside him, slowly spinning his massive body around, searching for Sharon inside the circle. Sharon's spirit floated to the edge, but she could not cross the salt circle.

I looked from Sharon to the demon and back again.

Sharon was visible to us, but the Incubus couldn't see her.

He slammed his foot down, shaking the entire house before bellowing, "Witch! Where is she? Bring her back to me, NOW!"

The thin glass windows in the china cabinet shattered with his booming voice, along with a few of the crystal pieces inside. The chandelier shook, several of the crystal beads exploding. Glass blew around the room, whipping past me and Penny, slicing at our arms and faces before dropping to the floor. We each threw our hands up to shield our eyes.

"Quick! Say the spell!" I screamed.

Me, Cressy, and Penny stood our ground, arms down by our sides, facing the demon. We quickly formed energy balls in our hands. The room became brighter and brighter as each ball formed. We said, then repeated the incantation

"Goddess, goddess of the night, take this demon from our sight,
strip him from our world, make right.
Purge him from our world's domain, send him back from where
he came.
Send him back, from where he fell, send INCUBUS through the
gates of HELL!"

On the last word of the spell, we threw our energy balls at the demon. He opened his mouth, and an ear-shattering screech tore through the room as each of the energy balls hit its mark. Blackjack fled from under the sofa, through the kitchen, and out the cat door. Penny clamped her hands to her ears, pressing her eyes closed. Even the spirits in the room, Sharon and Cressy put their hands to their ears.

I quickly opened the bottle of holy water and threw the entire contents, then the bottle, onto Incubus. The demon screamed, his voice carrying through the house and shaking it to its foundations.

His screams turned to wails and then to whimpers as the holy water sunk into his skin and his body dissipated. His body broke apart, steamy smoke rising at all the places the energy balls and holy water had hit until there was nothing left inside the circle.

Except for Sharon.

FIFTY-FIVE

ALEXANDRA

The four of us stood, staring at the space the demon had occupied only moments before. Our breathing slowed in unison to a semi-normal rate. "Excellent job, ladies," Cressy said softly.

My entire body felt shaky and numb. I was afraid if I moved, I'd crumple to the floor.

Penny shook out her hair, bits of glass falling onto the floor. She fell to her knees, then onto her back, ignoring the pieces of shattered glass digging into her. She lay, staring at the ceiling, her hands clasped over her heart, chest moving up and down with her ragged breath.

With shaky steps, I moved toward the circle. "Sharon, are you ok?"

Sharon's spirit, still captured within, slowly turned toward me. "The spell you cast... he... he couldn't see me after. What happened?"

"We cast a spell to separate the two of you forever. He

should never come after you again," I whispered, then watched as ghostly tears formed in Sharon's eyes.

"Never? Can you promise?" Sharon clasped her hands in front of her in a prayer position.

I nodded my head and smiled. "That should really do the trick, I promise." Relief flooded my body. I took a deep breath.

It was over.

Almost.

"Oh, Alex, I can't thank you enough. You don't know what this means to me." Sharon's ghostly tears streamed down her cheeks and disappeared. "Can I go back to my body now?"

The smile slid off my face as I shook my head. A couple of pieces of shattered crystal fell from my hair to the floor. "No, Sharon, I'm afraid I can't let you do that. That body belongs to Betty Burke, and she needs it back."

Sharon wailed. "Nooooo, please Alex, I don't want to be dead! I want to live! With John! I love him!"

My heart sped up again, and a sharp pain burned through my chest."I'm so sorry, Sharon. I can't let that happen. You died when the Incubus possessed your husband, and you need to go to your afterlife, where you belong. And..." I paused, "Betty Burke needs her body back."

Sharon's wailing calmed to a sniffle.

"I've never seen my afterlife, Alex. I've just been on the run - hiding - either in the darkest places I could find, or...."

"...in whatever body was available..." I finished her sentence.

"Yes, exactly."

Cressy stepped toward the circle. "Sharon, I know this is difficult, but if you will allow me, I would like to call on someone special to escort you to your afterlife, which I'm sure is the most beautiful place you could ever imagine."

"Heaven?" Sharon sniffed.

Cressy chuckled. "It will be whatever you imagine heaven to be, my dear."

"I imagine it to be rather beautiful."

"Then it shall be."

"Okay." Sharon wiped at the tears on her face. "Will there be a big, beautiful house for me there? With a pool, and a butler? Like I had in my last life?"

Cressy laughed. "Absolutely, if that's what you imagine your heaven to be."

Sharon nodded, then looked at me. "I've been running from... *him*... for so long, I never had the chance to experience a beautiful afterlife. Thank you, Alex." She paused, then looked up at Cressy. "I'm ready to go now."

I could barely see Cressy and Sharon through my tears. Penny stood up, swiping at the tears sliding down her cheeks.

"You'll never have to run again. I promise you, Sharon." I could barely get the words out as sobs wracked my body. Cressy nodded at me, then turned toward Sharon and closed his eyes. I could see his lips move, but couldn't hear his words.

Wisps of white milky clouds appear inside the circle. Faint at first, then taking shape. Sharon pulled back, momentarily afraid, her eyes big, her breathing shallow.

She gasped as a spirit fully formed and stood before her. *Mitch Myles.*

"Cressy! You summoned Mitch?" My voice shook.

"Indeed. Who better to escort Sharon to her new home than her one true love?"

Mitch smiled at Sharon, reaching for her.

"*Mitch!*" She ran toward him, into his arms. Mitch held her close, his eyes closed.

Cressy stood beside me, one arm draped around my shoulder. Sobs wracked my body. A mix of joy and relief.

Mitch opened his eyes, looked at me, and slowly smiled.

"It was you, wasn't it?" I asked. "You somehow changed the article we found about you and allowed me to call the Sanatorium and come see you."

Mitch nodded.

"But how...?" I asked. Mitch slowly shook his head, pressing one finger against his lips.

Then, I just knew.

It was his secret to keep, not mine to know.

Not yet, anyway.

I smiled at him through my tears.

"Ready to go home, kids?" Cressy asked the reunited duo. They both turned toward him and smiled.

"We're ready," Sharon said softly, looking into Mitch's eyes.

Mitch stroked Sharon's hair before kissing her.

My heart was so full. My lungs could finally draw a full breath. I made a space in the salt circle and stood back to let Cressy in. He paused and took my face in his hands. "I'm proud of you, little girl," he whispered.

My body shook. "Th... thank you, Cress. We couldn't have done it without you."

He smiled, stepping into the circle. I poured fresh salt and closed the circle once again.

Cressy, Sharon, and Mitch held hands.

"Ready, my dears?"

"Ready."

They disappeared.

CHAPTER
FIFTY-SIX

BLAKE

"Alex? Alex? Are you there?" I yelled into the phone, pacing the room and running my hands through my hair for the umpteenth time as I listened to the goings on at Alex's home over the past hour. I heard the screaming, glass breaking, chanting, and the God-awful shriek of the demon as he met his demise.

I could feel myself aging by the second.

I had never felt more helpless in my life.

If anything happened to Alexandra, I'd never forgive myself for not being there for her.

I glanced over at John Middleton, seated on the floor, staring down at the bodies of Betty and Jack Burke. Both had a weak pulse, and he could feel small breaths coming from *his Sharon*, so he had no reason to perform CPR. His attempts at shaking her awake did nothing, so he just sat helplessly beside her.

I stopped pacing when Alex answered the phone.

"I'm here. Did you hear all of that?" she asked.

302

"Alex! Oh, thank God. Yes, I heard everything. Are you okay? I can't believe you did it! Is Sharon gone now, or will she come back here to Betty's body?"

"She's gone."

"Ok, but... what about Betty and Jack...?" Betty stirred, then Jack beside her. John sprang forward, taking Betty's shoulders in his hands. He shook her lightly.

"Sharon! Sharon? Wake up!"

Betty stirred, her eyes fluttering open. She stared up at Dr. Middleton, her brows furrowing. "Who are you? Where am I?"

"Sharon, it's me! It's John!"

She peered at him and replied, "Who's Sharon?"

John slumped, releasing his grasp on her shoulders. She flopped back on the floor. He backed away, his back hitting the edge of the bed. Tears sprung from his eyes as he held his head in his hands.

I moved toward them, still gripping the phone. "Betty! Betty Burke! Can you hear me?" I shouted.

Betty peered at me. "Sheriff Blake? What's going on?" Jack stirred beside her and opened his eyes. When he saw me standing over him, he gasped. His eyes opened wide, snapping his head toward Betty. Seeing her, he sprang up.

"Betty! Betty, are you ok?"

"Jack? What happened? What are we doing here?"

Jack scooped her up and gave her a big squeeze, voice choked up, "Oh thank God, you're back. Oh, Betty, I've missed you so much."

Smiling, I stood up and put the phone to my ear. "Did you hear that, Alex? They're back. *Betty and Jack*. Together."

Alex's voice was light but choppy. I knew she was crying, but she also sounded relieved. "I heard. Th... thank the Goddess."

Jack helped Betty shakily to her feet. She shook her head and stretched, glancing at John. "Jack, who is this man?" She glanced around. "And why are we all in a hotel room together?"

John slumped. "You don't remember me?" Sharon shook her head and John held his head in his hands. "It's true, then. Sharon's spirit really had walked into Betty's body. Just like Alexandra said."

"What is he talking about?" Betty looked at John, then Jack and me, then around the room, her brow crinkling.

She stopped short when her gaze hit the hotel room mirror.

She grabbed at her hair, then glanced down at the gold lame' bomber jacket, white tennis skirt, and 4-inch gold pumps. "Jack! Why is my hair blonde? And why am I wearing this outfit?"

She looked at her husband, eyes wide.

Jack and I started laughing.

Moments later, our laughter was joined by John's.

"Oh, Betty. My Betty, have I got a story for you..." Jack said as he hugged his wife.

FIFTY-SEVEN

ALEXANDRA

Penny and I flopped onto the kitchen table chairs. The kitchen had fared better from the interior tornado than the living and dining rooms had. Only a couple of panes of glass were shattered in the dividing French door, and a few things had blown off the kitchen counter, but it was much neater than the disaster I normally called my living room.

I poured a rich burgundy wine into two large glasses and didn't stop until the glasses were nearly full. The heady scent of the wine pulled me in before taking a much-needed sip. "We did it! Oh, my Goddess, I can't believe we did it!" We clinked our glasses together and drew a long gulp of the rich, red liquid pleasure.

"I can't believe that, even for a moment, you thought you could do this on your own!" Penny reached over and slapped me on the shoulder. I laughed. "I mean, I know you're a great witch, but even you have to admit, this was a doozy!"

"I completely agree. I'm so glad you were here. And Cressy." I reached for Penny's hand and squeezed.

"Yes, I'm glad too. Despite almost dying in a tornado and being fire-bombed by a massive demon, tonight was a total blast." Penny bobbed her head, copper curls bouncing.

"I agree. I couldn't have done this without you, Pen." Tears stung my eyes. I brushed at them absently and smiled at my friend.

"But we need to talk about forming a coven, Alex. I mean, I truly hope we never have to face another demon like... *what's his name*..." her voice dropped to a whisper, not wanting to say the demon's name out loud, or at all. "Therefore, I officially wish to commemorate this moment, the formation of the newly established Castle Point Coven. And I also vote for Alexandra Heale as the High Priestess!" Penny clinked her glass against mine and drew a long sip of wine.

I coughed, laughing and choking on my wine. "Umm, don't you require someone to second that nomination?" Just then, we heard the cat door open. Blackjack slipped into the kitchen and sauntered to the table. He jumped up on an available chair between us, glancing from one to the other, raising his nose in the air, sniffing, sneezing, and farting. Then he hopped onto my lap and exuberantly rubbed up against me. I scooped him up, hugging him close.

"Blackjack seconds the nomination!" Penny raised her glass once again. "The Castle Point Coven is duly formed!"

I laughed and rolled my eyes, stroking Blackjack's fur. "You did great, you old cantankerous thing. Although I was worried you'd be sucked into the vortex for a minute there." Purring loudly, Blackjack settled onto my lap.

"He makes a good third for our coven, don't you think?"

Penny reached over and stroked Blackjack's glossy coat. He looked up at her, sneezed, then farted, again. The stench of rotting fish permeated the air. We laughed, holding our noses.

"I think he just told you what he thinks about that idea." I waved a hand over Blackjack's butt.

"Well, Castle Point has a lot of witches to choose from, so Blackjack can play mascot instead." Penny ruffled his head. Blackjack ducked and peered at Penny, green eyes piercing. "Accept the love, you ol' cranky pants. Goddess knows you make it hard to love you."

I was hardly listening to Penny, my mind reeling at the thought of forming a coven. A giddy nervousness crept up my spine. "The question is, will we be able to convince any of them to join? I mean, our powers are greater in numbers, but so is our chance of being caught..." I crinkled my brow. "Besides, I may not even be around to be part of a coven..." I said, my voice a whisper.

"You think Blake would still arrest you after what you've done? I mean, now that Betty is Betty and Jack is Jack and everything has returned to 'normal'?" Penny, air-quoting the last word, pursed her lips, peering at me.

"Let's just hope he decides not to. However, I have a small suitcase packed, just in case..."

"Ahh, that's a good witch. Got your broomstick handy for a quick getaway?" Penny smirked. I shrugged.

The warmth of the wine spread a fluid coat of relaxation through my body. I took another deep sip, welcoming the heat. "Yeah, something like that." I thought of the invisible glamor spell I had learned from Cressy so many years ago. I hadn't needed to use it since I was a child, hiding from my mother, but I had read the spell recently, to refresh my memory, just in case I would need it now. The glamor would hide me long enough to make a clean getaway, should the Sheriff come knocking.

At least, until I could perform a forgetting spell on him.

I took another swig of my wine, my thoughts flitting from saying goodbye to Blake forever, to my mother, and to whether or not I would ever get the chance to help her. I thought about the games I played - fun for me, frustrating for mom - when I would use the invisibility spell to escape her angry grasp when I was merely a young witch, coming into my powers.

She hated those games.

I thought they were a hoot. Until the spell wore off and she'd catch me. Then? not so fun.

My mother - indoctrinated in her lineage to believe witches were pure evil - was in a constant battle with me to keep my powers suppressed, for fear of losing her only child in the dungeons of Castle Dagon, or worse - the pyre.

Even though mom was sequestered in the Sanatorium - and trapped by a demon's curse - I just couldn't let that happen.

I couldn't let Blake or anyone else burn me on the pyre.

Who would take care of mom? Who would release the curse?

I mean, I hadn't been successful so far, but it wasn't for lack of trying.

A shrill ring burst through my mind, slamming me back into the room.

It came from the antique phone, hanging on the wall by the kitchen door.

A white-hot heat flooded my body. I pushed my chair back and stood up quickly, knocking the chair onto the floor, and Blackjack off my lap. I spilled my wine, the red liquid contents sloshing over the side of the glass, spreading across the tile floor in a bloody trail.

I pivoted in the phone's direction.

The shrill ring, louder this time, pierced my ears. I dropped my wine glass, shattering it on the tile floor, bits of glass skittering across the room, the bloody trail, now a pool.

I covered my ears.

Penny pushed her chair back in surprise, the legs scraping against the tile floor. "Alex! What the hell? Answer the damn thing! Why is it so loud?"

The phone was an antique wooden box, with two brass bells on the top, and a brass rotary dial on the front of the wooden housing, above a small black megaphone. The earpiece hung, dusty and unused, on a brass holder on the left side of the wooden case. A brass hand crank on the right. Small cobwebs, which had clung to the brass bells for years, floated away, released by the vibration of the disturbingly loud ring.

The phone rang again, the ring louder, shriller, and longer.

I stepped over the broken wine glass and puddle of wine and stood in front of the phone.

"Alex! Answer the phone!" Penny yelled again, hands covering her ears.

"Why is it ringing?" I stared blankly at the phone and shook. Blood drained from every body part and pooled at my feet. Tiny beads of sweat burst onto my temples.

"Because it's a phone! For the love of the Goddess, witch, answer it! Someone's calling you! What's the matter with you?" Penny moved toward me, jumping over the mess of wine.

"Pen, it shouldn't be ringing," I said between the shrill rings.

"What are you talking about?" Penny held her hands over her ears, her brow creased as she narrowed her eyes at me.

I turned toward her, my eyes wide.

"It's just a decoration, Pen. *It's not connected.*"

Penny froze. "What?" she breathed, her hands dropping to her side.

The phone rang again, and again the ring was louder, shriller, and longer.

I peered at the two brass bells on top of the phone that had, until now, been silent for decades. My mother had more modern equipment installed when I was just a girl, but kept the phone as part of her antique collection.

I placed my hand on the earpiece and slowly picked it off its cradle. I held it in the air for a moment, studied it, and pulled it toward my ear.

"He..hello?" I heard a loud scratchy sound on the other end, like severe static from an old dial radio.

I shuddered, and a freezing chill ran through me.

This sounded exactly like the call to the Seaside Sanatorium.

"M... Mitch? Is that you?"

A voice, very distant, faint, but still discernible, came through the static.

"*Alex...Alex...andra?*"

A chill ran through me, goose flesh forming on top of gooseflesh all over my body.

The voice was unmistakably my mother's.

"Mom?" I could barely get the word past a mouth full of quicksand. I tried again.

"Mom? Is that you?"

"He... lp... me, Alex... andra... heeeeellllp... me." Mom's voice was so distant, faint and hard to hear beyond the scratches and static.

Then the line went dead.

"Mom!" I shouted into the mouthpiece, but no reply came.

The earpiece fell silent.

Still holding it to my ear, I flicked at the brass hanger repeatedly, hoping for the sound of a connected line.

Nothing happened.

The phone was completely dead.

I hung up hurriedly, holding my hand on the earpiece, willing the phone to ring again.

It didn't.

I jumped when Penny laid her hands on my shoulders.

"Alex, what's going on?"

"That was my mother!" I forced the words over my thick tongue. "I need a drink".

"Go sit down," Penny commanded. She grabbed another wine glass from the kitchen cabinet and poured a large dose. I took the glass with shaky fingers and gulped the ruby liquid.

"I don't get it, Alex. Not only is your mom catatonic in a sanatorium two counties away, but she's also calling you over a disconnected phone. What in the Goddess's name is going on?" Penny took a long draw from her own wineglass, the liquid staining her lips a deep burgundy red.

"It had to be her spirit, Pen. It's just like when I called the Sanatorium, even though there was nobody really there. She somehow figured out a way to reach out to me from....." Cressy's words floated through my brain "... the abyss..."

Penny's eyes were enormous. "The abyss? Like, the

place Betty Burke had been hanging out in while Sharon had her body?"

"Yeah. I guess so." I took another long sip of wine, willing my hands to stop shaking.

"Why now? I mean, she's been under a demon's curse for years. Why reach out now? And how?" Penny took a long swig from her own glass, her hands also shaking.

"Maybe... maybe what we did tonight has something to do with it? I mean, it worked. Betty Burke came back from the abyss. Maybe my mom somehow knows what we did and reached out, just like Mitch Myles did."

An idea struck me and I sat back hard in my chair, slapping my hand on my forehead. The wine had thankfully cooled my nerves, but a rush of excitement tore through me.

"Pen, could you help me with something?"

Penny shook her head. "I know what you're thinking, Alex. But one demon banishing per day, that's my limit and I stay within it, witchy-poo."

I smiled, the heady gulps of wine calming my nerves. "Yes, but... I was hoping we could try..." I peered up at the ceiling. "*Strength in numbers* and all that..." I looked over at Penny, my eyes pleading with my copper-headed friend.

Penny took another sip of wine and nodded. "You want to try this on your mother, don't you? But, haven't you tried for... like... years to cut the ties of the demon who bound her?" Penny was the only person in Castle Point who knew the magical secrets surrounding my mother. Doc Holloway was there when my mother was committed to the sanatorium, but my best friend knew the truth behind why.

"Yes, but I have never tried it with another witch. I can't believe I haven't thought of this sooner, honestly." I pulled at the vial earring, staring at the remaining wine in my glass.

"What do you propose we do?" Pen asked. "Could we even get away with spell-casting while she's in the sanatorium?"

"Yes, actually. Her doctor knows nothing about the demon's curse, and mom doesn't appear to be a threat, so he's always been good about us being alone in her room. He'd never suspect me of spell-casting when I'm with her, because why would he? I'm sure he wouldn't suspect anything if there were two of us." I took another sip of the red liquid bliss. "Besides, we could cast a protection spell or two, so nobody hears what's going on in the room while we're there." My heart beat faster. A giddiness welled up inside me as I took another swig of wine and closed my eyes, the liquid courage grasping hold of my heart. "This could work, Penny!" I looked at Penny, who was smiling back at me.

"I'm game if you are! I mean, who am I to disobey the High Priestess of the Castle Point Coven?" Penny clinked her glass against mine and slugged back the last of her wine.

I laughed and shook my head. "Oh Goddess, help me. It doesn't sound like I have any choice in this High Priestess thing, does it?"

"None, witch." Penny got up and walked to the front entry. I followed. We smiled at each other and hugged for a long moment before breaking apart.

"Get any hits on my future, Pen?" I asked, a little hopeful.

"Still nothing. Sorry, Alex." Penny frowned. "But let's stay positive that Blake will keep his promise to you, okay?" I nodded. "And let's talk tomorrow. Make a plan to visit your mom." Penny smiled, and I nodded again, holding the door open for my friend.

The thunderstorm had ended, but the rain remained, only softer now. Bits of moonlight reflected off the puddled pathway. Penny's red hair seemed to curl tighter as the dampness hit. She flipped the hood of her jacket onto her head.

"Tomorrow it is unless I'm running for my life." I laughed nervously, clutching the door knob.

"Ha," Penny waved and walked to her car. I closed the door and said a silent prayer to the Goddess to protect me from Blake's handcuffs.

I had work to do.

Mom needed me.

CHAPTER

FIFTY-EIGHT

ALEXANDRA

I walked into the living room and was debating whether to clean up the disaster from the tornado or leave it until morning, when a knock at the door made me jump. I smiled. Penny must have forgotten something. I walked over to the door.

"What'd you forget, witch?" I said as I opened the door.

I froze when I saw Blake standing on the other side.

He rested one hand on the door frame, his other on one hip.

When he saw me, he smiled.

"Blake? What are you doing here?" My heart rate sped up and a hurricane of butterflies went crashing through my insides.

Was he here to arrest me?

I suddenly couldn't remember the words to the invisible glamor spell, and it wasn't like I could just disappear right in front of him.

My throat worked hard.

I tried to swallow but had forgotten how.

"Hi, Alex." Blake eyed me and stepped inside, closing the door behind him.

"You must have sped all the way back from Ellsworth." Heat flared through my chest and ears as I tried to keep my tone light.

Blake took a step closer.

I took a step back.

"I did, actually. Broke all the traffic laws, in fact." He took another step closer, shedding his stetson and jacket to the floor. Ribbons of rain clinging to his jacket ran in rivulets down the fabric, pooling on the floorboards.

"What about The Burkes? And Dr. Middleton?" I rubbed my sandpaper tongue on the roof of my mouth, trying to conjure even a drop of saliva.

"Betty and Jack drove home together, happy as clams."

"That's so great, Blake. I'm so happy for them. What about John?" I asked. Blake took another step closer to me, and I took another step back. My nerves were on fire.

I wanted to dash out the door.

"Dr. Middleton and I had a good chat. Apparently, he transferred to Lexington Psych after they suspended him from the hospital in San Antonio because of his 'obsessive nature toward female patients'. He was only hired at Lexington with the understanding he would work with male patients only. When Doc Holloway called him for a consult, he accepted, and promptly fell for Betty - er... Sharon. He stayed at the hotel in Ellsworth for the night and plans to go back to Lexington Sanatorium tomorrow."

"Sounds like he should be a patient there, not a doctor," I replied, my lips in a firm line. No wonder I felt something 'off' about him. He was harboring secrets when he arrived. I looked up at Blake, who was standing, hands on his hips, studying me. "Blake, why are you here?"

"I came to see you." He moved toward me, then glanced into the living room.

I followed his gaze.

Shattered glass, pictures, and candles were strewn about, a salt circle, still intact, in the middle of the room. I could still smell sulfur, mixed with a fire's sharp, filthy scent. I glanced at the fireplace, but it was out, cold charcoal logs spilling out into the room, ash coating the floor and furniture. I looked at Blake.

"You're a messy homeowner," he said simply.

I forced a smile."Maybe I should hire a housekeeper."

He grinned. "An army of housekeepers, more like it."

"Why did you come to see me, Blake?" My voice dropped to a whisper and tears stung my eyes. "You're here to arrest me, aren't you? Now that everything's back to normal..." I squeezed my eyes shut, tears spilling over and dropping to meet the pools of rain at our feet.

Blake grabbed one of my wrists.

I kept my eyes closed, waiting for the cold steel of his handcuffs to hit my skin.

Instead, I felt him pulling me into him and lifting my face with his other hand.

I opened my eyes and met his deep brown ones, staring into me.

My breath caught...

CHAPTER
FIFTY-NINE

BLAKE

My lips burned to taste Alex's mouth.

I felt her body stiffen.

I ignored it, pulling her into me.

She pushed me away.

"Blake! What the hell?" She stepped back, putting acres of distance between us.

The zipper of my pants, which, moments ago, threatened to give way, suddenly relaxed.

"I'm sorry, Alex. I thought..."

"You thought what, exactly?" She crossed her arms in front of her chest.

I extended my hand toward her. When she didn't move, I grasped her arm and unwound it from her chest, then slowly pumped her arm in a handshake.

"I thought I'd call a truce."

She eyes me suspiciously. "So, does this mean you won't arrest me?" She whispered, her warm hand still in mine.

"Consider your sentence served."

CHAPTER
SIXTY

ALEXANDRA

I was safe.

I would not rot in the belly of Castle Dagon.

And I didn't have to sleep with Blake to do it. Or marry him.

And I was thrilled about it.

I think.

I stopped cleaning long enough to squelch the flurry of mammoth butterflies in my stomach. Thoughts of his lips distracted me. I should have cleaned it up after Blake left, but chose to sleep instead.

He wanted me.

He took my breath away.

I kinda regretted making him stop.

Lost sleep over it, in fact.

I'll probably never sleep again.

I put enough food and water out for Blackjack to last the night. I finished packing the car with Cressy's grimoire, candles, herbs, oils, and salt.

319

Today was the day Penny and I were going to free mom from a demon's curse.

I clung to a small thread of hope that it would work, but part of me didn't believe it would. I tried to stay positive and root for Team Coven, Party of Two as I drove to Penny's.

Penny kissed Cathy goodbye on the front stoop of their home before getting into my car, her arms loaded with road snacks.

"Cathy ok with you going for the night?" I asked, grabbing snacks from her arms and tossing them into the back seat of the car.

"Yeah, well, she's ok with it I guess. I told her we have something important to do, and she would never question me about things that fall under the 'need-to-know' category." Penny ripped open a breakfast bar and took a large bite.

"I love that you two have such a great relationship. Kinda jealous about it, actually. Would be nice not to have to hide." I admitted as we drove to the offramp heading to Lexington.

"You will too. I know it. Someone is out there for you, Alex, who will love you for who you are." Penny smiled and touched my arm. Her grip tightened as she slammed back against the seat of the car, her eyes closed, and the breath rushed from her lungs.

"Penny? What's wrong?" I glanced at Penny, keeping one eye on the road. Penny let go of my arm and grinned.

"So... the sexy cop tried to get it on with you last night! Dish!"

My cheeks fired.

"That's cheating! And also, a super invasion of privacy on... like... every level!" I swatted at her.

Penny laughed. "I disconnected before getting to the

good stuff, don't you worry?" I shook my head, cheeks still blazing. "There was no good stuff, Pen, so you can relax."

"So, you didn't get some? That's a damn shame. But you're here, so, I guess this means he's not arresting you?" Penny teased.

"No. He called a truce, so I guess I'm safe. Well, I hope so. I still don't quite trust him. I can't put my finger on it, but let's just say I'm not letting my guard down." I relaxed in my seat, placing my hands in the sensible ten and two positions on the steering wheel.

"Probably smart," Penny said, staring at the road in front of us.

"Did you see anything else, Pen?" I asked quietly, not sure if I really wanted to hear the answer.

Penny paused. "No, nothing. Just what's already happened. Sorry, Alex. I don't know why your future is so... dark for me." Penny slumped into the seat and looked out the window.

"I guess maybe it's a need-to-know basis kind of thing. Although you certainly didn't need to know about Blake making a pass at me last night!" I coaxed a smile from my friend.

"Would you have told me if I hadn't seen it for myself?"

"No comment." I smiled. Penny laughed and handed me a bottle of water and some homemade nut mix. We spent the rest of the drive talking about mom.

WE ARRIVED at the Lexington County Psychiatric Sanatorium about two hours later. After parking and checking in with the front desk, we headed to mom's room.

I had mentally prepared a little speech to give to Dr. Joseph, should we see him in the halls. But he was out for the day.

Bonus.

Mom sat alone in her room, her chair turned toward the room. A light shiver ran through me, recalling the way Mitch Myles - or the ghost of him - was sitting in a chair the same way. I suddenly felt the need to reach for mom and feel the warmth of her skin against mine, just to be sure she wasn't an illusion.

"Mom, it's me. It's Alexandra." As usual, she gave me no response. "This is Penny, remember her?"

Penny knelt down beside mom and touched her arm, closing her eyes. When she opened them again, she looked up at me and shook her head.

No visions.

"Hi, Mrs. Heale. Remember me?" Penny spoke softly. Mom merely blinked and stared.

"Mom." I touched her arm. "I know you're in there. Do you remember calling me yesterday? On the old phone in the kitchen?" Still nothing. I sighed and looked at Pen. She got up and went to the bag of things I'd packed for the incantation, pulling out the Grimoire.

"What spell are we using?" she asked, flipping the pages.

"Lifting the Demon's Curse. I mean, it's the closest thing I could find to what's going on with her."

I flipped to the page. Penny read through the spell. "Geez. This will not be easy, Alex. Have you ever asked for Cressy's help?"

I paused, looking out at the view of the gardens. "Cressy can't help, Pen."

"Good Goddess, why the heck not? He's so powerful, even dead!"

"Because, Pen, the demon who put a curse on mom is the same demon who killed Cress."

Penny stared at me, wide-eyed. "Are you kidding me?"

"I'm afraid not."

"So, you're telling me that Cressy, - who is possibly the most powerful witch that ever came to Dagon County, was killed by the demon who also put this..." Penny waved her hand at my mom "... curse or spell or whatever, on your mom and you think *we* will have a better chance at killing it than Cressy did?" She stared at me, her mouth hanging open, head slowly shaking.

"Well, I'm hopeful, yes." I rubbed my hands across my face and through my hair. "Am I crazy?"

Penny closed her mouth and took my hands in hers. "Look, love, I get it. You want to help your mom. I'm just not sure that we have enough power between the two of us to do it."

I shrugged, struggling to hold back tears. "Worth a shot, at least?"

"Yeah, of course." Penny put a warm hand against my cheek. "Ok, let's get started."

WE STARTED by locking the door and placing a cloaking spell over the room. It was a simple spell that allowed us to work inside the room while everyone on the outside would be completely oblivious.

"What if her doctor or a nurse checks up on her?" Penny asked.

"The spell cloaks their thoughts too, so they won't even think about coming in here. For a while anyway," I said as I worked with Penny to set up the room.

"Ok, we have the candles, incense, the burner, salt... I think we're done." Penny looked up from the book and surveyed the room. We closed the drapes and moved Mom further into the room, and poured the salt around her chair. Black candles were outside the circle, their golden flame casting eerie shadows on the walls. The ingredients we needed were white ash, copal resin, and Burberry leaves burned in the small cauldron outside the circle.

"Great, thanks Pen. Let's do this." I took a deep breath and stood beside the circle, facing my mother. Penny took her place on the opposite side. We both closed our eyes and started the incantation in unison;

"Goddess of the North, South, East, West, hear our call, grant our request.
Free this woman from where she sleeps. Remove the demon's curse, we plead, and bring her back from the abyss."

We repeated the incantation three times.

Nothing was happening.

"Should we try calling Cressy, Alex?" Penny whispered.

My shoulders slumped. "No, I already know that he has no power over this demon's curse."

"Maybe let's just try again?" Penny asked, shrugging.

"Ok, sure." We tried again, repeating the incantation over and over and over. At first, nothing, no movement from Mom or anywhere in the room, the twist of smoke from the smoldering herbs diminishing.

Then, Mom shifted in her seat.

I gasped. "Penny look." Penny walked around to stand beside me.

"Oh my Goddess, Alex." Her breath caught. My breath quickened.

Although she was still staring straight ahead, expressionless, eyes blank but blinking her right hand moved. Tiny movements at first. Her fingers brushed against the arm of the chair. Then three of her fingers touched together at the tips, the movements becoming more defined, stronger somehow.

"Is she trying to write something?" Penny asked.

I watched the motion of her fingers with growing excitement and disbelief.

"Oh my Goddess, Penny, I think she is! Quick, grab the pad and pencil from my bag." Penny did so and handed them to me. Then she made a split in the salt circle so I could enter. I placed the pad of paper under Mom's hand, then grasped her hand, holding it as still as possible, and placed the pencil between her fingers.

When I let go, the pencil touched the paper, and she wrote. Gooseflesh threatened to burst through my clothing.

"What's she writing? Can you see?" Penny asked, peering at the paper from her spot outside the circle.

"It looks like... symbols." I peered down at the paper, to be sure. I stood up, my breath leaving my body.

The symbols were the same ones I had seen on Mitch Myles's cell walls.

Penny reached for me, ignoring her place outside the circle. "Alex! Alex, what is it?" She pushed against me, snapping me back into the room.

"It's the same symbols Mitch drew on the walls of his cell, Pen." I stumbled back a step, then bent over, grasping my knees. The room spun.

"Alex! Are you ok?"

I took a moment to catch my breath and stood up. "I think so." I looked over at Mom. The writing had stopped. The notepad and pencil fell to the floor.

Mom sat, staring straight ahead.

I stepped over to pick up the paper and pencil and studied the same repeated pattern of symbols as Mitch had shown me.

As I copied from his cell walls.

I stepped out of the circle, quickly dug through my bag, and retrieved the paper I had written the symbols on.

"Penny, look." I shoved the notepad and the paper toward her.

She took them, peering at the pages. "Alex, what do they mean?"

I shook my head. "I have no clue. The book in Castle Dagon wasn't any help."

"How do we find out?" Pen asked, handing the papers back to me.

I blew out a breath. "I really don't know, Pen. There's only one thing I'm certain of right now."

Penny perked up. "What's that?"

"Whatever we did today - together - got us closer to communicating with Mom than any of my past efforts ever did."

Penny threw her arms in the air, jubilant. "Score one for the Coven of Two!"

I laughed, relief, and excitement shivered through me.

"Yeah, Pen. And if we got this far today with the two of us, just think of what we could do if we had more..."

Penny smiled, punching a fist high in the air.

CHAPTER

SIXTY-ONE

THE WITCH HUNTERS

The Witch Hunters gathered again in the courtyard of CastleDagon under the dark of night. We formed a circle, bowed in reverence, and began chanting the ancient language in unison, calling upon the Earl Dagon and the Demon Vine to commune with us, in this, the holiest of places.

The GrandMaster raised his scepter, signaling us to stop. The courtyard fell quiet, the sound of crashing waves along the rocks a soothing background melody.

"Come forward, Blake, Pupil of Vine, and tell us of the witch." The Grand Master commanded.

I stepped out of the circle, pausing.

I thought of Alexandra, her powers, and what she was capable of.

My heart raced, and I bit my lip to suppress a smile.

Her powers will be mine.

Then I thought of the work she had done to help Betty and free Sharon's spirit.

Alex wasn't only beautiful, she was a smart, talented lady, with a heart as big as my stupid head.

But she was also a witch.

A witch who I felt a disturbing need to protect.

A witch who rejected me. Is probably afraid of me.

I grimaced.

"Come forward, I command thee!" The GrandMaster bellowed.

I stepped in front of our commander, my boss, Sheriff Roberts, and knelt before him. I bowed my head, the hood of my cloak masking my face.

"What have thou learned of the witch?" he asked. I paused again. Visions of Alex's smile and the thought of her lips rushed through my mind. The GrandMaster tapped his scepter on the rocky floor forcefully.

I moved my tongue around my mouth and then spoke; "She is a powerful witch, Commander, with many powers to be... obtained... she..." I paused again.

"Continue!" He tapped his scepter again. Despite the woolen cloak, a shiver crept up my spine.

"She is also in possession of the ancient language of Our Lord Demon Vine, Commander, and I fear she may find the interpretation.." An audible gasp spun around the room.

Beads of perspiration dotted my temples.

"This cannot be, Pupil. For if she can interpret our language, it would be the end of the followers of Vine." Another gasp fled through the room.

I swallowed hard.

"She must be stopped! Tell us! What is the witch's name?"

I squeezed my eyes shut and bit my lip.

I hoped Alex could forgive me.

If only there was a way...

Then my eyes flew open, my heart racing.

I raised my head, meeting the eyes of the High Commander.

"Her name is... *Penny*."

THE WITCHY ADVENTURE CONTINUES WITH:

"Castles & Cauldrons" Castle Point Witch Series Book 2 Preorder Available!

https://www.tammytyree.com/castle-point-series

Castle Point's nunnery is wreaking havoc on Alexandra Heale's personal property. The nuns, under the rule of an ancient demon, are acting anything but holy.

On top of that, Alexandra's best friend, Penny is missing, presumably kidnapped and being held by the Witch Hunters in the bowels of Castle Dagon.

Alexandra, now High Priestess of the underground witch population, is already at the mercy of Blake Sheraton, Deputy Sheriff sworn to uphold Earl Dagon's ancient law against the practice of witchcraft.

Battling another demon and a group of possessed nuns while trying to save her friend will surely cinch her fate.

Alexandra, torn between her love/hate feelings for Blake and her desire to exist, enlists the help of badass Master Herbalist and burgeoning witch, Theodora Cunningham to do the impossible; create a potion that would banish the demon and bring peace back to Castle Point.

If only they could do so without exposing themselves or the underground...

If you love the classic Witches of Practical Magic, the paranormal investigations of the Palmetto Point Witch Series by Wendy Wang, or the slow-burn romance and humor of The Witches of Hollow Cove by Kim Richardson, then you'll love this book!

"Castles & Cauldrons" is the intensely gratifying, edge-of-your-seat second book in the Castle Point Paranormal Witch series, written by award-winning author, Tammy Tyree!

Preorder here! https://www.tammytyree.com/

FOR READERS

Thank you for reading!

BONUS SCENE!!
    "The day Alexandra met Cressy"
    https://dl.bookfunnel.com/viik9fjpq1

If you enjoyed this book, please leave a review on your favorite platform on my website here:
    https://www.tammytyree.com/review

If you found spelling mistakes or niggly plot points, please email the author directly: tammy@tammytyree.com

If you'd like to join my ARC/Beta Reader group, please email me directly at tammy@tammytyree.com

Don't miss out on a single new release!
    Sign up and we'll make sure you hear about every new book Tammy Tyree publishes as soon as it hits the stores.

https://books2read.com/author/tammy-tyree/
subscribe/1/308381/

FOR AUTHORS

Are you an author, looking to up-level your career, your writing, or your time? The Author Revolution Academy has everything you need to succeed!**

Aspiring & Emerging Author Courses

Are you working toward getting your very first book out? Maybe you have a small (but growing backlist of titles)... If so, look no further. These courses are the best fit for you.

The Story Cure: http://bit.ly/410XVqW
Plan Your Series Challenge: http://bit.ly/3GFAv27
Indie Publishing Fundamentals: http://bit.ly/3GDrd6W

Prolific Author Course

Ready to take self-publishing to the next level? Rapid Release Roadmap is the course to get it done. Learn how to plan, write, publish, and promote 4 books (or more) every single year in this one-of-a-kind course!

Rapid Release Road Map: http://bit.ly/3o8b8zu

Millionaire Author Courses

Want to learn how to apply the Law of Attraction and manifestation techniques to your author career? Look no further! These courses (or membership) are just what you're looking for!

Millionaire Author Challenge: http://bit.ly/43osfNP

Millionaire Author Manifestation: http://bit.ly/3KoY5RQ

Abundant Author Activation: http://bit.ly/3MA2Iew

**Affiliate links

ABOUT THE AUTHOR

Tammy Tyree is a retired Board Certified Clinical Hypnotherapist and award-winning author of paranormal suspense and memoir.

Most of her professional career was dealing with entity attachments and demonic possession, which she thought was rather fun. Now, she works alongside International Bestselling author Carissa Andrews to up-level the lives of aspiring authors to manifest millionaire author careers.

She has four adult children and one incredibly perfect granddaughter whom she sees and spoils regularly.

You can follow Tammy on Facebook and Instagram, and visit her website at www.tammytyree.com

facebook.com/TammyTyreeAuthor

instagram.com/tammytyreeauthor

tiktok.com/@tammytyreeauthor